# Out of Body

A Magical Misfits Mystery

Lina Hansen

Literary Wanderlust | Denver, Colorado

Published in the United States by Literary Wanderlust LLC, Denver, Colorado. www.LiteraryWanderlust.com

ISBN Paperback: 978-1-956615-35-7
ISBN Digital: 978-1-956615-36-4

Printed in the United States of America

# Dedication

To my parents, for giving me books.

# 1

## BARE BONES

At the end of a long, muddy hike, the last thing I fancied was a pile of human bones. How could I be so sure the sorry remains didn't belong to a sheep, a cow, or another farm animal that perished during our recent heatwave? The skull was a dead giveaway. With empty eye sockets and dodgy dentistry, it grinned from among the nettles crowding the wooden stile.

"Come on, Myr, almost there." Chris skimmed the steps with annoying ease. "Good job too. I guess we've earned our dinner."

He landed in the sodden grass of the next field, the tip of his walking boot only inches away from the greenery. And the skeletal parts, discolored and desolate.

I blew aside the strawberry strands of hair that obscured my vision and blinked. Unfortunately, the skull was still there, and so were the bones that first trapped my attention. Despite being flattened and cut in places, the weeds hid the mess pretty well; one needed to stand close by or observe the fence from a particular angle to notice anything. Trust me to be the lucky one.

"Fancy some of Greg's spareribs Southern style?" Chris

asked. "With corn, not grits. Can't stomach the stuff. A baked potato with garlic butter wouldn't go amiss either. Or a grilled tomato. What do you reckon?"

I ogled the femur lurking among the vegetation, its prominent hip joint unmistakably human. As if I needed more proof that I had somehow stumbled over another crime scene. A wave of nausea rolled through my stomach. It was starting all over again.

"I reckon we might have a problem." A drop of water hit my exposed neck and trickled down my spine, making me shiver. "Eek, wet."

"Don't tell me it's piddling already." Chris squinted at the sullen summer sky, heavy with racing clouds. "Mh, the worst should hold off for a little while longer, but we better hurry up. Chop-chop, onwards and upwards."

I stood rooted to the spot. Another day of this unsettled weather and the nettles would have regrown dense enough to veil the grisly sight. Whose stupid idea had it been to go hiking today?

Mine, of course.

"Are you coming, or what? It's a bog-standard stile, not a bouldering challenge." Chris's mobile brows slanted.

My gaze got sucked in by a beige shape half-hidden behind a clump of grass. "Uh, don't move. You might step on the pelvis."

Chris's brow flew into full V-mode. "What?" Dutifully, he froze and scanned the perimeter in visible and increasing confusion.

My heart skipped a beat. It was entirely possible that my fickle magical skills had asserted themselves, and I was suffering illusions or visions. Or something. Not that second sight was my strength. To be honest, nothing was. Instead, I got ambushed by magic at the most inopportune moments and wouldn't have given myself more than two stars for my hexing skills. It didn't matter, since the few other supernatural beings left behind on planet Earth weren't any better. If anything, they were worse.

Chris, who had been scything through the nettles with the sole of his mud-spattered boot, froze and gingerly put down his foot. "Oh, blast."

"Do you see it, then?"

"I spy with my little eye a bunch of human bones if that's what you mean."

Not a vision, then. Relief buoyed my chest, but only for a moment. "Okay, just checking. Let me join you." I climbed over the barrier and landed next to the man who had in the space of not even two weeks become a rock in my life. He held aside the nettles with a branch, and together we examined the sad leftovers scattered among the drippy foliage.

"Could be worse, I suppose," Chris said.

"How?"

"Our bony friend here has been dead for a while."

My nausea increased. So far, I had only been confronted with reasonably fresh corpses. While a skeleton was the other extreme, Chris had a point. The phase in between was a lot more revolting.

My helpful brain dragged in a lesson from my previous run-ins with dead bodies. "We must call the police. And try not to disturb things too much."

With a curt nod, Chris withdrew a few feet away toward the public footpath, a trampled line of mud and unruly grass. It continued across a field dotted with grazing sheep, the spire of Avebury's church rising in the distance like the needle of a compass.

"Sounds like a plan," Chris said. "You'd better alert your tame copper."

"Sarah's anything but tame and you know that. Let's hope she's around."

I fumbled in the pocket of my windbreaker until my fingers touched something fluffy, fished out the smartphone, and eyed its neon-pink fake fur cover with disgust. The bimboistic gizmo that attracted lint like a fuzzy magnet was a gift from my cousin

Daisy. Most likely, she had meant well.

I thumbed a number and listened to the ringtone. Sergeant Sarah Widdlethorpe of the Wiltshire CID was a busy woman, so I wasn't surprised when my call landed in her mailbox. "Sarah, it's Myrtle. Call me ASAP, please. I found some bones. Human, I'm afraid."

That would get her attention. But I couldn't shake off that little voice worming away in my conscience, telling me to try harder.

"Should I perhaps try the police switchboard? With my luck, bloody Diloff gets roped in."

Chris rolled his eyes. "What, DI Dickhead? Blast, no. The bones have been knocking around for a while, they can wait a bit longer."

It was hard, but I managed not to glance at the nettles. "You know what? I don't think the skeleton's been here all that long. With that heatwave we've had even something as robust as a nettle will wilt and expose ...uh, stuff."

"Good thinking, Myr. This is a dumping site, not a crime scene. Means there's even less of a hurry."

"Okay."

My relief was only short-lived. More mercantile considerations jostled for space. The tourist trade in idyllic Avebury had taken a hit when my friend Jenna's grandmother Dot Wytchett, aka the solstice killer, caused murderous mayhem with her poisoned wine—hexed poisoned wine, to be precise.

Wild thoughts chased each other through my head, but only one made it past my lips. "Chris, could this be one of Dot's victims?"

My companion eyed the nettles in disgust. "Nah. Told you already, these bones are too clean for a fresh death. Or do you smell anything?"

I had forgotten about my nausea. Now it returned with a vengeance. I forced my gaze away from the pelvis, half-covered by the dense greenery that whiffed of nothing more sinister than moist soil and rotting leaves.

"No."

Another thought muscled to the forefront of my mind. The nausea cranked up a notch. "But in that case, someone must've stored the body before dumping the bones. That's sick."

Chris reached out and caressed my cheek. "Myr, you worry too much. Let's go. There's really nothing else we can do for this sorry specimen. No point in getting wet."

He was right, but somehow my legs refused to cooperate. "I'd just hate to find out the hard way that it's my problem after all. Or a problem for the coven. Like it was last time."

Chris raked his hand through his thick, black curls. "Ah, I get it. Someone needed to rid themselves of their skeleton in the cupboard in a hurry and used Dot's body count as a smokescreen." He winked.

"Oi, show some respect. This was a human being. Or... Hey, could it be a model skeleton? My old GP had one. Used to frighten me something rotten whenever Mum took me for my jabs. Sarah will have my guts for garters if I cause a stir over nothing."

"No way, sorry. These bones are too weathered to be artificial."

*Drip.*

As one, we gazed skyward. The heavens had shrouded themselves in a menacing shade of gray, only a brighter streak in the west showed the sun was still hanging in there.

"We *really* need to make a move," Chris said.

"I know. Let's hope no one runs into Skelly in the meantime. Someone with heart problems, for example."

"Unlikely many people will be out hiking now, not when it's about to bucket again. They'll all head for a nice warm pub, and I suggest we join them. If Sarah wants statements, she knows where the Whacky Bramble is."

"Sounds like a plan."

We turned our backs on the latest fiasco and headed for the

village.

—

Twice, I swung around, reassuring myself the unwelcome find wouldn't be visible from the trail. It wasn't. Nettles, bushes, and a fence complete with a stile but no bones, thank the soggy heavens.

Chris was pulling away from me, either desperate to leave the remains behind or hankering after the type of comfort that comes in a glass and contains alcohol. Perhaps, it was a bit of both.

"I don't think I fancy ribs anymore," he said once I caught up with him.

"How can you even consider food?"

"I'm considering *not* having it. What I need is a large glass of Greg's excellent Malbec. Medicinal purposes, you know?"

"Nice try."

"Well, you've done it again. Found a corpse, I mean."

"Oh, it's my fault now, is it?"

I lengthened my stride to keep up with the pace he was setting. Tall for a woman I might be, but his legs were still longer than mine, which made for an unfair advantage. Moving helped, though. Blood returned to my chilled limbs, and the skeleton's ghastly afterimage lost its grip on my memories. Despite the worsening weather, my mood climbed out of the pits. The sheep mimicked our determined progress; kicking up clods of soil, they bounded across the field, bleating loudly.

The pub came into view the same moment the sporadic drops segued into a drizzle, which soon became a full-blown downpour. The benches and tables in front of the Whacky Bramble counted down the last meters as I scurried for the entrance, for once ahead of my partner. With a bow, I opened the door. Warm air gushed out in an aromatic welcome, saturated with the greasy, yeasty smells that, for me, make up the essence of a decent pub.

The view to the bar was obscured by a steaming horde of people, most of them holding glasses in their hands. Taller than even Chris and built like a linebacker, Greg, our temp landlord from across the big pond, calmly served the thirsty evening crowd.

"Myrtle, Chris, over here." On the other side of the public bar, an elderly gentleman flapped his arms like an overexcited crane. His thick glasses flashed, reflecting the glare of the recessed spotlights over the counter. "Come and join us."

"Us" turned out to be a handful of coven members hogging seats in front of the fire that billowed smoky heat into the room. Single file, Chris and I wormed our way through the throng, headed for the table occupied by Damian, his wife Rosie, Colonel Elmsworth, and the melting remains of their drinks.

"You're a lifesaver." I shrugged out of my soggy windbreaker, trying not to blacken anybody's eye with my elbows. With a grateful groan, I sank onto the hard wooden seat Damian had pulled out for me. "Evening, Rosie. Hi, Colonel."

Frantic yapping broke out at my feet, and I twitched my legs away from the Chihuahua's sharp teeth.

"Shut up, Buster," the Colonel said, his sandy mustache bristling. "Sorry about that."

Chris bent over me. "What are you having?"

Despite all the water outside, my throat was parched from our mad dash. Or, perhaps, it was a late onset of shock. "I don't care. As long as it's warm and wet."

A fresh volley of yipping and snarling exploded under the table. The Colonel crouched, remarkably agile for a man in his seventies, and scolded his irascible pet.

"With or without?" Chris's hand was a warm weight on my shoulder.

Good question. Combubble it all, after the sight in the nettles I deserved a treat. "With. Actually, I think a mug of Greg's brandied hot chocolate would do me nicely. And an extra helping of marshmallows. Uh, what about dinner?"

"Ask me again later."

"Why don't we have a drink now, then go home and decide? We can always call in for food or return here. I want a hot shower before I eat anything."

"On it." Chris gave my shoulder a gentle squeeze and withdrew.

Across the table, Rosie tutted. "Your tee is totally soaked, dear. Can't say I enjoyed our heatwave, but this take on a British summer isn't my thing either."

Concern was pulling surplus lines into Rosie's thin face. She wasn't that old—mid-sixties was my best bet—but the big C had stamped its mark on her gentle features.

"I'll survive. First, I need a pick-me-up. We had a nasty surprise at the end of our hike." I bit my tongue, but the words were out.

The Colonel lifted a bushy brow. "Hah, Pete's bull has escaped again, has he? That critter is turning into a real menace."

"Uh, thankfully not."

"Did you take the Windmill Hill path?" Rosie asked. "Damian and I walked there this morning. It's so totally enchanting, even without our special brand of magic. Oops, sorry." Rosie covered her mouth with her hand and tossed a nervous glance at the other guests.

She needn't have worried. The place was much too noisy for anyone to have overheard. If they did, at worst they would mistake us for Wiccans or Druids. The pagans were all over the village, especially so soon after the solstice.

Her first statement, however, had me sitting up straight. "Uh, you hiked on the hill path this morning? We came the same way. Did you notice anything...odd at the last stile? The one you reach shortly after crossing the stone bridge over the brook?"

The Colonel tossed me a hooded look. But he kept quiet.

Rosie furrowed her forehead. "No, why? Oh, you mean the nettles? Amazing how they've grown back so quickly. I collected a bagful before we returned to our car. Nettle infusion does wonders for my hair."

With a smile, she fluffed up her cobwebby white strands, still short from the chemo she'd endured earlier this year. I had no idea whether her hair truly had grown, but that wasn't the point. For Rosie to be able to gather weeds at the stile and do so without noticing any remains, they must've been dumped after her visit.

Would she have missed them? Possible, but unlikely. In places, the nettles had been flattened and cut, especially close to the pelvis. A shame I didn't take a photo.

Chris and Damian returned with the drinks and our conversation turned to more mundane matters. Only later, back in the private living room of my bed and breakfast, the aptly named Witch's Retreat, did I get to voice the lost thoughts straying through my head.

"Chris, I'm pretty sure Skelly was dumped this afternoon."

He looked up from the leaflet advertising Indian cuisine delivered by Mukherjee's Mobile Mahal. The shower had washed away this afternoon's misgivings together with the sweat and grime, and we were both hungry again.

"Is that a more or less intelligent guess, a statement, or a prophecy?" he asked.

"I'll give you more or less."

He grinned.

"Neither. Just good old-fashioned sleuthing."

"Apropos sleuth, did Sarah call back?"

"Nope. Tried her number twice already. If I don't hear from her soonish, I'll have to ring the cop shop proper. Let's hope it doesn't come to that. I really don't want to poke our favorite DI into action."

Chris grunted. "Wait until tomorrow. While it's pissing down, the bones are safe enough. And you still haven't told me what triggered your brainwave."

"Rosie and Damian hiked the same trail, and she plucked nettles for her infusion. Had our bony friend been in residence, she would've noticed. She's pretty observant, you know?"

"Mh." Chris drummed a sonata on the coffee table with his long, slender fingers.

The noise woke up Tiddles, my geriatric tortoiseshell cat, who yawned and arched her back in the knitting basket. My Aunt Eve's basket, I wasn't into knitting. After auntie's untimely demise, I hadn't known what to do with her half-finished handiwork, so I simply kept matters as they were. Tiddles, originally auntie's pet, was now in possession. My gaze strayed to the top shelf that housed auntie's eco-friendly urn, decorated with cute paw prints that walked up one side and came down the back. She would have approved of the arrangement. Of that, I was sure.

My gaze found the bucket-sized fake terracotta pot hovering at seat level. When it came to Petty, my magical zombie primula, I was a lot less sure what auntie's view on the subject might have been.

The plant's nubby green leaves and pink blossoms were rustling and swishing as if tossed by an invisible wind. It was the little flower's way of talking. How I wished I could understand her better.

*Zing.* A fat spark fired from a blossom and winked out on the tabletop.

"Somehow, I don't think she's buying your theory," Chris said. The warmth in his grin made me go all mushy inside.

"Since when do you speak primula?"

"I don't."

"Me neither. Shame, really. Anyway, Sarah needs to know about the timing. Cripes, why does she always go MIA on me when I need her most?"

Chris snapped his fingers and rummaged in the pocket of his jeans. "Here's something to take your mind off bones and crime scenes. Your housekeepers left a message at reception. From the German bloke digging into your witchy background."

I sat up. "Schlüsselblum?"

"Doesn't he have a first name?"

"That's even harder to pronounce. What does he want?"

"No idea. Since you stormed upstairs without looking, I picked up the message for you."

"Oh, cool, he must've found something."

Chris retrieved a crumpled scrap of paper from his pockets and read. "Looks like he wants you to ring back. Something's wrong."

# 2

## POT SHOT

My alarm went off at seven in the morning, shockingly early after a night filled with broken dreams and a nameless disquiet. Blinking away the fuzziness in my brain, I sat, the movement bouncing Tiddles off my duvet. She flicked her tail and stalked from the bedroom. But my furry friend couldn't fool me. She'd be back for her breakfast before I could say "pussycat."

Instead, I said, "Chris?"

No reaction from the dark, curly mop of hair nestled in the other pillow. A tender wave of warmth flooded my core and washed away the cobwebs of my night.

Chris and I had agreed to take it easy on the romance, past relationships having left their scars. Three murdered visitors and Dot's attack on the coven later, and my resolutions crumbled. Shamelessly, I threw myself into his arms, where I was most welcome. Twelve—no, thirteen days into our new relationship, I somehow didn't trust my good luck. But here he was, by my side.

My lover was witty, cute, and sexy—and my feet were cold. Mr. cute and sexy Lentulus had done it again and hogged my duvet. That was the downside of sharing my bed with somebody other than the grumpy feline who now padded back into the room and let rip a throaty yowl.

Chris stirred and lifted his tousled head. With bleary eyes, he stared at the mottled animal approaching the bed, her claws clicking on the sanded floorboards.

He sank back with a groan. "What time?"

"Too early for verbs, I guess. Just gone seven."

"Nggh," Chris said and pulled his, or rather, my pillow over his head. I gave him a poke, and he grabbed my hand. "Come here, Myr."

I was about to do just that when my smartphone resting on the white wicker washing basket exploded into a slow-mo version of "Smoke on the Water."

"Congratulations, perfect timing." I swung my legs over the side of the bed onto the downy runner. "That's got to be Schlüsselblum, returning my call."

I picked up the vibrating gadget and checked the number. Not Germany, but an unknown caller. If this was another scam attack from "IT Mumbai", I'd give them an earful.

"Witch's Retreat B&B, Myrtle Coldron speaking."

"Tell me it isn't true." Most of the time, Sarah spoke in level tones. Not so today, but I couldn't blame her.

"Good morning to you, too. Are you referring to my message about the bones we found? The message I left yesterday?"

"Sorry, I was drowning in paperwork, so I turned the damn phone off. Then it went on the blink. Next time, call the switchboard or ring in an emergency. We can't have bodies lying around unattended."

Hopefully, there wouldn't be a next time. "Trust me, I would've raised hell had the body been ...uh, fresh. This one could wait."

Sarah sighed. "Do me a favor and don't discover any more corpses, okay?"

"My feelings entirely. Actually, neither your switchboard

nor the emergency number were an option."

"Why not?"

"Your superstar of a boss."

"Ah, true. Right, what exactly are we talking about?"

"A skeleton. Well, a heap of human bones. We found them at the end of our hike."

"As one does," Sarah said, her tone acerbic. "Where exactly?"

"Quite close to the village, on the Windmill Hill path."

A groan wormed into my ear. "You'll have to show me. I don't know my way around all that fresh countryside of yours. How about if I pick you up in, say, two hours? It'll take a while to kick the SOCO and our pathologist into action. I love that chap. He's all sunshine and roses."

"You do that. Don't come here, though. Too many nosy neighbors, not to mention my housekeepers. I'll wait for you at the corner to Nightingale Lane." I rang off and rubbed my eyes as if that would ban the grisly images of yesterday's find.

"Sarah, I presume?" Propped up on the pillows, Chris bounced me a sympathetic smile, his eyes open and alert.

The cat chose that moment to race across the duvet and hop onto the windowsill, where she then sat, tail flicking from left to right. Between the chartreuse curtains, the windowpane showed, covered in ribbons of rainwater.

"Yup, and guess who gets to venture forth in this weather and act the tourist guide for the coppers?" I fetched the packet of kibble from the shelf and let the pellets rattle into a metal bowl.

"Brrp." Tiddles slipped off the sill and stuck her face into the bowl, the tail a pennant over her bony rump. Energetic crunching followed. Better to keep some cat food in the bedroom than to traipse all the way to the kitchen in my dressing gown. It might shock the guests.

Chris laughed. "Off you go into the shower. Or do you want to try Schlüsselblum now? The continent's an hour ahead."

I weighed the phone in my hand. "I'd rather put something

in my stomach before I do that. And talk to the Simpkinses. It'd be typical if one of them peppered the message with an 'urgent' and a 'problem' rather than Schlüsselblum."

"Wouldn't put it past them. The ladies are fantastic, but they relish their little dramas." He regarded me with a twinkle in his night-black eyes. "Might join you, actually."

"Since when are you into breakfast chit-chat?"

"I'm not. I was talking about a joint shower. More ecological—besides other things."

Those "other things" kept us pleasurably occupied for a while until we made our way downstairs, drawn by the aroma of toast wafting from the kitchen.

I left Chris to read his daily in the breakfast room and entered the kitchen through the connecting door.

*Bang.*

A white vehicle rolled past the kitchen windows and drove off. Marty Wytchett, doing his delivery round. He'd left his greasy goodies behind—batteries of eggs and enough sausages, bacon, and black pudding to clog the arteries of a full tour group. Alma and Cecily were busy cramming the bonanza into the two commercial fridges.

*You really, really must talk to Jenna.*

Yes, I needed to get hold of Marty's sister, but I wanted to help, not crowd her. The sad business with her murderous grandmother had left my friend confused and hurting. To the point the entire village tiptoed around her as if she were made of glass. I hadn't seen her in days.

Alma, her hair freshly poodle-permed, her stocky body clad in a sapphire nylon house frock, banged the fridge door shut. She faced me with a frown on her forehead. "Will you have time to fetch the tomatoes and mushrooms? Last lot's gone moldy without guests to eat them."

Thankfully, that was about to change.

"Yes, but not before midday. I've got an appointment first." With the police. Hopefully, the business with the bones would be sorted before the local rumor mill kicked off.

"Good," Cecily, sporting a hairdo similar to her sister's and wearing a pink nylon house frock, fished for a pan and banged it onto the stove. "Scrambled for Mr. Lentulus, as usual?"

I nodded. The Simpkins sisters had taken Chris's overnight stays at the Witch's Retreat in their stride. If anything, they seemed to approve of the union. Why did I even care about their opinion? The answer was straightforward. I liked them a lot and not only because I couldn't run the B&B without them, especially not with a wedding party due this afternoon.

I opened the fridge and removed the skimmed milk. To ease the strain on my waistline, I had switched to muesli, fruits, and yogurt to replace the greasy delights offered by Alma and Cecily. Cereals were much healthier, but latest by eleven I would be circling the snack cabinet. Hopefully, babysitting the cops would keep me away from sugary temptations.

"Our guests will arrive around four, right?" I poured the milk into a bowl and reached for the strawberries.

"Well, sort of," Cecily said. "They come from all over the country, so I don't think they'll show up together. Shall we wait for them?"

"Nah, don't worry. I'll be here. If there's a problem, I'll call. Apropos call—thanks for passing on the message about Herr Schlüsselblum. Who of you actually spoke to him?"

"Me," Alma said. "Bit stressed, that man. Mumbled something about a discovery, a problem, and things being urgent." She leaned against the kitchen counter, a glint in her shrewd eyes. "He didn't say what it was all about, though. Did you get hold of him?"

*Ugh. Kiss goodbye the hope the ladies might have put a disaster spin on their message.*

"Not yet. I'll try again later."

Cecily was whipping the eggs into a froth. "Something to do with that stuff you took over from your aunt? Is he trying to find more dividends, then?" Her tone was deceptively casual.

As much as I liked the Simpkins sisters, the coven's existence and matters such as Team Schlüsselblum's efforts to throw more light on the history of the last witches were on their "must-never-know" list. Diversion tactics were called for.

"Descendants of the families who once lived in Avebury? Yes, that as well. I'll sort it out with him, thanks. I'm more concerned about the arrangements for our wedding party."

"The barbecue in the garden?" Alma asked.

"Yes. Between Linda's customers, ours, and the group from the pub, there'll be quite a squeeze."

"You forgot the lot staying in Calston," Alma said.

She was right. I had forgotten them.

Cecily sucked her teeth and pointed at the drippy windowpane. "Forecast looks naf. Not ideal for wedding receptions."

Alma placed an onion on the chopping board. "If you ask me, the vicar shouldn't have let them marry in our church. They're no locals. That man's looking after so many parishes, he doesn't care anymore."

Cecily threw a furtive glance at the window, as if she was expecting surplus ears to lurk in our backyard. "He should. Have you heard? They say our guests are from the Mafia."

Alma huffed and hacked the onions into perfect little cubes. I swallowed the sigh that longed to escape. Even without the bones, the village rumor mill was running hot already.

"They're into Italian cooking. That doesn't make them criminals. You better tell your friends that. I mean, whoever mentioned the bit about the Mafia."

"No smoke without fire." Alma attacked a tomato.

"There'll be trouble. Mark my words." With that cheerful comment, Cecily switched on the water kettle. Once it had finished wobbling and steaming, she filled a pot with fragrant Lapsang-Souchong for Chris and a cafetière with my beloved craft coffee. She placed it on a tray, together with my muesli, a rack of toast, and some low-fat cream cheese. "Here you are,

Myrtle. Is that really all you're going to eat?"

I tossed her a wicked grin. "I'll try my best." With that, I escaped into my living room.

—

While a downpour rattled onto the gravel outside, gloom ruled supreme in my private space. As if to compensate, the place was filled with the happy lemon scent of my primrose familiar, squatting on the parquet since her fake terracotta pot was too big for the windowsill.

"Hey, Petty, how's life?"

The pot rose in a swirl of pink sparks and floated across to the seating area in an unspoken invitation. I placed my tray on the coffee table and gently nudged aside the cat, stretched out to her full length on the settee.

"Brr?"

"Sorry, sweets, but I wish to sit down. And I also wish to point out this is my sofa."

Tiddles tossed me a baleful glare and clambered into her knitting basket. I savored my coffee, watching the primula dip her flowers and pop the occasional spark that winked out of sight on the wooden floor.

"I hope your night was better than mine. These blasted bones gave me nightmares. Unless it was the curry. Mukherjee's uses far too much ghee."

The plant pot leaned toward me, as if keen to learn more.

"Nah, must've been to do with the skeleton. It's silly really, but I've got this hunch something's quite wrong, and it's something to do with the coven. Again. Does that make sense?"

The pot rose and landed on the coffee table.

"Last time I only worked out the coven was in trouble when it was much too late. Seriously, I can't make the same mistake twice."

The lemony scent increased. Like a soothing balm, it entered my nostrils and filled my body with calm. I reached out and fingered a leaf, sturdy and fragile all at once, like the rest of my astonishing floral friend. "Thank you, that helps. I'll cope. Somehow."

Petty stilled. The next moment, a rap sounded on the windowpane.

I groaned. Couldn't a woman enjoy five minutes of peace here? I headed across and opened the window to a gust of warm, wet air.

"Myrtle?" The Colonel was waiting in the car park, geared up in olive boots, tan rain poncho, and a floppy hat that dripped water from its brim. Buster, wearing a checkered doggie raincoat and looking sorry for himself, cowered beside his master.

"Morning, Colonel, why don't you come inside for a cuppa? My back door is always open. Well, during daytime it is."

"Thank you, too kind, but we have a date with the V.E.T." He directed a meaningful glance at his hound. "Just wanted to take him out for a quick walk so he can let off some steam."

Fat chance.

The Colonel looked left and then right. "Uh, I've a confession to make."

"You hexed something by mistake?"

"What? No. Not to the best of my knowledge."

"Jolly good."

"It's to do with your, eh ...nettles. I couldn't resist and went to the stile."

His words kicked straight into my belly. "Don't tell me the dratted bones have disappeared."

Elmsworth barked a laugh. "No, they were there. What a sorry sight. I know, I know, rather nosy of me."

"It's fine. Means, I won't take the cops on a wild goose chase later."

"Ah, that would've been my next question. You can tell them someone shot at me while I searched the stile."

"What?" My brain conjured up images of Western-style gunslingers. "Why would anyone want to hurt you?"

"Either someone's a lousy shot, or they were aiming for Buster. They hit a tree a few meters to my left. Used an air rifle. I reckon I was being warned off the remains."

"Did you see anyone?"

The rain stopped from one second to the next, and the sun peeped out from behind a cloud. Colonel Elmsworth removed his hat and shook it out.

"No, since I took cover sharpish. There's no point in a counter-attack when one doesn't carry a weapon. Unfortunately, the shooter was clever enough not to move. In the end, I left, using the bushes as a cover. I came straight here since I reckoned you'd rope in that detective sergeant you're friendly with, right?"

"Correct."

"Good. The cops need to know about the shots. What is this place coming to?" He bent down to pat the Chihuahua's head. Buster, fully in character, growled.

"I wonder whether the moron with the gun is the murderer." Elmsworth's sandy mustache bristled with righteous indignation.

"Colonel, I'm not even sure there's been a murder. Let the police sort things out. We've enough on our hands. I'll pass on your news, promised."

For a moment, I was tempted to tell him about Schlüsselblum's cryptic message. But there was no point in sharing something that might turn out to be nothing worse than yet another dead end to the foray into the coven's convoluted history.

"Good, thanks. And you're right about having enough to do. We're trying our best, Damian, Rosie, and I. Doesn't stop certain coven members from *still* holding back information that belongs in our database."

*Tell me something new.*

"Not much we can do about that. We'll simply have to stick to our plan."

The plan was to have Chris program the database that would contain the coven's lore, currently scattered among its members, and then enter the text from the two remaining grimoires, the Coldron recipe book and the Wytchett's laundry list. Those witches wanting the access code for the database would have to submit their own legacy first.

So far the theory.

"One of these days, someone's gonna catch a cold, not knowing how hexing works. But I'm preaching to the converted. Give my regards to your friendly copper." Elmsworth slapped his hat back on, gave me a determined nod, and marched off, his retreat covered by a parting snarl from Buster.

—

The Colonel left, but the echo of his words circled in my ears. Aunt Eve in her urn and Dot dying in a prison hospital already had "caught a cold." Setting up a database to map our magical skylles was a step in the right direction, but quite a few coven members continued to guard their precious heirlooms like broody hens.

Magic didn't come easy. With a sigh, I closed the window.

"Guess, I'd better get cracking." I sat and spooned cereal that tasted of cardboard. To top the culinary experience, the strawberries rivaled the raindrops in taste. That's assuming raindrops can be sour. Naturally, the toast and coffee had gone cold.

Preoccupied with my less than delicious breakfast, it took me a while until the silence in the room registered. I glanced up and regarded the primula, still and mute like any ordinary houseplant. Something bristly brushed the back of my throat.

"Petty?"

The blossoms turned my way.

"You okay?"

The leaves drooped.

"Is it about Elmsworth?"

Petty's leaves and blossoms rustled, and the pot shifted back and forth.

"Mh, not sure I understand you. Do you want to come with me? Is that it?"

The pot bounced and landed again in a shower of sparks.

"Sorry little one, won't work."

Petty vanished, only to reappear immediately afterward.

"No, not even if you go invisible. It's just not feasible. How about a visit to the farm later? You like Jen and Marty, don't you?"

The pot bobbed up and down, which I knew meant a yes. I stroked the velvety blossoms of my miracle plant and was just about to leave the room when she jerked, dipped, and banged her pot on the table.

"Sorry, you can't come with me, and I need to get ready."

A wild rushing and rustling of stalks were the response, a clear sign of agitation. Whatever Petty's problem might be, I couldn't deal with it now. I had hardly enough time to clean my teeth and say a temporary goodbye to Chris before meeting Sarah.

# 3

## OLD FRIENDS

Sarah nudged the nettles aside with her foot, clad in a smart, black ankle boot. Luckily, Colonel Elmsworth was right and the bones were still around.

"Sometimes I wonder what made me choose such a crap profession," Sarah said. "Seriously."

Detective Constable Cameron, who had been speaking on the phone, cut the connection. "The SOCO is on his way. The pathologist is …there."

He pointed out a male figure trotting up from the street, carrying what appeared to be a metal briefcase.

Once the guy had clambered across the stile, he gave us the briefest of greetings before he groaned to his knees and examined the remains in the greenery.

"I pronounce this fellow to be quite dead," was his unsurprising conclusion, proffered a short while later in a gruff-sounding voice. "Before I can tell you how long he's been that way, I need to get him to the lab. For it's a he, in case you didn't notice."

"The pelvis gives it away," Cameron said, the teeth in his

swarthy face as white as his shirt. "It's too narrow for a female."

The pathologist, still crouching on the ground, clapped a slow applause.

"What can you tell us about the state this guy's in?" Sarah asked.

"State? He's dead. Given the degradation of the bones, we're talking quite some time."

I could almost see numbers counting down on Sarah's forehead as she wrestled with her self-control. "I'm referring to the fact the remains are all over the place. Femur next to the skull, the pelvis on top of these ribs here, that sort of thing."

"A deceased contortionist?" was the sour response.

Sarah pinched the bridge of her nose. "Ms. Coldron has given me reason to believe the skeleton might've been dumped at some point yesterday mid-morning or early afternoon."

The pathologist snorted. "Coldron? Oh, you're the female who keeps finding dead bodies for us. Congratulations. Don't do it again."

What a cheerful sod. I slapped a five-star smile on my face, hoping it might counterbalance Sarah's murderous expression. Not that the doctor took any notice of either of us. Instead, he prodded the skull with a gloved finger.

Then he looked up. "To answer your implied question, Sergeant Widdlethorpe, yes, chappie died somewhere else quite a while ago, decomposed, and ended up in our backyard courtesy of some unknown idiot. This doesn't have to be a local crime. Doesn't even have to be a crime, which means I'll be wasting my time."

Sarah sighed. "Okay. As soon as our SOCO friends are done taking their pictures, this shambles is all yours, Doc. When do you think I could have some prelims?"

The pathologist, still crawling around on all fours, growled up at her. "Since this guy isn't exactly fresh, there's no urgency. It's not that I'm not busy, you know?"

Sarah sighed once more before she waved me aside, away

from the bone doctor and a snickering Constable Cameron. "Okay, Myr. Thanks for this."

"You mean finding another body and adding to your workload?"

"You only did your civic duty. No need for you to be involved any further, though. We'll take it from here."

"Last time, my involvement proved quite useful, didn't it?"

"True. However, I prefer to solve my cases myself. Should it be necessary, I'll call. Hang on, there's one last thing you can do for me." She pulled her notebook from the pocket of her taupe raincoat. "I know where the Ragworts live, but I require the address of that Colonel ...what's his name again?"

"James Elmsworth. And you'll find him in Ouagadougou Cottage, 17 Main Street."

Sarah raised a well-shaped brow. Raindrops glistened in her spiked, dark-brown hair. "That's an address and a half."

"If I understand him correctly, he spent part of his service years in Africa. He's a lovely man. His Chihuahua isn't quite so nice. Still, no reason to take potshots at the creature."

"No, unless somebody worried Fido might make off with a bone." She pocketed her notebook.

"The least you can do is pass on Doc Sunshine's ruling on the bones, once he's deigned to do his job. Can't say I was overjoyed when I found Skelly yesterday, so it's sort of personal."

Sarah turned her face at the heavens, got a drop in her eye and blinked it away. "Okay, okay. I'll most likely regret this later, but if I can, I'll let you know."

Cameron stepped up. "Sarge, is it okay if I drive Ms. Coldron back to her B&B? She came out here especially for us. And I could talk to that Colonel while I'm in the village."

"You do that. Here's the address." She ripped a page from her notebook and handed it over.

On another occasion, we would have embraced. But since she was working, all I did was wave at my friend and follow DC Cameron to the police car.

—

Fifteen minutes later, I said goodbye to the constable and headed for the Witch's Retreat, slowly, to give myself time to mull things over. If Sarah seriously believed she could shut me out, she'd have to think twice. As a responsible business owner in Avebury, my obligation was to protect the village from further harm. As the leader of the local coven, I needed to rule out a connection between the skeleton, the shooting, and our merry gang of magical misfits. It was bad enough somebody had dumped a skeleton on our doorstep. Either the same culprit or yet another moronic git then used Elmsworth and his hound for target practice.

All of this meant only one thing—by foul or fair means, I would have to keep an eye on the investigation, even if it was only to reassure myself that my hunch was wrong and neither the misfits nor the village were in trouble.

*Right? Right.*

Arguing with myself never took long. After all, I was a sensible person who listened to the voice of reason.

Once inside the B&B, I checked my messages, but Schlüsselblum hadn't called. I thumbed his number and was pressing the phone to my ear when the landline at reception rang.

"Oh, rats." I swiped the call away and dashed across. "Witch's Retreat B&B, Myrtle speaking?"

"Ah, so pleased to get hold of you in person." The voice was cultured and not without an undertone of amusement. So, why did it send spider feet skittering down my spine?

"I beg your pardon?"

"No need to. I simply wanted to check how you were doing and whether you found the time to reconsider your position?"

I stared at the handset, listened to the unctuous tones of false sympathy dribbling from the speaker, and wondered how much of the plot I was missing. It had to be a fair-sized chunk, as I couldn't work out for the life of me what the caller was on about. And who he might be. Though the oily voice sounded vaguely familiar.

Miller perhaps, the funeral director who'd looked so well after my aunt? When talking about my position, was he referring to a funeral that still hadn't happened, almost three months later? But Miller had genuinely cared, helped me cope with my grief, and he never sounded like the parody of a used-car dealer.

"Hello?"

"Who are you?"

"Ah, frightfully sorry. I keep making that mistake. I assume people will recognize me. Of course, you're so right. Our acquaintance is of a fleeting nature. How I wished we could rectify that."

I gave the guy on the phone a mental downgrade from car dealer to snake oil salesman. A clever move, since it finally helped me put a name to the voice. I was talking to Chris's uncle Bob Ignatius, the man whose lackey caused the accident that killed my parents, the man who pissed off my aunt so badly, she twisted her magic, killing herself in the process.

"Mr. Ignatius, I told you to leave me alone."

Chris's uncle laughed. "Ah, always so charming, so charming. I didn't want to impose my presence too soon. I fully understand it isn't appreciated. But I'd really, really like to hear a better answer than no."

"For that, you can wait until hell freezes over. Have a nice life—"

"Shouldn't you care about the well-being of your tribe? There've been some disconcerting developments lately, I hear."

My stomach plummeted to the wooden floor, polished and spotless courtesy of the Simpkins sisters.

Slap-bang, here was a good reason for my bad hunch. Bob Ignatius, scion of the witch hunters and top UK entrepreneur, had wanted first my aunt and now me to hex for him, supposedly to gain an edge on the competition. How foolish of me to assume the man would ever take no for an answer.

"What are you trying to achieve with your skeleton stunt? And shooting at the Colonel was downright idiotic. Just so you know, we've involved the police."

"Skeleton? Uh …my dear Ms. Coldron, rest assured that I do nothing without an ulterior motive. However, I told you before how much I resent unnecessary violence. Shooting people falls squarely into that category."

Translate that into "I never get my hands dirty." But he sounded quite determined. "You didn't shoot at Elmsworth? Or, rather, have a minion gun for him?"

"No, Ms. Coldron, I did not. As you phrased it so aptly, that would be idiotic. Not conducive to our business relationship at all. We could do wonders together, you and I. Of course, I would make it worth your while."

Keenness had crept into the smarmy voice, and an alarm bell was clanging away in my head. This conversation had to end. Like now.

"Mr. Ignatius, I hate repeating myself. No matter what you throw at me, neither I nor the coven will, in any form or fashion, cooperate with you. Ever."

"Sure, sure. I'll send you a number where you can reach me should you change your mind."

"I won't. Don't call again."

I pressed the off button and sucked in a deep breath to calm my galloping heart. The conversation replayed in my head, and I winced. By jumping to conclusions and verbalizing my suspicions about the skeleton, I had played into his hand. At least, the call hadn't been completely in vain since Ignatius had denied responsibility for the shooting, and his refusal had a genuine ring to it.

The relief lasted only an instant. What if an Ignatius minion, going beyond their brief, shot at the Colonel? That sort of thing happened before.

Unless I had totally the wrong end of the stick, and there

was a second villain on the set while Ignatius played jolly mind games.

I slammed my fist on the reception counter. Pain shot up my arm.

*Ow.*

I needed a sounding board, someone who could help me unknot my thoughts. Chris would be coding and was out of reach. Who else could I ask?

The answer pinged in immediately afterward—Jenna. Involving her would help distract my friend from her gran's crimes. Perfect.

I swung around—and barreled into Alma, who staggered backward from the impact.

"Oops, so sorry. On my way out again."

She rubbed her arms and gave me a lopsided grin. "Takes more than a little bounce to shake me. One of these days you'll break a leg with all that hustling about. Oh, what about the tomatoes and mushrooms?"

Nothing could be further from my mind than grocery shopping. However, the Riders of the Apocalypse would most likely descend on the Witch's Retreat if we ran out of frying matter. "Cripes, forgot. All right, I'll go now."

I bolted for the back door, Alma's "drive carefully," drifting after me.

As if I ever did anything else.

—

Returned from my foray at the greengrocer's, I set the blinker for Tadpole Lane and Wytchett Farm. Just as I turned the steering wheel, a silver sports car materialized from absolutely bloody nowhere, shot past me, and cut into my lane, with only inches between its taillights and my minivan's front bumper.

I stomped on the brakes and leaned on the horn. My heartbeat zoomed into the stratosphere. In the back of the van, something crashed. The other car sped away, unconcerned.

"Tosser." Of course, I'd forgotten to memorize the number plate.

A fruity aroma filled the van's interior. No detective skills were needed to deduce that at least one tomato crate had taken a hit.

Spot-on. Safely arrived at my destination, I found the contents of two crates of mushrooms rolling around on the floor while a case of tomatoes had smooshed into the front of the cargo compartment. It was smeared in a reddish goo that dripped down the panel and pooled on the mat.

Relax, my inner voice said.

Since the order had been placed with the largesse typical of the Simpkins sisters, there was enough left to feed hungry guests for days to come. I turned my back on my soiled vehicle, walked up to the front door of Wytchett Farm, and banged the knocker. Nothing happened for quite a while, but that wasn't unusual. While waiting, I counted only one pair of mud-encrusted wellington boots standing on the stoop, which meant Jenna and the kids were out, but her brother was most likely in. The next moment, the door swung inward and a bleary-eyed Marty appeared. His auburn hair was even more disheveled than usual, his clothes rumpled, which told me the man must've been enjoying a well-deserved nap.

"Oops, now I've woken you up. Jenna and the twins aren't here, I suppose?"

Marty scratched his bristly cheek and suppressed a yawn. "Nope, sorry. As to waking me up, I'm glad you came. I caught some Z's as Greg would say and plain forgot to set my alarm. Uh, do come in. Fancy a coffee? I need one, otherwise I'll never get my head cleared."

Jenna's brother stepped back from the entrance, and I followed him along the corridor into a kitchen filled with a fading potpourri of exotic aromas. I couldn't stop my gaze from slipping across to the door in the far corner, hidden behind gaudy aprons. Below lurked a basement full of shadows, a place that had seen my darkest hour when I almost lost Petty.

Water bubbled and the aroma of coffee percolating pushed the ghosts aside. Marty was never very talkative, but today he was downright subdued.

"What's wrong?"

Marty reached for two blue mugs hanging from the shelf and poured. "Cream? You don't take sugar, right?"

"Yes, please. And no, I don't. Marty—"

He waved at one of the hardwood chairs and dropped onto the other with a groan as if he was in his dotage, not his late thirties.

I sat.

"She's gone." He looked up and raised his hands. "Ack, should have phrased this differently. She'll be back, don't you worry. That's typical Jen. When the going gets too rough, she runs. At least this time I know where she is. With a friend in Weston-super-Mare and only for a few days. She called me yesterday evening. The boys are loving it."

He sipped his coffee, the weariness in his ruddy face at odds with his words.

An imaginary icy fist grabbed my heart and squeezed. *Damn Dot. Damn her many times over.*

Jenna was gifted but vulnerable, the reason she now carried her grandmother's murders on her frail shoulders.

"How can I help?" Gone were this afternoon's niggly little nuisances. Gone was my worry over the skeleton, Ignatius, and the shooting. Here, I had found real trouble and a friend in need. Two friends, actually.

Marty placed his coffee on the table and smiled at me with his kind, warm eyes. No matter what storm might shake the roof of the Wytchetts's farmstead, this man would always be around to nail the shingles back down.

"Nah, better leave her be. She'll come round. See, four days ago Gran died without ever waking up, and that sent her off."

The fist squeezed my heart again. Dottie had sneaked out

like the coward she was, leaving her family to face the music. Was I surprised? Not really.

"You're bothered about something, aren't you? Want to share?"

Marty possessed no magical skylles. At least that's what he claimed, but I'd always found him to be amazingly empathic. "Mh. You heard about the bones?"

"The ones you and Chris discovered? Mel and the Colonel called me earlier. The news is all over Avebury. Nobody seems to be missing, though." He sipped his coffee and frowned. "Mel wonders whether someone's trying to put another spanner into the local business. After what Gran did, it won't take much to scare the tourists away again."

This time, the icy fist punched straight into my belly. "That was one reason for coming. You wouldn't believe who rang me."

Jenna's brother raised a questioning brow.

"Chris's uncle. Bob Ignatius. Wants me to consider his proposal for a magical cooperation between the misfits and himself. The nerve of him. What you just told me fits. He'd do anything to cause trouble for us, hoping I'll cave in."

"You mean he dumped the skeleton?"

"Possibly, though he didn't admit it in so many words. We don't need more headlines screaming murder, do we?"

"True. No, we don't. Can't see the man getting his hands dirty, though."

"No, but he employs minions who then ignore their instructions. Ignatius acted cagey over the skeleton but claims he didn't order the shooting, and there I'm tempted to believe him. Uh, you know what I'm referring to, yes?"

"Yup, the Colonel complained at length. Nasty, that. Guess if we find out who dumped the skeleton, we'll most likely nail the shooter."

"The pathologist seems to think the bones are old and the poor chap could've died anywhere. Which would explain why nobody's missing."

Marty poured more coffee. "Bad news about Ignatius, but I reckon we'll just have to wait and see what the cops say."

I would pay for all that caffeine tonight. Oh well, the brew tasted delicious, the cream coming fresh from Marty's cows.

"I don't want to be caught napping again, especially not with that tosser breathing down my neck."

"Not much you can do, is there? As you say yourself, the dead fellow could be an import. Though...."

Jenna's brother was a great guy, but he chewed his thoughts as pensively as his cows their cud. "Tell me."

"Why don't you talk to the curator of the museum? If anyone's savvy about bones, it's him. He's got a whole cellar full. Failing that, try Jedd, the director of the so-called Society for the Promotion of Neolithic Wiltshire. Bit of a mouthful, innit? Anyway, he might be able to help, though he's a right bastard."

"What do you mean by that?"

"Treats his interns like dirt—you know about the society's intern scheme?"

"Not much."

"He makes them do all sorts of rum jobs totally unrelated to their studies. Easier on the budget, see? He's as ambitious as they come, that chap. Sucks up to management. And he drives like a maniac."

It appeared I might already have run into that charmer. "Not sure I want to talk to him."

"Me neither, but he's pretty clued up when it comes to historical stuff. Gotta be careful, though. It'd be suspicious if you just marched into the society's local offices. Or the museum. Unless you know these guys?"

"I'm afraid I don't, no."

"In that case, you'll need someone to introduce you. Won't be me, for sure. Not much time for museums and stuff." He grinned. "Though I took the boys once."

That was excellent advice, just what I had come for. "That's easy. Since she took over Knick-Knack's, my cousin's all pally with the local crowd and knows absolutely everything there is to know. Seriously, Daisy can give MI6 a run for its money." She hadn't actually bought the shop yet, but with me backing the offer, the sale was a formality.

He nodded. "Good one. That'll work."

All fired up, I thanked Marty and, filled with a renewed sense of purpose, drove to the gift shop.

# 4

## SLEUTHING AWAY

The cowbells over the entrance to Knick-Knack's announced my arrival with their usual ear-splitting clamor. As if lured by an invisible force, my gaze found the mass-produced country wines, dips, and jams now filling the shelves. They weren't on a par with the delicacies cooked up by the local Women's Institute, but it would take a while until customers would dare to buy those again. Otherwise, the choice of goods hadn't changed. They ranged from souvenirs to blankets, scarves, and soaps. Their scents filled the room with an aromatic blend of antique rose and sandalwood, chased by just the teensiest trace of saltpeter from the stone walls. As I headed for the cash desk, I let my fingers trail over a soft mohair plaid in lovely pastel colors.

I checked the price tag.

*Ouch.* Expensive.

"Can I help you?" a voice behind the counter chirped.

My cousin, perfect makeup, perfect outfit, perfect everything, jumped up and put aside her book. Upside down, I couldn't make out much of the title, but the handsome man, his frilly shirt open at the chest, a swooning female sagging against his impressive pectorals, screamed historical romance.

"Oh, there you are. I was wondering where you'd got to. Mrs. Mornings insists the police have been around again. Something to do with that skeleton?"

The blasted neighbors. Next time, Sarah would have to pick me up in Swindon. Or Scotland. Not that there would be a next time.

Hopefully.

"Yes, Sarah and Constable Cameron wanted to take a peek. Honestly, I wonder how our friendly co-witch gets anything done when she's on gossip patrol all day."

My cousin giggled. "She's not a bad sort. Just a tick intense."

That was one way of describing the woman. "Okay, she's handed in her stuff, unlike some others. Makes a pleasant change. Uh, Daisy, apropos sharing, I need a favor from you."

Daisy toyed with the fluffy tip of her auburn braid. "I get it, you're sleuthing again," she said in her breathless little girl voice. "Super. What can I do?"

Behind my cousin's shapely front and spaniel eyes hid a maze of a mind that I suspected—not for the first time—to be a lot sharper than she let on.

"I want this business with the bones sorted. It's bothering me. I mean, I can at least check if the thing is local. Taken from the museum, for example. Marty suggested I should talk to the curator and quiz him about the bones in his cellar. Could be someone nicked a few."

"Ugh, gruesome." Daisy shuddered with gory delight. "But there's something more to it, right? Something you're not telling."

She batted her caked lashes. Oh yes, my cousin wasn't the ditz she pretended to be.

"Guess who called."

"Search me."

"Chris's uncle. Bob Ignatius."

Daisy's eyes widened. "Oh."

"Exactly. Still wants me to hex for him. If he's somehow involved, I can't just sit on my bum."

"Fair enough. So, what do you want me to do?"

"How well do you know this curator? Or the director of this strange promo society?"

"Jedd? I've heard about him. He such an …There's, like, new management at head office or something, and he's trying to show off. Pip says so."

"Who's Pip?"

"Oh, one of this year's interns at the society. There's three of them, all rather nice."

A deceptive mildness had crept into Daisy's tone, and there was a predatory gleam in her eyes. I deduced Pip had to be male and felt sorry for him. And for Greg, Daisy's partner.

"So, you don't know Jedd in person?"

"Nah. Can't say I'm sorry about that."

"Mh. And the curator?"

"Ah yes, Hagbottom-Smythe. Bit of a fuddy-duddy, though I haven't met him either. He doesn't seem to be much of a shopper. Hey, Mel arranged the Open Day with him. Why don't you try her? She'd still be helping out at the manor. I think the woman who normally does the tours is sick. All you have to do is scoot across." Daisy hooked a thumb over her shoulder in the vague direction of the manor.

Just then, the cowbells jangled discordantly, and a group of hikers entered. I blew Daisy a grateful air kiss and left her to deal with her customers.

—

Tudor by origin, Avebury Manor had weathered the centuries remarkably unfazed. A dizzying variety of chimney stacks and gables added a whimsical touch to the grayish building. The house had never been a grand lord's seat; three floors was the limit of its aspirations. But the place was quirky, well-suited to the village.

I picked my way along the uneven stones of the garden path, framed by rows of fragrant lavender. The head gardener, a wizened and sour-faced man in his sixties, and his young helper were hard at work, trimming those parts of the plants that had gone leggy. As I passed by, the head gardener rose, straightened, and held his back with a groan.

Then, he waved his pruning shears around. "Cal? Wakey, wakey. You gonna fetch the seedlings this century?"

"Actually, I think—"

"Stop rabbiting on about what you think. Just get them."

"Sure." As he passed, the young man bounced me a conspiratorial grin.

"Is it bad?" I asked *sotto voce*.

"He's okay, really. Only his back giving him gyp. Among us three, I think I drew the winner." He winked and sprinted off.

The head gardener turned his back on the path, which suited me just fine.

I entered the manor. To my right, the flagstone corridor gave access to a living room whose furniture and wallpaper bounced the visitor straight back to the Twenties. A gauzy figure flitted past the shelves, stopped, and waved a dimpled hand.

"Hello, Myr."

"Hi, Mel."

My fellow witch emerged from behind the chunky wireless radio that added subdued vintage jazz to the ambiance. Mel's generous curves were set off with filmy robes and glittery scarves. Bracelets and hoop earrings jangled as she fluttered around, so much more light-footed than I would ever be.

"What are you up to these days?"

"By that, you're referring to my run-in with Skelly, correct? Everyone else is."

She played with the amber beads resting on her ample bosom. "Eh, yes. No need to explain about Ignatius and your reason for popping over. Daisy already gave me chapter and verse. There aren't any visitors around, so talk as freely as you like."

"Great stuff. You seem to know this museum chappie. What's his name again?"

"Hagbottom-Smythe?"

"Him, yes. It would be decidedly odd if I just waltzed in and enquired about his bone collection."

Mel snickered. "He's a bit of a zany character and rather full of himself, so a frontal approach won't work, no. He's certainly proud of his collection. Trouble is, the volunteers keep unearthing so many things, they're out of display space. The latest finds are from the Bronze Age, I believe."

Could the skeleton be that old? If that were the case, the pathologist would bend poor Sarah's ear.

"This might be nothing worse than a silly hoax," Mel said.

"Not if Ignatius is involved, no."

"True. Right-oh, let me see if Smithey bites. Uh, what shall I tell him?"

"That I found the bones and want to help the police, I guess." *Urgh.* Guilty of illicit sleuthing. Given a bit of luck, Sarah would never learn about my shenanigans, otherwise my bum would be on the hot griddle.

Mel picked up an authentic-looking rotary phone and walked to the window, the cable trailing behind. The person, presumably the curator, at the other end of the conversation took some convincing, but I couldn't blame him. I really was winging it. Fortunately, Mel could talk the hind leg off a donkey.

She placed the receiver in its cradle. "Right, Smithey— Hagbottom-Smythe will talk to you. He's a bit upset, but that's normal, so ignore the ramblings. Flatter him about his research, drool over his exhibits, and you'll have him eating from your hand."

*The things I do for the coven...*

I thanked Mel for her help and left the manor. Outside, watery sunshine mellowed the scene, and the temperature was warm enough for me to shrug out of my fleece. The two gardeners were still at work, the older raking the lawn, the younger man pushing a wheelbarrow full of clippings around the corner of the old house.

From the church tower issued a series of melancholic bongs. Noon already, and I still hadn't touched base with Schlüsselblum. He was a busy man. All witching matters had to be conducted outside work hours. No wonder we kept missing each other. I left him another message and cursed the fact we couldn't send emails like ordinary people.

But that was one of the things Chris had warned us about. "You never know who reads your emails, especially if you use free providers."

Nothing the coven did would ever be safe, exposure a constant threat. However, mulling about the unfairness of fate would get me exactly nowhere, so I made my way to the museum.

———

At the far end of the courtyard, a handful of tourists had decided it was summer and time for an outdoor lunch. I passed the stripey umbrellas and made my way to the short part of the L-shaped building that housed the Magic Mushroom Café and the museum, both hunkering under a cap of weathered thatch. The structure gave off strong barn vibes, which it must have been at some point in its patchy past. The double glass doors, propped open with a cannonball, didn't sit quite right with the rural theme, nor did the raised voices drifting through an open window.

"Seriously, what's Mel thinking? I don't lose my bones. Ever," grumbled a male bass that could only belong to Gag ...no, Hagbottom-Smythe.

"Of course not, John." Higher and more strident, the voice sounded familiar. My synapses clicked. That had to be Anna Hutchinson, the churchwarden. She had sharp gray eyes, a long nose, and—having been born in this place—cared little for newcomers.

"And who's that Coldron person she's sending across?"

"She's a newbie. Runs the Witch's Retreat. It appears she's found some. Human remains. I mean."

"So what. That's a problem for the gang in blue, not for me."

He was right, and I needed to make up my mind; I couldn't remain where I was, halfway in and halfway out of the museum. The way those two were going on told me now wasn't the time to announce my presence. Instead, I might glean some intel by listening in. Since the glass door reflected an entrance area filled only with exhibition panels, not people, Anna and the curator must be somewhere deeper into the building. I slipped inside, hiding behind the first panel I found. A whole fleet of them snaked their way through the museum, guiding the visitor to the glass cases at the back, which was where Anna and the curator must be standing. Owed to some great acoustics, they were conveniently out of sight but not out of hearing.

The panel also hid a heap of cardboard cartons, which I hit with a muffled *whoomph*.

*Rats.* I held my breath.

"Well, seems like the coppers have already turned up. Ms. Coldron was seen leaving in a squad car this morning," Anna said with relish.

"If that woman's been arrested, why should I talk to her?" Hagbottom-Smythe asked. "I've got more important things to do. Like categorizing the arrow tips. If I ever get the time, that is. Guess who's in charge of stopping Peter's rookies from messing things up? It's typical, really. He has a bright idea, and I'm the one to make it work."

Oh dear, someone was feeling sorry for himself. I peeped through the gap beside the panel, but I only caught a glimpse of Anna's blazer-clad back, close to a dusty showcase.

"Annoying, isn't it? Though I think Ms. Coldron's quite friendly with the cops. Must've come in handy when her guest was murdered." That last tasty morsel was served in a voice quivering with the sort of excitement that spoke of thrill rather than compassion.

Hagbottom-Smythe groaned. "Oh, she's the niece of the nosy parker who set up the posh B&B and fell from the attic, right? Took over, did she? Well, if her guests keep getting offed, she won't last long. Certainly not if she cliques with the rest of these blasted newbies. I don't understand why the Wytchetts or Mel even bother talking to them."

*Note to self—don't listen in on conversations. You might not like what you get to hear about yourself.* Dust tickled my nose, and I struggled to suppress a sneeze. The tickling became an explosion. I froze, ready to bolt.

"What was that?" Anna asked.

"Rats in the thatch, most likely."

I sent the grumpy curator a mental blessing.

"Heavens, John, you really got up on the wrong foot today."

"No, I didn't."

"Sure, sure. Your facts are still wrong. All those newcomers have local roots."

"You mean, as in their gardens? Ho, ho, ho."

Father Christmas had nothing on him.

"Don't be silly. I'm talking about their ancestors. Check the church annals. Or those gravestones at the back. Coldron, Cowslip, Asher—they used to live in the area." Anna's voice had taken on a lecturing tone.

*Uh-oh.* We'd have to watch that woman.

"Dearest Anna, that was over four hundred years ago. Anyway, I spent time I don't have and checked our cellar. All my remains are present and accounted for."

"Take it as a warning. If I were you, I'd be a tad more careful with the keys."

"What about them?"

"You leave them lying around."

"Ah, bah. Nothing's ever happened. That's because there's

nothing worth stealing, neither up here nor in the basement. Everything halfway valuable gets snapped up by the county museum. Tell me, who came up with the silly idea that because there's a heap of bones lying around, they should be mine?"

Footsteps came closer, and in a rush of lukewarm air, a man blurred past my panel. I squeezed against the stack of boxes, but the latest arrival wasn't interested in the exhibits.

"Oh, there you are, John." The man had a pleasant tenor. "When I nipped across earlier, I only found your intern."

"My intern? Your intern more likely. I should have hired a temp from the local agency as I wanted to. That Nina person is useless. I don't know what they teach at university these days, but it doesn't seem to include typing skills."

"Careful, John," Anna pleaded. "She's in the office. She might hear you."

"So what," Hagbottom-Smythe said. But he had lowered his voice. "And what on earth made you think that Pip bloke is cut out for the tourist info? I've spent ages training him, and what does he remember? Zilch. It's like talking to a brick wall." The curator's volumes were on the rise again.

It didn't take a Sherlock to deduce the newcomer had to be Jedd, the infamous director of the promo society.

"Well, with most of our voluntary helpers on cruises to the Galapagos Islands, or walking trips in Transylvania, I had to find a stopgap," Jedd said. "Why don't you ask the boy who helps in the garden? Maybe he's more competent."

"What?" Hagbottom-Smythe's voice had gained significant decibels. "And start all over again? With the under-gardener? You must be joking. Your fault if you let your pensioners leave during high season."

"Well, they *are* volunteers. Happens every year, in case you didn't notice. This time, we're actually lucky there aren't that many tourists around."

My leg muscles tingled. Standing still for so long was taking its toll. I shifted, mindful of not making more noise.

"Anyway, the feedback forms have come in, and the visitors love our service. That's why I came. I wanted to thank you." The director's voice might be pleasant, but there was a false charm dripping from his words that reminded me of Ignatius.

"Pah," said Hagbottom-Smythe. "They have no clue what to expect." He paused for a moment. "Has something been done about that stone? Has it finally been cordoned off?"

"The one you think might be wonky? It's fine, really, but to humor you, Anna'll ask the tourists not to touch that one. Should be safe enough."

"They shouldn't be allowed to do that anywhere," Anna said. "I hate it."

"That's our unique selling point," Jedd said. "You can touch the stones. You don't need a blasted telescope like you do at Stonehenge."

"Hah, if they touch the wobbly one, it'll be the last thing they do." The curator was back in shouting mode. "Told you before, it must be blocked off."

"John, it's all in hand. We can't bar the tourists from our main attraction if we want them to return. Listen, I wanted to go through the feedback with you and discuss how we can improve the tours. The visitors love all those tiny details. Like, how the ancients could dig out nine-foot ditches without spades, that sort of thing."

"But that's my job," Anna wailed. "I spent hours on the analysis. I coordinate the tours, so I should also ensure—"

"Yes, yes, my dear. Excellent job, well done. I'll take it from here. HQ wants to see suggestions pronto, so we better shift gears."

A phone shrilled.

"Oh no, it's these fake mafiosi again." Stress vibrated in Anna's voice. "They won't marry in my church. No way. Excuse me."

A second later, determined footsteps clacked past me and faded outside.

"Fake mafiosi?" The curator asked. "At least she doesn't have interns."

"She's a decent enough secretary, but with ideas above her station. Now, if you don't mind, let's discuss …"

I didn't get the rest of the sentence. The curator had found his match in Jedd, who must have been frog-marching him away if the shuffling of feet on the concrete floor and the curator's protests were anything to judge by.

My muscles softened with relief, and I slumped against the panel. Which wobbled in its stand and tilted.

Heat surged through my body. I grabbed one side of the board and pulled it toward me, its stand scraping across the cement floor until it steadied once more.

I strained to listen, white noise rushing through my ears. At the back of the exhibition, a door slammed shut. They hadn't heard me.

*Get out, now.* Occasionally, my inner voice could be useful, so I fled from the building into the feeble sunshine.

# 5

## SPAGHETTI JUNCTION

Phone pressed to my ear, I headed for the Magic Mushroom Café. Since Hagbottom-Smythe wasn't missing any bones, there really was no point in bothering him. The young woman answering my call was most understanding and promised to pass on the message about the emergency I'd faked. Schlüsselblum still being incommunicado, the next point on my agenda was a snack.

I would never make a great detective. How did these people survive endless hours of stakeouts in cars that were alternatively freezing or boiling, with only junk food to keep them going? Not my idea of a good life. Sleuthing also was time-consuming. Afternoon sneaked up on me while I was busy talking to people and snooping on the curator. Soon, my guests would arrive.

First things first—my late lunch.

A nasty wind was gusting around the umbrellas, so I chose a table indoors, where I sipped my coffee and savored a crispy, creamy chicken sandwich washed down with a mocha latte. Munching along, I dug around in my purse for a good old-fashioned notepad and pen for my notes. Multi-tasking, that's me.

Unfortunately, some grease transferred from my fingers to the top sheet, so I ripped it off and started afresh.

Okay, so the curator wasn't missing any exhibits, which was a shame since it left me in an investigative limbo. Nobody in the village had gone AWOL, either. I still liked the theory about Chris's uncle stirring up trouble. Not that I liked the notion as such, but his involvement made sense when not much else did.

I noted Ignatius's name and doodled a skull and crossbones.

With the last bite into my sandwich, my teeth snagged a piece of lettuce, so I dropped my notes and removed the greenery, hopefully without smearing too much mayonnaise over my face.

Where was I? Ah, Bob Ignatius. Even if the skeleton originated from somewhere else, someone *did* dump it, and since Chris's uncle never soiled his hands, he would have used a helper, who then got creative. That was my best, my only starting point for the moment.

Could Jedd be that minion? Like Ignatius, he struck me as being an unsavory character, but he too seemed to suffer from a delegation complex, which meant he was just as unlikely to do things himself. His interns, then? Perhaps one of them belonged to a gun club?

I doodled a revolver.

Nah, that notion was as far-fetched as it was difficult to verify.

Hagbottom-Smythe I dismissed. The man came across as cranky, petulant, and a tough one to handle, and it was unlikely Ignatius would employ him. Anna the churchwarden I didn't know well enough, so I added a starburst of question marks to her name.

I stared at my sheet and my mood curdled. All I'd gotten for my troubles were greasy notes, questionable suspects, and an acid stomach.

My phone rapped away as I emptied my cup. Chris was supposed to have fixed the blasted thing, but it kept changing ringtones.

"Myrtle Coldron, Witch's Retreat B&B?"

"Hello, Myrtle. Sorry for stringing you on, life's a bit hectic at the moment. Thought I'd better call while I can," Schlüsselblum said. His English was immaculate, though pronounced too crisply for a native speaker.

"Schl ...eh, Jochen, great to hear from you." Somehow, my hand holding the phone had gone sweaty.

"*Tut mir echt leid.* Unfortunately, I don't have all the facts yet. We're still checking stuff. But I wanted to put you in the picture."

"That's great. Let me guess. Either you ran out of sources, or you found a source that tells us there's no way we'll ever find out what really happened back then."

"Oh, nothing like that. It's not about our history. Well, not in the way you think." On Schlüsselblum's side someone complained in German. It sounded stressed.

"Hang on," Schlüsselblum said. "*Was zum Kuckuck ist jetzt wieder los? Ich bin am Telefon, Mensch.*"

A swift exchange took place, something about budgets. Budgets caused trouble the world over.

The door slammed. A sigh fluttered into my ear.

"Jochen?"

"These days not even my coffee break is safe anymore. Right—"

Determined knocks rang out in the background. "Ack, here's another one. This doesn't work. I'll call you back, okay? Tonight, I should know more." With that, Schlüsselblum was gone, leaving me staring at my smeared phone. What the heck had the man dug up now?

—

The snack a leaden mass in my stomach, I returned to my minivan—only to find its cherry-red roof splotchy with bird poop. Since the van's interior was already covered in caked tomato, why not mess up the rest? Quietly seething, I swung myself into the driver's seat. I was backing out of my space when an engine growled, a horn tooted, and a silver vehicle shot past the back of my van. My heart jumped into my throat, and I jerked at the wheel, nearly ramming the car next to me.

A split second later, tires screeched, the horn went ballistic, and someone screamed.

*Right. That's it.*

I yanked up the handbrake, slammed out of my van, and dashed along the line of parked vehicles until I spotted a low-slung silver sports car, nosing its way into a group of young mothers, kids in prams, and wide-eyed toddlers, some of them bawling. The mothers hauled abuse at the driver, but the car sped away, spraying them with gravel, and was gone in a heartbeat.

"Are you okay?" I asked the nearest woman, who had one kid in a kangaroo sling and a second on the way. Like the others, she wore long swirly skirts and plenty of jewelry. I'd seen them before. They lived in the next village.

"Yeah, guess so, thanks. That man's nuts. He nearly flattened my feet." Her cheeks were flushed, and there was a dangerous glint in her eyes.

"Got his number this time," said another woman, triumphantly waving a scrap of paper. "I'll call the cops."

"Good." I rummaged in my purse for my business card. "This lunatic needs to be taken off the streets. Here's my card. If you need a witness, call me."

"Ta. High time Mister Bigshot Jedd learns a lesson or two."

*Why am I not surprised?* "You know him?"

"After our first run-in with the tosser, I asked around a bit and found out who he was. Likes to live in the fast lane, that one."

"Not for much longer." We grinned at each other.

On my way home, I was singing along with the radio, pleased the obnoxious director wouldn't get away with murder.

———

My upbeat mood carried me through an annoying stint of car cleaning and lasted until I reached the parlor. "Girls, I'm back."

Tiddles opened one greenish rheumy eye, twitched the tip of her tail, and that was as much as I could expect for a greeting. Petty, however, bobbed around me, leaves rustling, stalks whispering, and sparks shooting from the blooms. A few touched my skin. They were as light as a feather, neither warm nor cold. My miracle plant landed on the coffee table and banged her pot twice.

"Okay, you have my attention. What is it?"

The stems with the blooms collapsed and drooped over the rim in a parody of desperation.

"You're tired? Or pissed off because I don't get it? Sorry, I had a hell of a day, and it isn't over yet. Actually, I just wanted to say hello. And relax for a moment."

The flowers shot back up, sparks whizzing in all directions. Again, my primula rapped on the table, only once this time. Next, she zipped to the shelf and hovered in front of the recipe book.

"Ah, the familiar desires the mighty witch to study her grimoire."

More fireworks and agitated greenery, which probably meant yes. Since she'd gone to so much bother, I pulled the tome from the shelf and dropped back onto the settee with a groan. I wouldn't get the timeout I craved. Familiars were supposed to support budding witches and help them grow. There had to be a reason for Petty's outlandish behavior, which meant I'd better pay attention.

I opened the Coldron grimoire lying on my knees. "Any suggestion what I should look for?" Slowly, I leafed through the pages, stopping as soon as Petty banged on the table.

What did we have there? Ah, chocolate chip biscuits, one of auntie's recipes. The trick was to add chili, which gave them a kick.

"Sweetie, I have no time for baking."

The blooms drooped, and the pot nudged the recipe book a few times.

Inspiration struck. "Okay, I think I know what you want."

*Rustle, spark.* The blooms stood to attention.

Once again, I flipped through the recipes my aunt and grandmother had left behind until I hit the empty pages in the middle, where the hexed image I had found and lost must still be lurking. Petty rose and hovered in the airspace over the book where she fired a salvo of sparks. Okay, I might not be the most accomplished practitioner on the planet, but even I got it.

"You're telling me the recipe book's hiding more information than the one image I found."

*Rustle.*

"You're most likely right. These pages aren't really blank, just a bit hexed. But don't ask me how to lift the spell that hides the content, for I don't know."

The flowers drooped.

"Sure, I've done it once. But that was more or less by accident. Someone got murdered in front of my eyes, and I was stressed out. If knowledge comes at the cost of lives, I seriously don't want to find out what else is in here."

The leaves followed the blooms' example and sagged. Then the whole greenery sprung back up, and Petty rapped her pot on the table, twice this time. A twinge squeezed my temples. Petty might mean well, but her magical acrobatics were only one damned thing after a lot of others.

"Sweetie, I mean it. Unless there's something other than homicide to power me up, the blank pages will remain blank." When I glanced at my primula, she was parked on the table, unmoving and giving me the distinct impression she might be peeved.

Defeated, I collapsed against the backrest of the sofa. Would I ever get on top of my paranormal skylles? Would I even want to?

A sonorous bonging sounded through the house, and otherworldly challenges dropped into the recesses of my mind. My guests had arrived ahead of time.

I jumped up and checked my face in the mirror over the mantelpiece. Makeup around gray-blue eyes okay-ish, fly-away strawberry hair not brilliant but not off either, but the white blouse didn't compliment a pale face where my freckles stood out like fly-poo. Tough, it would have to do. I hurried into the corridor the same moment the bell gonged again. Having plastered a welcoming smile on my face, I threw open the door.

Framed by the hanging geraniums, a blonde woman stood on my porch, wearing a pinstripe suit, a black fedora, and carrying a violin case.

—

Hours later, I gargled, spat out the mouthwash, and ran my tongue along my teeth. Smooth and clean, as they should be. "That'll be one heck of a hen party," I said.

"Mh," said Chris from the bedroom.

"My eyes pretty much popped when the first guest showed up. In full Mafia gear. Took me a moment to recover. She, of course, laughed her head off."

"Mh?"

"Glad Alma and Cecily weren't there. They wouldn't have been amused."

"Mh."

"Ta-dah," I sort of half-jumped, half-danced from the bathroom in my new nightie. Fashioned of apricot lace and for once not bought at an outlet, it was fiendishly expensive and somewhat see-through. But that was the desired effect.

A silver shaft of moonlight penetrated the slit between the curtains and slashed across the duvet. Earlier, the rain had been pelting the windowpanes, April masking as summer.

Chris was in the bed. A frown on his forehead, he was tapping away at the tablet on his chest. Sadly, said chest was covered in a profusion of dark hair. What others might find manly was a tick too wild for my taste, but then you can't have everything. The rest of his body was just fine. More than that, actually.

The ploy worked. Chris looked up, a grin tugging at his thin lips. "What's that? The village pond version of Swan Lake? Racy outfit, though."

"Thanks a bunch." I slipped under the crisp sheets and turned over, smiling at him. He smiled in return and put the tablet away. We were making progress.

"You shouldn't be coding in bed. No one's expecting you to do miracles. Not when we suck at this stuff ourselves."

"Compared to yours truly, you lot are experts. I couldn't hex if my life depended on it. You can. Especially if your life depends on it. Were you talking about your wedding party earlier?"

"Ye-es. Did you listen at all? Mafia Cookery Club they're called."

"Original name."

"Hah, yes. I'm not sure their gangster outfits will go down well with the locals. Some of the residents suffer from a distinct lack of British humor."

"Uh, are they going to marry wearing costume? I vow to cherish this violin case in good and in bad times, or words to that effect?"

"Of course not. It's just for the hen and stag party. Everyone celebrating together, which'll have the tongues a-wagging even faster than they already are."

Chris crossed his arms behind his head and stared at the ceiling. His special scent, musky and reminding me of incense, drifted across. My libido twitched. It would have to wait a bit. My head was still too full of my day.

"That conversation I mentioned over dinner, the one between the curator and Anna, our churchwarden extraordinaire ..."

"I gather you don't like the woman."

"So far, I didn't have much to do with her. But my guests told me she's doing absolutely everything to block the marriage."

"Surely, that's not her decision."

"No, but she's in charge of the arrangements and is making their lives difficult. Well, I've given them the address of Anna's doggie parlor. They'll be visiting tomorrow and have a word with her in person."

He sank back into the pillows and groaned. "You won't make friends that way."

"She doesn't want any of us newbies for a friend. Anyway, back to the conversation. That director, Jedd, is a real macho tosser, but I can't see for the life of me how he fits into the picture. If only Hagbottom-Smythe were missing a few bones."

Chris tickled my cheek, and I batted his hand away. "You're doing pretty well. Your theory that unc's trying to put you under pressure makes sense, though it's not his style to squeeze people at the first attempt. I would've expected him not to heat the tongs until much later. He'd definitely hire local talent, that's for sure."

"He was pretty vague about the skeleton, but adamant about not being involved in the shooting, and I believe him. Must've been the minion. Whoever they are."

"Slowly. Don't jump to conclusions. You're good at that."

"I'm not. I mean—"

"Myr, relax. Come here," he said in a voice that sent my pulse into overdrive and pushed the theories, images, and worries zipping through my overactive brain far, far away.

—

That night I had the first dream.

It was one of those where I knew I was dreaming, but couldn't wake up. Not a nightmare. Just—odd. There I was, walking along. The morning dew wet the soles of my feet, and a fizzy greenness filled the air. An endless expanse of grassland filled my view, with trees somewhere on the horizon. But no matter how much I walked, I wasn't getting any closer. I sped up—same result.

This is silly, I thought, there's no point. Better wake up now.

But I didn't. Instead, I plodded on until I suddenly was floating—no, I wasn't. I was still walking, or at least my body was, while my brain drifted away from its shell, like a hot-air balloon lifting, slowly, majestically. A pleasant sensation, one that filled my inner being with a contented glow. I was glad to let the ground below me shrink, enjoyed myself rising toward the pale blue of the heavens. Below, my body plodded on, a stalwart little soldier ...

It was fading. Though fading was the wrong word. The colors were still there, but my body was becoming translucent.

Now, that was super daft. It was high time I woke up.

So, I did.

# 6

## ALL THAT REMAINS

The mellowness from my dream lingered and, with it, enough fizzy energy to tackle another day. Chris was already rummaging around in the bathroom, and Tiddles had annexed his space in the bed, her furry side rising and falling in a slow rhythm. Since she wasn't shouting the house down, the Simpkins sisters must have fed her. I blinked at the alarm clock. Half-past seven in the morning. Early, but not too early to check for messages from Jochen. I could swear last night's bizarre dream was triggered by my subconscious angst about his discovery. Knowledge was the best antidote to uncertainty.

I fumbled for the smartphone on my nightstand, but it flumped onto the floor. With a groan, I bent over, fishing for the darn thing, when Chris returned to the bedroom.

"I'm out of T-shirts," he complained. "Forgot to bring a few last night. Seriously, living in two places fries my brain. Eh, what are you up to?"

"Schlüsselblum never rang back."

"You reckon he's hiding under the carpet?"

If I hadn't been hanging half in, half out of bed, that

comment would have merited a pillow in the face. It certainly didn't warrant a reply. I straightened, thumbed the call open and, on the other side of the British Channel, a phone rang.

Chris threw himself next to me, the movement bouncing poor Tiddles from her resting place on the mattress.

"Merow." She arched her back, the tip of her pink tongue protruding sideways from her muzzle.

"Sorry, cat," Chris said. "Perhaps he's stumbled over a love potion?" He nuzzled my neck, and I swatted him away. The ringtone in my ear ended in a beep.

"You're a sex maniac. That's what you are."

Hang on. Was I on voicemail now? "Jochen? Myrtle here. Please ignore my previous comment. Uh, I'm dying for your news. Can we talk today? Take care."

I disconnected, but I couldn't switch off the heatwave surging through my body. "Blast, what if he heard that? And you give it a rest."

I threw a pillow at Chris, who was doubling over with laughter. Wiping his eyes, he said, "Well, let's hope the guy's got a sense of humor."

The phone spat out a jingly tune. Incoming call. My stomach dropped two floors and my mouth went dry. Professional calmness looked different.

*You can do this.*

"Witch's Retreat B&B, good morning. Jochen?"

"Crystal Dawn B&B, Linda here. Is that you, Myr?"

"Yes. Hi." Rats. It would've been less stressy if Jochen were the caller. At least, I'd know whether he'd heard my comment.

"Hi, yourself. Sorry to bother you so early, but do you have a moment?"

My fellow witch took shape in my mind. Tall, with straight dark hair, and clad mostly in black, she radiated Morticia Addams vibes—assuming Morticia ever wore trousers.

Chris was nuzzling my neck again, so I swatted at his hand. "Sure."

"Good. It'll sound weird, but—you haven't come across any spare violin cases, by any chance?"

"I ...no."

"It's the wedding party. My lot turned up yesterday in full hitman gear ...uh, hit woman, I guess. Or person. Well, whatever. They all carried black cases with Mafia Italian Cookery Club written on them in drippy scarlet letters."

"Mine did too. It's how they transport their spices and stuff, apparently. Gave them the idea for their hen and stag combo."

"It appears they've gone AWOL. I'm talking about the violin cases, by the way. We kept them with the empty luggage in the shed. Now they're gone. Luggage's still there."

"Is your shed locked?"

"Of course not. Well, usually it isn't necessary. At least not with the solstice behind us."

She had a point there. With fewer people around, break-ins were less likely. "Odd."

"Very. We'll have to report this, but I thought I'd better check with you first."

"I haven't been down yet. I'll have a look and call you back later."

"You do that. Cheers."

Chris was closing the last button on his tight black jeans as I put the phone away.

"I'll be at my place," he said. "Had a really cool idea last night, and I want to try something. And wash my T-shirts. How about lunch at the café?"

"Sounds good."

He bent over me and mumbled, "Sex maniac at your service."

I was still searching for a comeback when he strode from the room, chased by my cat.

—

I showered and then stared at the contents of my wardrobe for absolute ages—with summer gone MIA, I might never wear my shift dresses again. In the end, I settled once more on jeans and a blue T-shirt with a colorful scarf to brighten the outfit. While dressing, a couple of pale pink rose petals caught my attention, lying scattered under the bed.

Rose petals? I picked them up, a feathery weight in my hand. The essence of my magic manifested in bright red petals, not this washed-out pastel. Somehow, they must have blown in through the window. I brushed them into the paper basket, went downstairs, and checked the storage. No problem there: thirteen violin cases rested peacefully next to each other.

In the kitchen, however, all wasn't well.

"Did you hear about them stolen cases?" Alma asked.

"Linda rang me. No worries, ours are still *in situ*, I just checked."

"Institute?" Cecily asked, perplexity crowding her forehead.

"Sorry, I'm talking posh. All violin cases are here."

Her brow cleared. "Ah. But since you lock up at night these days, how could they've been stolen?"

It would've been nice if the ladies kept the backdoor secured during daytime, but as usual, I wanted too much. I bit into a tomato. "I didn't think so, but I needed to make sure."

"With or without violin cases, these people are a real fright," Alma said. "Saw them in Main Street yesterday evening. Gave me the creeps."

"I guess they were enjoying themselves," I said mildly.

Alma pursed her lips and the fine wrinkles around her mouth sharpened. "Huh. Let's hope the vicar knows what he's doing. People aren't happy, I tell you."

From the breakfast room came the sound of shuffling feet, voices, and laughter.

"My, my, early risers, are we?" Cecily cracked the door to the conservatory open. "No gangster thingamajigs."

"I'll get their orders. Weirdos or not, they're paying guests." Alma grabbed her pencil and pad and marched into the breakfast room.

The phone in my pocket rang. My stomach lurched in response and sent up an air bubble tasting of tomato. That could only be Schlüsselblum.

"Witch's Retreat, Myrtle speaking."

"You didn't show up yesterday," a peeved voice drilled into my ear—the curator.

"I'm frightfully sorry. Something got in the way. I rang your office to let you know."

"Nobody told me."

He would inevitably take it out on the intern, and I felt a trifle guilty. "Sorry, perhaps I didn't make myself clear. How can I help?"

"Mel said you were searching for missing skeletons. Yesterday, everything was fine."

*Oh?*

"Someone's stolen a skeleton during the night?"

His voice segued from peeved to pissed-off. "How am I supposed to know when it happened? I don't have the time to count my exhibits every day."

I shifted on a chair that seemed to be covered in ants. "Of course not."

"The prehistorical remains are all there, but we also have remains from later eras. Why, I don't know. They just hog space. The time it takes to keep that place organized is unbelievable."

"I understand it must be a nightmare. But I appreciate you contacting me immediately."

"So, you should." I must have hit the right mixture of admiration and servility; his tone sounded marginally friendlier.

"See, that one was part of a project I oversaw a couple of years ago. The dovecote needed some repairs, and when we exposed the foundations, we found an old burial."

My mind projected an image of the dovecote. It sat in the middle of the car park, halfway between the manor and the museum. I zipped past it a few times yesterday. "How old is old for you?"

He laughed, a surprisingly pleasant sound. "Nice one. Seventeenth century. Mostly we found scattered bones, but there was one complete skeleton plus a few minor items. I had it all labeled and stored in the cellar. And it's missing now."

"That's ...fascinating."

It was. More than that. In the sixteen hundreds, the witch hunters had been active. I couldn't sit on the chair anymore and jumped up.

"It is, isn't it?" The curator must have caught the genuine interest in my voice. He was almost purring down the phone. "And there's more. Why don't you come over? I'll show you."

———

With the guests of all seven rooms having arrived at once, even Alma and Cecily were taxed to their limits, so I joined the fray, boiled tea and eggs, prepared coffee, dashed back and forth between kitchen and conservatory to fill up the buffet, and chatted with the culinary mobsters. Hagbottom-Smythe and my sleuthing would have to wait a little longer. Once the guests were busy with their breakfasts and the Simpkins sisters back in control, I grabbed the watering can and barreled through the saloon-style doors into the corridor—where I slammed into an invisible obstacle.

My heartbeat spiked until a rustling and a faint scent of lemons reassured me it was only my magical plant. At least she had remembered to cloak.

"Petty, I told you not to come out here." Waggling the can, I steadied my somewhat ragged breathing. "Look here, food is on its way. Let's go back to the parlor."

Laughter sounded from the conservatory, followed by footsteps.

"Now."

With a *whoosh*, something pushed past me, and the door at the back of the corridor banged open. I followed suit, panting.

In the living room, Petty exploded into view right in front of my eyes. I jumped backward and bumped my shin on a sofa leg.

"Ouch, for heaven's sake, what *are* you up to?"

The pot zipped up and down, leaves rustling and flowers opening and closing rapidly. My magical plant shot around me, coming full circle until she stopped at eye height. A sharp, peppery aroma I'd never noticed before hit my nostrils.

"Petty?"

She floated her pot along my arm, her leaves tickling my skin, raising goosebumps. The touch wasn't unpleasant, but then her agitation grew worse, the leaves rushing as if a mini-tornado were raging in the plant pot. Sparks and petals dropped to the floor as Petty shot toward the coffee table and banged against the surface. Then she sat still, her foliage limp like a drooping bunny ear.

I heaved a deep sigh and counted. Once I reached ten, my breath came more evenly.

"Are you ill?" The bottom dropped out of my stomach. "Please, Petty, don't be ill."

I stroked the nubby leaves, ran my fingers over the silky-smooth surface of the blooms. One leaf caressed my hand. Lemon aroma hung in the air. That scent I was familiar with. It signaled happiness or pleasure. But underneath lurked something else. Something acrid and wrong.

I withdrew my hand and extracted the recipe book from the shelf. Great Aunt Petunia made very few references to familiars in the grimoire. She didn't seem to have created one; her grandmother's familiar was the "last of its kind." She commented on the "gyft of invisibility" and that "only the strong ones" had it. But otherwise, familiars weren't something she felt like writing about. Not even in the section at the back, which I usually avoided—the section I had marked with a black string of wool—the part of the grimoire containing the more in-depth instructions on hexing.

Today, I went straight to the scary part.

"How to revyve a dead animalle or plant." Well, I'd done

that already.

"How to change the physical appearance of an object." I'd done that as well. No need for a repeat performance.

Now, we were getting into the area where lots of little skulls loomed, the part my aunt had studied far too diligently for her own good. The headlines looked harmless enough, but page by page a queasy sensation was spreading from my stomach.

"How to self-defend against malice" came right at the end, and my gaze slipped away from the old tome, unable to read on. Instead, it came to rest on my aunt's urn, and the queasiness deepened until I could take it no longer. I snapped the book shut, since the answers I was seeking were not to be found within. At least not in the section where the text was actually visible.

Jenna knew about familiars; she could help me.

*But she isn't here.*

Petty's soft rustle interrupted my musings. She had shifted across, hovered over the book, and used the edge of her pot to knock it open—on an empty page. The pot kept hovering, dropping the occasional spark.

"Don't worry, I got it. What I want to know is in here. Well, we'll have to make it visible then. I've done it once. I can do it again," I said with more optimism than I felt.

It worked, though. Petty popped a pink spark and launched herself toward her favorite place in front of the window, where she turned her blossoms at the weak sunlight.

Even if my mood lightened somewhat, a nagging disquiet burrowed deep into my chest. A shadow had touched my sunny little plant, and I didn't know who or what might be casting it.

*Don't be such a wuss.* My inner voice wasn't all that good with pep talks, but at least it kicked me into action. I left Petty to her sunbathing, reveling briefly in the lemony scent, free now of any trace of the peculiar pepper aroma. Then, I drove to the museum.

—

Other than the rows of panels, one of which had given me shelter, the museum housed glass cases full of arrow tips, reconstructions of the henge, or even the sad bones of a small child, curled up as if to protect itself from prying eyes. Hagbottom-Smythe was nowhere in sight, so I knocked on the office door and entered.

Three people turned as one. One was female, wearing nerdy black-rim glasses and a micro-skirt. Two young men, one sporting a stylish blond fringe, the other wearing his mousy brown hair in a no-nonsense cut, kept her company. The brown-haired one I recognized for the gardener's helper.

"Hi," he said, smiling.

"Hi, yourself. I'm Myrtle Coldron. Mr. Hagbottom-Smythe wanted a chat," I said in a voice that sounded a tick too preppy in my ears.

The girl hooked a thumb over her left shoulder, where an opening arched in the wall. "I'm Nina. He's down in the cellar. Keeps resurfacing to call people. Poor reception down there. I don't know what's wrong, but I think he's lost something."

The young man I hadn't met said, "Most likely his brain. Oops." The latter was directed at me.

I wasn't so good at the poker face. As an ex-teacher, I really should do better, but I hadn't been in the job long enough.

"Sorry," he said with a cocky grin, which indicated he was anything but. Nina giggled.

Cal, the gardening intern, pulled a face. "Give it a rest, Pip. So far, chappie treated *me* okay—"

"Lucky you."

"I wasn't finished. I don't like the way he's treating Nina, but—"

"No need to go protective on me. I'm a big girl." Nina picked up a letter opener and prodded her finger nails.

"Can I finish a sentence here?"

Pip shrugged. Nina sniggered.

Cal dew a deep breath. "What I'm trying to say is Jedd's much worse than old Saggybottoms. Promised us the world, and now? Just look at us. It's modern slavery, that's what it is. If it weren't for Joe, the job would be impossible. I mean, come on. My family's in the business. I know my plants, management experience is what I need. I'll tell you—"

Pip rolled his eyes. "Blah, blah. Give it a rest. I'm sick and tired of your Robin Hood complex. Nothing ever comes out of it. Apart from trouble. Want my advice? Suck it up, do something about it, or drop out. I'm all for option two."

"Listen—"

Nina flapped an elegant hand at the open archway. "Off you go, Ms. Coldron, this might take a while."

"Thanks."

I climbed down a set of rough concrete stairs that led into a storeroom crammed with metal shelves. Ancient strip lighting on the ceiling tried its best to illuminate inconspicuous boxes of all shapes and sizes, marked with little stickers.

"Hello?" My shout reverberated through the stuffy air.

"What?" A head stuck out from behind the shelf at the back. "Who are you?"

"I'm Myrtle. You wanted to show me something. Frightfully sorry, I got held up."

"Punctuality is a virtue, young lady," the curator grumbled.

I couldn't exactly tell him my magical plant suffered from a paranormal bug, which meant I had to consult my spell book for treatments. "This sort of thing always happens when one is on a deadline, doesn't it?"

"Bah. Come over here. You won't see anything otherwise."

I had pictured him being mid-sized and rotund, and I was right on that front, though he wasn't wearing a suit as imagined, but a pair of nondescript beige canvas trousers and a white shirt.

The curator pushed up his wire-frame glasses. "We keep the remains in this corner. Humans, animals, everything that doesn't get nicked by the larger museums in the area. They only leave us the dregs." A frown appeared on his forehead, and his lips puckered, making him look like a sulking cherub.

He pointed at a container on the top shelf. "All skeletons are labeled and properly stored. Including those remains we found under the dovecote. "

Hagbottom-Smythe reached up and, with some grunting, pulled a cardboard box from the shelf, which he then placed on a metal table. He raised his chin at the gap where the box had been. "We stack them two rows deep. I don't know what made me check when all the prehistoric ones were untouched. But I did, and that's when I realized somebody had removed the specimen behind."

"Why would they nick that particular one?"

He shrugged. "No idea. Maybe because its container was smaller than the others, easier to carry. They're all different sizes. I have to use what I can find."

"I see. And what exactly was in there?"

Hagbottom-Smythe pursed his pouty lips again. "That's what's annoying me. A prime specimen. Complete. You seldom get them like that. And, what's more, we found some items with it, as I told you."

"Items?"

"I'll show you." The curator donned his gloves and gingerly lifted the lid off the box. Inside, the gray-beige dome of a skull lurked among old newspapers and plastic bags. "Here, we only found the skull and a few of the long bones. And parts of something we believe to be a bronze mirror. See?"

The curator was fiddling with a plastic bag and triumphantly pushed a misshapen and discolored object at me.

"Uh, that's a mirror?"

"Yes, yes, I assure you. Back then, it would've been valuable. No shops around the corner, where you could just buy them. The mirror buried with the missing skeleton was in much better condition. It was in a metal box, that's why. Such a shame. Anyway, look at this." He rummaged in the carton some more and retrieved a lump of rock with etchings on one side. It reminded me of—

"A prehistoric clay tablet? I've seen those." In my Swindon bank box. The famous plaques of the witches. Indistinguishable from hundreds and thousands of the things found all over Wiltshire.

"Indeed. The missing skeleton had three. Plus, that mirror."

"I guess it was already pretty unusual to get buried under the dovecote. Or was it built over their resting place in later years?"

Hagbottom-Smythe was gingerly re-packing the skeletal parts and their accouterments. "No, the structure was erected somewhere between 1533 and 1550. Carbon dating won't give you the exact year, but those mirrors weren't available in the fifteen hundreds. I'd say these people were buried at least half a century later."

I was right. We were back to the era of the witch hunts. "Why would they end up in such a strange resting place?"

The box went back onto the shelf. "Young woman, I recommend you read up on the local history. Not enough that these pagans are all over the place now, but around the end of the sixteenth century or thereabouts, a group of early environmentalists settled here. Called themselves Earth Wardens and believed they could do magic. Ah, bah. Got themselves killed, that's all. And buried in unhallowed ground. Under the dovecote, for example. Pah."

The skeleton must have belonged to a witch.

Shoved by the curator, the box slid into the spot at the back, and I forced myself to shelve his amazing revelation for later. "Why would anyone want to steal one of your relics?"

"Remains, young lady. I have no idea." Hagbottom-Smythe frowned. "Of course, it'll suit Jedd. He thinks I'm a doddery old codger. He's been making noises to management about synergies if one person oversees all attractions. Guess which person that would be?" His voice was no longer grumpy; it was downright bitter. "So, if I'm seen to be losing my marbles together with my exhibits ...Anyway, I want my skeleton back. Do you think you could help?"

Despite his attitude issues, Hagbottom-Smythe wasn't a bad sort. In any case, anyone on the receiving end of Jedd's schemes deserved my help, so I made supportive noises and promised I would pass on the news to my friend Sarah. It seemed likely that my skeleton and his were the same. That seemed to cheer him up, since he invited me to return for a more detailed tour another day, which I accepted. Once outside the museum, my smartphone pinged.

I had two messages. One from Sarah.

The other was from Jochen.

# 7

## A ROCK AND A HARD PLACE

Not ready for Schlüsselblum, I listened to Sarah's voice message first.

"Myrtle? That skeleton of yours is hundreds of years old, the pathologist says. Gave me an earful for wasting his expertise. As if. Doc only found out so fast because of a coin caked to the inside of the skull. Apparently, he has a pal who's into coins and between them and an x-ray unit they managed a dating. Early seventeenth century. Any idea who might've mislaid a bunch of historical bones? We can discuss over a glass of wine. Give me a shout. Cheers."

Oh, now I had the license to meddle again, did I? Luckily, I'd been busy doing the things Sarah'd told me not to do, so I messaged her the contact details of the museum.

One problem taken care of, I sucked in a balloon-load of air and then thumbed open the second missive.

"Hello, Myrtle, thanks for calling. We're still having issues with our source. Hopefully, there'll be more for you later today. Oh—give my regards to your sex maniac. He's a fortunate man, whoever he is."

Can humans go chili-faced in an instant? My cheeks were burning for sure.

I shoved the phone back into my purse and headed for the public toilets behind the museum. While the fly-specked mirror added surplus freckles to my face, it also reflected a beetroot complexion.

*Eek.*

The icy tap water took care of the flush, but I found only scratchy paper towels to pat myself dry. Presentable once more, I left for the café to share the results of my sleuthing with the maniac.

—

"I can think of better ways to cause trouble for you lot than stealing a skeleton complete with grave gifts, dumping it in the countryside, and guarding it at gunpoint," Chris said. "And why top the crackpot act by nicking a bunch of phony violin cases? Even if someone's acting on dear Uncle Bob's orders, they'll soon find themselves fired. Mustard?"

We were sitting in the shadow of a red and white striped umbrella. Being its usual unpredictable self, the weather had turned sunny and warm, and I was boiling in my jeans.

"Yes, please." As far as I was concerned, there never could be enough mustard on a pork pie.

"Oh, one more thing." I shot a nervous glance at our environment. While the tables were filling fast, ours sat in a corner, the nearest seats as yet unoccupied.

"I talked to the curator." I gave Chris the short version of the man's lecture. "Those bones must've belonged to a witch."

He speared a pickled onion and chewed pensively. A dark lock curled into his forehead, highlighting his night-black eyes, their corners crinkling with amusement. With the five o'clock shadow he sported at high noon and his favorite all-black outfit, my man was hotter than the mustard.

"You're probably right, but does it change anything? As

warnings go, the skeleton stunt is pointless. Unc doesn't do pointless. Ever. And none of his minions would act that stupid. At least, not for long. There's got to be stuff we don't see."

"Mh." I bit into my pork pie, which was exactly as it should be, the crust crispy and brown, the inside moist and savory.

As usual, Chris's reasoning was sound. Trust me to think of complications. "What if we've got things wrong, and it's not about the bones, but the grave gifts? I wonder what happened to them. There was nothing looking remotely like a mirror or a plaque."

"Might've been hidden among the nettles."

"I'll ask Sarah, though I'm sure she would've said something. Like she mentioned the coin. No, I'd say someone's nicked them."

"Why?"

"Search me. Despite popular opinion, witches aren't mind-readers. Well, I'm not."

The next moment, awareness struck like lightning from clear blue skies. Plaques. Witches. Of course, that was it.

"Ah, let me guess. You've had an inspiration."

Seriously, my poker face sucked. "What if your uncle is after the magical plaques of the witches? He was last time."

"He surely wants them, be it to cause you grief or to use them for blackmail." Chris played the piano on the tabletop, his long fingers drumming on the wood. "Let's assume your skeleton really belonged a magical being, and let's also assume uncle knew it, then the obvious thing to do would be to keep the bones and grave gifts and blackmail you over the lot." The drumming got more pronounced. "There's no point in dumping the skeleton. Unless ...you better check up on your plaques. Make sure they're still there. Actually ..."

"Your sentences are trailing."

"It's because my thoughts are all over the place. What if that's exactly what my uncle wants you to do? Drive to Swindon to check the box in the vault, I mean."

"And then what? Somebody skulks around the corner and bops me over the noddle?"

"Unlikely, but it's probably a bad idea to go in person. Send someone else. And make them wear a hard hat."

"Very funny."

Last week, I'd visited the bank, following up on a hunch that Dot might have had a go at our relics. She hadn't. According to the records, no one had accessed the box apart from me, and it also hadn't been moved. I knew, because I'd placed two of my hairs underneath. Thin and light, they were hard to spot.

"I'll call the bank." My phone was already out, and after endless minutes spent listening to canned music, I had the facts. "The last person to take out the box was me a week ago. No one's been asking questions. No strangers trying to sneak into the vault."

"I suppose that's good news, though it doesn't help us with this bizarre business." Chris reached for his second can of Irn Bru.

How anyone would fancy a lemonade that tasted of mouthwash was beyond me.

"Almost too bizarre for unc, to be honest."

"If not your uncle, who else could be behind this charade? I'm suffering from a severe lack of suspects."

Chris licked mustard off his lip. "You're the sleuth here. I'm only acting as the sidekick."

"Thank you, Dr. Watson. Let's be methodical, then." I counted suspects off my fingers. "Jedd? He's playing power games and might've lifted the skeleton to cause problems for Hagbottom-Smythe. But why disappear the grave gifts?"

"If they've been stolen. You don't know that yet."

"I'm pretty sure they are. However, the Colonel's the problem. Why would Jedd shoot at him? And why steal the violin cases?"

Chris shrugged. "Who else do we have?"

"The interns. Could be one of them acting up or executing

Jedd's orders. Though neither of them seems happy with management, and I can't blame them. Why would they even help Jedd? Why take potshots at the Colonel? Why keep the mirror and the clay tablets and steal the cases?"

"Because they don't like management?"

"But the skeleton theft is a problem for Hagbottom-Smythe, not Jedd."

"True. What about the curator? He might be throwing smoke grenades."

"Why would he implicate himself when Jedd's already trying to pull the rug from under him? The guy sounded genuinely worried. Plus, that museum's quite the open house. Chappie leaves his keys lying around all the time, so anyone can help themselves."

"Okay, how about Jedd or an intern acting on his behalf sneaking away an exhibit to implicate the curator? Or an intern is acting under their own steam because they don't like this Smythe guy. They then dump the bones in public, but keep the tablets and the mirror, either to sell them or cause more problems later. That's assuming those items really are missing. While this makes a little more sense than the theory involving my uncle, we still have the teensy problem with the shooting and the missing violin cases."

"It's wild, I admit."

Chris finished his pie and brushed off his hands. "Told you. I don't think we have the full picture."

*Whoomph.* Somewhere close by, something heavy had fallen over.

Shrieking loudly, the rooks launched for the skies. Conversations stopped. The world fell silent. Not for long, though. When high-pitched screams erupted from the henge, I sprang up from my seat. No magic was needed to tell me what had happened.

"The wonky standing stone. Quick." I pelted past the café and slammed through the gate that gave access to the henge.

The grass was still wet from all that rain, and I slid to a stop, praying my hunch was wrong and the noise harmless. A minor earthquake, for example.

Chris arrived at my side. "Oh, crap."

One could say that.

Like the broken bracelet of a giant, the loose circle of craggy rocks that formed part of the outer henge arched away from us, into the open plain. The circle started close to the pub, from where spectators were now running up, smartphones in their hands. The spaces between the stones had always been uneven, but one gap was a lot wider than before. The boulder that had filled it lay on the ground; dark mud splashed all over the grass like so much soy sauce.

Yet more spectators arrived, crowding the fallen rock. Some shouted at their phones, hopefully calling for help. Some gaped in slack-jawed terror. The more beastly ones were taking photos of the fallen stone—

The stone.

Slate gray, cracked in places and speckled with yellowed and rusty lichens, it had been one of the tallest on the henge, like a finger admonishing the tourists to show some respect. Unlike the others, its base was narrow and not buried as deeply. The recent rain and the resulting mud must have further loosened its base. With no barrier warning people off, the boulder was an accident waiting to happen.

My gaze slid over the rock, its flank dotted by red sprinkles that might or might not be lichen. There was something buried under the stone, something small and white.

My throat tightened. A hand? I swallowed and forced myself to look harder.

Thankfully, I wasn't looking at a body part, but a shoe. Relief welled up, only to get sucked away again. Next to the stone and the ruined shoe lay a human shape, unmoving, silent.

I balled my fists and squeezed my eyes shut. Not again. Not another dead person.

Chris wrapped his arm around me. "Myr, are you okay? Would you like to sit down?"

I leaned into his spicy warmth. This was all too much.

Behind my back, the babble changed, got excited, and cheering broke out. I swung around and opened my eyes in time to witness the shape on the ground reach for helping hands, rise, and shake their head. Long blonde hair cascaded over a dark hoodie.

A woman. A living woman, wearing one white shoe.

The adrenaline in my system ebbed away, leaving me weak-kneed and hot.

*She's alive. Everything's okay.*

The pockets of my jeans vibrated, followed by the theme music of the Midsomer Murders. With trembling hands, I fumbled for my smartphone and checked the caller ID.

Sarah's phone seemed to work again.

"Myr, we're getting distress signals from that little hellhole you call a village. You don't happen to know what's gone wrong this time?"

I cleared a rather dry throat. "Standing stone. Only it's no longer standing. We were having lunch at the café, heard it fall, and ran across. We as in Chris and I."

"How on Earth do you manage to always—never mind. Any casualties?"

"A woman was down, but she's moving. Doesn't look as if she's badly injured."

"Can you find out how she's doing?"

I mouthed "Sarah" at Chris. He was one of those amazing people who could read between the lines, even unspoken ones. He headed for the group, passing the rock with the squashed shoe underneath. The red splotches were nothing worse than lichen. I could see that now.

"Chris is checking. Hold on."

"Ambulance and a squad car are on their way. Myr, I need your help. Someone's broken into Lu's laundry, and I can't cut myself in half. If things aren't too bad at your end, I can go there without too much of a guilty conscience. But I don't want to leave Cameron in the lurch. He's still wet behind the ears."

"Let's hear what Chris says, but I think she's fine.

My sweaty hand clutching the phone, I watched Chris join the group that had formed around the blonde woman. Standing on one leg, she was supported by two of her friends.

Something sharp and hot knifed my chest. I knew the trio. Had seen them at breakfast this morning. The culinary mobsters. My guests.

"Myr?"

"Hang on a sec." I headed for the group by the rock.

"Are you okay? You're making funny noises."

"I'm on the move. That woman …She's staying at the Witch's Retreat."

Sarah groaned. "Not another one."

I joined the hobby chefs who had formed a protective body bubble around their friend. She was pasty white, trying to smile, but not quite succeeding. Chris switched off the torch he'd used to check her eyes, apparently satisfied with the result.

"Iz hugged the stone, and the blasted thing keeled over," the nearest chef, a woman called Jade, said. "Bang. Just like that. If she hadn't jumped out of the way, she'd be dead." Her voice ended with a little hiccup.

"But she isn't." I gave Jade's hand a gentle squeeze. It was cold and clammy, but I don't think mine was any better.

"I heard that," Sarah's voice in my ear said. "How's the victim, then?"

"She's talking. No visible injuries, but she's rather white in the face. Shock, most likely. Yes, Chris is making her bend over. That stone has always been loose, but it shouldn't have fallen like that. This is no accident, I tell you. Someone's after my guests."

There was a roaring in my ears. "It's starting all over again." My voice sounded funny, distant.

"Uh, what? Calm down, Myr, please. I need you in control. Can you do that?"

"I'll try."

"Good. Please relax, okay? We don't know what's going on yet. This might well be a coincidence. Was that stone not cordoned off?" Sarah's voice was stable in a way the rock hadn't been. The roaring in my ears faded.

"No, that's the whole point. I'll explain things to Cameron when he comes."

Sarah sighed. "Fine. You do that. In the meantime, don't do anything you might regret later. I'll be back as soon as I can. Take care." She disconnected.

"Who're you talking to?" Jade asked.

"The police. They're sending an ambulance and an officer. We'll need to wait for him to arrive."

As if on cue, a siren yowled at the traffic.

"Ah." Jade passed on the news to her friends, who were fluttering around like a flock of hawk-struck sparrows.

Wearing two anoraks, her teeth shattering, Isobel was holding on to Chris.

"Iz here is doing great," he said soothingly. "She jumped immediately when she noticed the stone was moving. Doesn't have a scratch on her."

Iz ground her teeth, which effectively stopped them from chattering. She looked up and gave him a watery smile. "Heavens, that was so scary. I hugged the thing because that's supposed to bring luck and it teetered. I thought I'd bought the ticket."

It appeared no one had bothered to pass on the message about not hugging the stones.

An angry glint crept into Isobel's pale blue eyes. "Why wasn't there a warning sign? This is criminal."

Was I overreacting? The rock's tumble might be nothing more than an accident caused by negligence and crass stupidity, not someone targeting me or my guests.

"Am I now liable for damages?" Isobel asked.

"No way. This isn't your fault. I'm truly sorry you had such a fright. People touch these stones all the time, and nothing ever happened. Let me have a look at that rock."

Powered by curiosity—and naked self-interest—I retraced my steps to the toppled standing stone, now the center of a good-sized crowd. The sneaker seemed to be the only casualty: mangled and twisted, the shoe's front part was pinned down by the rock, the sole sticking up into the air.

"Somebody's been digging here," a man in hiking gear said. He pointed at the hole where the stone had stood.

My stomach curled into a bristly ball. "You reckon?"

"Oh yes, there are shovel marks on the ground. And look at all that soil scattered about." He flapped his hands at the dark streaks I noticed earlier.

My heartbeat ratcheted up. I'd known it. This wasn't an accident. Someone had rigged the stone to fall, in which case we were talking about attempted murder after all. Preparing the trap would be reasonably straightforward. Dig a hole and rely on gravity. Since the marks left behind by the shovel were crisp, the deed must've been committed after the latest downpour and finding out when the rain stopped should be easy.

*Nothing you can do until the police are here.*

Unfortunately, with the entertainment over, some tourists were already wandering off.

"Uh, sorry, could you wait here, please?" I had to shout to make myself heard. "The police might need your statement."

Wrong move.

The response to my request reminded me of a gardening session, where I lifted a clump of grass and uncovered a wiggly ball of woodlice. The insects scuttled away in all directions as fast as their little legs could carry them. Today's gawkers were no better, even if they had fewer feet.

In the end, only the culinary mobsters and the hiker who noticed the shovel marks stayed behind to be interviewed by

Constable Cameron. Since I didn't intend to air my assorted theories in the open, I agreed to join him and Sarah at the cop shop in Swindon, to "help with the investigation."

Wasn't that the term they used for suspects?

# 8

## CURIOUSER AND CURIOUSER

In every detective novel I'd ever read, the coffee at the cop shop sucked, but reality was even worse. A cautious sip of the lukewarm brew left a vile smear on my tongue, rusty and bitter, with curdled milk thrown in for good measure.

"Ugh."

"I know," Sarah said. "Sorry, I thought even the ersatz caffeine might help a bit. Didn't realize the milk's off again. Let's get you something decent to drink. In the meantime, try these."

She wriggled a plate of chocolate chip cookies fresh from the box. They were about the only attractive thing in a room decked out in institutional whites and grays. Even Constable Cameron—white shirt, dark trousers—and Sarah in her oyster-colored pantsuit had gone gecko on me.

"I'll sort it out." The constable creaked open the door and left the room.

Sarah bounced me an intense look. "Okay, about these observations you wish to share in confidence. In my official capacity as detective sergeant, I can only hope you haven't been snooping."

I widened my eyes and pointed at my chest. "*Moi?* Would I do that?"

"All the time. It's no surprise, really. Your village's been in the spotlight, and you can't afford to let that happen again. I'd be amazed if you didn't suffer from the same gut feeling that keeps bugging me."

"Such as?"

"Something's very wrong and about to get worse. My twitchy gut is the reason we're sitting here. Friends or not, I seldom involve civilians in police matters."

"Unless said civilians are hard to get rid of and proved to be helpful in the past."

"Something along these lines," Sarah said.

We grinned at each other.

"Actually, I covered my back and cleared it with the DCI. He likes you. Thinks you might give us the local insight we need in this case. He shares my concerns and wants me to nip things in the bud. Without wasting time, human resources, or money, of course."

"I'll do my best."

Cameron returned with a water jug and three glasses, which he filled and passed around. I downed my drink in one go. It smacked of chlorine.

"Okay, where shall I start?" Not with Bob Ignatius, he was strictly off-limits. The rest of the dodgy lineup was less of an issue.

"Wherever you like." Sarah sipped at her water and pulled a face. "Was the drinks machine on the blink again?"

"Am I a detective constable?" Cameron asked.

Sarah placed the glass on the table. "Once I knew the bones were old, I was ready to let things drop. My inbox is about to explode. I've no burning desire for more cases. But that standing stone business bothers me. A lot."

I snarfed a cookie. "I'm not sure what the heck's going on, but something certainly is. Everybody, including the interns, hates the director, Jedd. The curator, Hagbottom-Smythe, is a bit of an eccentric, but seems to be more or less accepted, even by most of the interns."

Sarah sighed. "Which interns?"

"There are three of them. The young woman in the museum and two blokes. They study business administration or something like that. The director has organized placements for them, and, to phrase it politely, they don't seem to be happy about their lot."

"It's a hard life," Cameron said.

"I don't think they're our biggest problem. Yesterday, I overheard a fascinating conversation between the curator and the director concerning the standing stone."

"Hang on." Sarah raised her chin at the constable. "Take some notes, please. And you, I won't even ask how and why you 'overheard' stuff."

Cameron prodded his tablet into action and tapped away merrily while I recalled my observations.

"Hmm," Sarah said after I'd finished. "Okay, let me ensure I understand this. There's a feud between the guy who runs the museum and the other guy who runs what exactly?"

"The promo society. Think committee in charge of marketing Wiltshire's Neolithic past, which means mostly us and Stonehenge. They coordinate the guided tours, the ticket shop, develop themed hiking trails, that sort of thing. Didn't know them, so I had to google things. They operate mainly with volunteers. Shoestring budgets. Sounds familiar, I guess."

Sarah and Cameron grimaced.

"Jedd reports to the board, which is somewhere in the area. Marlborough, I believe."

Cameron's fingers flitted over the surface of his tablet. "That would make Jedd Hagbottom-Smythe's boss, right? When I interviewed him, he sounded as if he were in charge."

"Uh, not quite. From what I understand, the man's keen to take over the whole shebang, but he isn't there yet. The manor and the museum remain independent. But Jedd's definitely flexing his muscles. Fires off new ideas left, right, and center. Cue the intern scheme."

"Nothing like a bit of one-upmanship in a small village to keep the blood flowing," Sarah said. "And that standing stone, which is no longer standing, might be the result. That's at least something to run with."

"But, guess what. DI Diloff doesn't agree," Cameron said. "He wants us to steer clear of the village."

That didn't come as a big surprise.

Sarah toyed with her glass. "Before I even consider doing that, I need to be sure we don't have a bigger problem in the making. Which I fear we do. Based on Myrtle's intel, I like both the director and the curator for the standing stone incident, assuming it wasn't an accident. Oh, and those interns go on the list, for sure."

"Looks like somebody's been digging," Cameron said. "And as Ms. Coldron quite rightly suggested, it must've happened once the rain had stopped."

"Yes, but establishing facts is what the techies are there for. Plus, we need to ensure we're not missing someone. For I also see some problems with these two gentlemen." She gave Cameron an encouraging nod.

He placed aside his tablet. "While that Jedd guy might've nicked the skeleton to make his rival look bad, loosening the standing stone would put him squat in the limelight, since he refused to block the blasted thing off. Plus, he doesn't seem to be the physical type. The curator knows his way around shovels. And he really hates the other guy's guts."

"Exactly." Sarah crunched on a cookie.

"However, I can't see him disappearing the skeleton," Cameron said. "

"Let's assume the curator wants to cause trouble for the director, since he's a doucheface," Sarah said. "So, he dumps the skeleton to confuse us stupid coppers and then loosens the stone to prove a point over the lacking safety measures." Her frown told me what she thought of her theory. Not much.

I didn't either. "Look, Mr. Hagbottom-Smythe might be as cranky as hell, but to my mind, he's no criminal. And you'd need to be just that if you're ready to drop rocks on innocent people. Iz, she's my guest, had a pretty narrow escape. I shudder to think what would've happened had a pensioner been guiding this morning."

"Aye to that," Cameron said.

A gloomy silence settled on the room, broken only by crunching noises.

Sarah was the first to speak again. "Well, it always boils down to motive and opportunity. We're doing halfway okay on the motives—Jedd wants to take over the curator's job, and the curator wants the director out of his hair. However, we're not doing so well on the opportunities. First, we don't know when exactly the skeleton was stolen, even if, thanks to you, Myr, we have an idea when it might've been dumped. Neither of these two blokes was anywhere near the stone when it fell, but that doesn't matter, since the deed was done the night before."

Cameron nicked the last cookie, the bugger. "Trouble is, both gentlemen must be busy. I can't see either of them hanging around in the bushes, practicing with their guns."

"Uh, nearly forgot that one." Sarah groaned. "Though it might be unrelated. I really need that incident report. Perhaps we're lucky, and the fall was an accident after all."

"You won't get anything soon, Sarge. Scene Of Crime's running a skeleton staff."

"Bloody holidays."

Both police officers scowled in shared frustration. I filled up my glass.

"Anybody else you care to share?" Sarah asked.

Once more, Ignatius's specter flickered through my mind, but I kept my mouth zipped shut. The violin cases surfaced next. Another little nugget that had been left by the wayside. "There's something else, but it's really whacky."

Sarah curled her fingers in a gimme gesture.

"My current guests belong to a cookery club. The Mafia Italian Cookery Club, to be precise. Quite a large group, so they had to spread out all over the area. A handful stays at the Crystal Dawn."

Sarah snorted. "The Mob staying at a New Age B&B. Nice one."

"Hey, Linda's fine. Anyway, they stored their violin cases in her shed, and this morning they were gone."

Cameron, who had been taking notes again, looked up from his tablet. "Violin cases?"

"Yes, containing their condiments and stuff. With the name of their club printed on the surface in drippy scarlet letters. They're going to have a mob-themed stag and hen do, followed by a barbecue reception."

"Oh, they're getting married," Sarah said.

"Didn't I tell you? No, I didn't, sorry. Yes, at the local church."

"I see." She scrunched her forehead. "I really didn't need burglars and crazy chefs on top of everything else. Since nobody has called in the theft, technically, it isn't part of the case."

"I know. But you asked."

"So, I did. Foolish me. Makes me wonder whether there might be more than one fruitcake on the loose."

Cameron pretended to hit his forehead with his tablet. "Multiple perps. That would explain a few inconsistencies."

Sarah pointed a well-manicured fingernail at her subaltern. "Unless someone's escalating, of course. Starts small with lifting skeletons and cases, then graduates to almost killing people. "

"With all respect, Sarge, that doesn't work. The timings don't fit. If the theft only happened this morning, it came after the skeleton and the shooting. And most likely after somebody acted mole in the henge, since that hole must have been dug latest last night. If it was dug, that is."

Sarah ran her hand through her spiky hairdo. Whatever gel

she used withstood the assault admirably well. "Which makes me think we're either missing some suspects, or there aren't any, because Diloff has won the lottery, is right for once, and there is no case. Only an unlucky mix of craziness."

"Those bones didn't walk away under their own steam," I said. "Colonel Elmsworth knows a gun report when he hears one. The cookery club hasn't just mislaid their violins. I talked to them this morning. And I saw the spade marks at the accident site with my own eyes."

Cameron placed his tablet on the table and slouched in his seat. "Anything else?"

I searched my mind and ended up back in the museum, behind a panel. We'd forgotten someone. "Crikey, Cameron, who did you interview so far?"

"Lemme see. Both the curator and the director showed up on the scene, so I quizzed them. Hagbottom-Smythe was useless, just kept ranting and raving about Jedd's gross negligence. Jedd played it all cool and tried to shift the blame. Claims your guest is at fault, shouldn't have hugged the stone. Typical management behavior."

"Did you talk to the churchwarden by any chance?"

Sarah massaged her temples. "Has one of your chefs taken a dive off the bell tower?"

"Not to the best of my knowledge. But Anna puts in the hours for the society. She organizes the tours, coordinates the volunteers, and presumably also the interns. Jedd might be in charge, but she's working her socks off to make things happen. Does it in her spare time as well, when she isn't at her dog parlor. He treated her like crap. Were I in her shoes, I would've sorted him out a long time ago."

Cameron hid a snort behind his hand. "We'll talk to her tomorrow."

"Nope, we'll have to wait." Sarah pressed her hands firmly on the tabletop. Next, she pulled a face and wiped her palms. "Diloff will have a hissy fit if I sally forth without knowing for sure the fall of the rock is premeditated. While this is all very interesting as a milieu study, it doesn't give us much in terms of evidence. We need something more conclusive."

"In other words, it's a shame nobody's died yet," I said.

"Believe me, that's exactly the scenario I'm trying to prevent. Before I have that report in my hot, sweaty hands, I can't do much. Though I bet you my enormous salary, the findings will be vague, and no one any wiser."

"Accident-ruling. Then, that'll be it," Cameron said.

"Yes," Sarah said. "To dump a historical skeleton next to a hiking path is moronic, but not exactly criminal. Shooting at people is illegal, but nobody's been hurt. As for those thefts, even if we were involved, there's not much we can do."

Sarah didn't look happy when she finished speaking. Cameron switched off his tablet with a sigh.

"Budgets and reports aside, what is your gut telling you?" I asked.

"Still the same. I don't like this. Not one bit."

"Aye," said Cameron.

Sarah tapped her well-manicured fingers together. "Myrtle, I can't—and won't ask you to stick your pointy nose into this muddle. But if you feel the urge to listen to rumors about murderous bell-ringers, or other unsavory types in your village, be my guest."

"The churchwarden doesn't ring any bells, but I get your drift." We smiled at each other in perfect understanding.

Then she pointed a finger at me. "To make myself very clear, you're not acting in an official capacity. Don't interrogate people, just listen. Somebody might know something that turns out to be useful. Don't take unnecessary risks like meeting with your churchwarden on your own. One never knows. Toxic people come in all shapes and sizes."

—

I had followed Cameron's squad car to Swindon in my minivan, so I returned to Avebury under my own steam. No way would I wait for information to find me, since that would take way too long. I craved some peace of mind, which meant shaking some trees, which meant talking to Anna. But not now, not after a day like this. Better to catch her tomorrow, in her church.

Instead, I drove to Tadpole Lane to see if Jenna was back and could help me with my sick familiar.

I was out of luck. Wytchett Farm met my advances with stony silence.

*Rats.*

Too edgy to return home empty-handed, I weighed my options. There had to be something else I could do, both about the weird incidents and my Petty. Rosie always gave excellent advice and had plenty of ideas. Right now, I was straight out of them, so I headed for Field's View.

The front garden of Chez Ragworts still bore the scars from the building works, with planks flattening the grass, and plastic sheeting scattered all over the place. The tangle of roses covering the portico might have been mangled by the removal gang, but they still embraced me with their heady scent when I stepped up and pushed on yet another blasted bell button.

Big Ben chimed in the recesses of the house as I stood and stared at the front door, its brown panel dented and scratched. Second time lucky, this door swung open, and Rosie's face appeared. She looked tired. Moving house had taken its toll.

"Hello Myrtle, what a coincidence. Damian wants to have a word with you."

"Oh? No problem. I actually came to see you."

Her smile an instant youth tonic for her face, she said, "Anything you need, my dear."

I followed Rosie into a living room smelling of fresh paint, where I refused an offer of cake—the pie and police cookies had curbed even my amazing appetite. The tea I accepted and installed myself on a sofa so saggy it immediately sucked me into its chintzy depths.

Damian chose that moment to emerge from his den in the cellar. He too was gray-faced, the lines in his face more prominent than ever.

"Hullo Myrtle. Looks like we ought to get ourselves a new settee."

I rearranged my limbs with as much dignity as I could muster. At least I wasn't wearing a skirt. I shared my news about the standing stone incident. The Ragworts had heard about it via the village jungle drums but didn't know the details, so I filled them in.

"Spent the afternoon with Sarah. She shares my fear that something nefarious might be afoot, but because of their budget issues, she can't do much."

"So, she's given you a license to sleuth?" Damian asked with a twinkle behind his thick glasses.

The man was way too perceptive for his own good. "Not exactly. But she'd appreciate insider information, starting with the churchwarden." That wasn't quite the truth, but not too far removed from it, either.

Rosie appeared with the tea tray. And homemade jam tarts. Everyone was conspiring against me today.

"Anna?" she asked. "Oh dear, can't say I'm her biggest fan. The woman suffers from a severe case of village queenism. Thinks everything revolves around her, and gets upset when that doesn't happen."

She sat down and arranged her batik skirt around her bony knees. "I understand rather a lot of us newbies arrived here recently, but most of the villagers are ever so nice. Anna almost put us off buying our lovely house."

"In what respect?"

"Oh, at the time she was helping out at the estate agent's and took us on a few viewings. I wondered whether she actually wanted to sell something. She was so full of vitriol all the time."

Damian harrumphed. "Farmhouse smells in that property, dry rot in the other, though we found nothing amiss. This house she never even told us about. We found out from Marty Wytchett that it was on the market."

"Rumor has it her dog parlor isn't exactly flourishing, that's why she keeps taking on odd jobs." Rosie turned the cup around on the saucer. "She seems to be frightfully intense with everything she does and eventually gets complimented out the front door. She's no longer working for the estate agent, for example. I feel sorry for her."

"Hah," said her husband. "Wasted effort, if you ask me. Sorry to change topics, but did Jochen get hold of you? He said he rang, but you were on voicemail."

"Ack, while I was with the coppers, I turned my phone off. I completely forgot to check my messages."

"No problems. He contacted us. He's going to courier a reference I'll then have to verify."

"Reference?"

"A copy of an old article. Just like in the good old times at the library." Damian's eyes twinkled once more, and the grayness left his face.

"All this cloak and dagger stuff," Rosie said. "It's just ever so impractical. Never mind, can't be helped, I guess. Jam tart?" She wriggled the plate in front of my nose, and my fingers ignored my good intentions and grabbed one. The tart melted in my mouth, leaving behind a sticky coating that tasted of raspberry. "Sorry for roping you into this chaotic business."

"But I love to help, you know that. Jochen wanted what he called a fresh pair of expert eyes."

I reached for the second jam tart. "How long will that missive take to get here?"

"Theoretically, it should arrive tomorrow."

"Let's keep our fingers crossed. Did he drop any hint of what this might be about? So far, he's been super-vague."

"Not in so many words. He only mentioned one thing."

"And?" Rosie and I chorused.

Damian adjusted his glasses. "Well, as odd as this may sound, Jochen muttered something about a curse."

# 9

## HIDDEN TREASURES

Hey ho, a curse. Since we were supposed to be witches, maledictions definitely fit the bill. Such a shame I had no slots free in my calendar to deal with yet another manifestation of our blasted guerrilla magic.

"You're joking, right?" Rosie said, her kind eyes worried.

Damian took off his glasses and pinched the bridge of his nose. "Sounds cheesy, doesn't it? Jochen is still hoping he might be wrong. Especially since the source isn't very specific. Only that there is a curse."

"Doing what to whom?" I asked. "And how?"

"I said we don't know yet," Damian snapped.

*Whoa, what's wrong with the guy?*

He sagged in his chair. "Oh, sorry, I shouldn't take it out on you. I didn't get a wink of sleep last night because of that blasted leak. Not your fault, I know."

"There's a wet patch in the ceiling where the shower sits above," Rosie explained. "We keep telling the plumbers they must've botched something, but they won't listen. They want us to wait until next week and see if what they call a minor issue persists. It's not minor. It's wet. We stayed up into the small hours, trying to fix things."

"Please, don't stress. I understand. We don't happen to have a plumber among the coven members, do we?"

We didn't. We had a farmer, business owners, homemakers, a lawyer, a pest control specialist, and quite a few retirees, like my two friends here and Colonel Elmsworth. Plus, a handful of preschoolers and schoolkids. But no plumbers.

"We'll be fine," Damian said, not convincing anyone.

I finished my tea and rose. "Thanks for letting me vent and passing on the message about the curse. I guess there's nothing we can do for the moment."

Damian levered himself from his seat and gripped my hand. "I'm so sorry, Myrtle."

"Damian, it's fine. Water in the house is beyond shite. Makes you feel totally vulnerable."

"I guess with renovations that sort of thing is to be expected. Everything will sort itself out, eventually. Same with that curse. There's always a way."

Rosie might be right, but somehow, I was fresh out of optimism.

—

At the Witch's Retreat, I found the house muted with the chefs out, the Simpkinses gone, and the latest salesperson not due until tomorrow. That suited me fine, since it would give me the time I needed to coax the recipe book into spitting out invisible cures for magical plants. At the back of my mind, the word "curse" blinked in huge neon letters, but I pulled a mental curtain on the show. I had it up to here with today's disasters.

I opened the door to the parlor—and found Daisy snoring gently in the red armchair, Tiddles curled up in her lap. As quiet as I'd been, my arrival woke both sleepers.

"Who—What—"

The cat growled, shifted, and then snoozed off again. Cats

can sleep through anything.

"It's me. Sorry, had I known you were there, I'd left you in peace."

Daisy stretched and yawned. "No worries, but gimme a moment. It's been a hell of a day."

Yes, one could say that.

A surreptitious check of my watch revealed it was seven o'clock, and the church tower chimed its agreement only seconds later. The hell of a day had lasted even longer than I'd thought.

Petty, waiting in her favorite space by the window, rustled her leaves and fired off a greeting. Lush as ever, her foliage shone with health and the blooms bobbed cheerfully. Even her scent, balmy and buoyant, was just as it should be. An invisible load tumbled off my heart. My miracle plant looked and smelled okay.

"Is she ill?" Daisy asked.

The load rolled back up. "Uh, what do you mean?"

"When I came in, she whizzed around me. Suddenly, her greenery flopped. And she smelled like, sour? I patted the leaves, and once I'd talked to her for a while, she sort of calmed down."

Daisy turned toward the primrose, now rising from the floor boosted by a twinkly cloud. "Hey, little one, what's wrong with you?"

*Zap.* One spark landed on my cousin's nose. She sneezed and laughed. "That tickles."

"That's exactly how she acted this morning. And she made me read the recipe book. Trouble is, whatever she wants me to find seems to be hidden in the empty pages."

Daisy's eyes widened to the point I feared they might pop out, cartoon-style. "Ooh, she did that to you as well? She guided me to the grimoire and made me flip pages until she plonked her pot on the first empty bit."

"I reckon she doesn't know where exactly the information is hidden, just that it's in there somewhere. And I've no inkling of how to get at it."

"Oh, gosh, what could be wrong with poor Petty? Should we go and see a gardener? I mean, it could be something harmless. Mites, fungus—"

"For that, we don't need the recipe book."

"Hmm. True. Oh, how about if she's allergic to magic?"

I couldn't help it. I burst out laughing.

Daisy pouted. "What I'm saying is she might be allergic to our magic. I mean, it's pretty crap. Are you allergic, Petty?"

My primula sailed across to the coffee table and rapped twice.

"That's a new one," Daisy said.

"Actually, she's been doing that for a while, but it's getting more frequent."

Daisy twirled one of her auburn locks around a slender finger, the nail painted a sparkly orange. "Hey, sorry Petty, we don't speak plant."

*Rap. Rap.*

"A shame. She doesn't speak English either," my cousin said.

*Rap.* Followed by wild rustling.

"If I didn't know better, I would say she's, like, trying to communicate?"

"Daisy, she's always been doing that. With the scent, the sparks, her leaves and blossoms. That's not new. This banging is. Ditto the odd smell."

More lock twirling. "You know what this reminds me of?"

Big chocolate brown eyes blinked at me, like a spaniel begging for treats. The hair slipped from my cousin's finger and curled effortlessly onto a shoulder covered in baby-blue angora. I'd say it was too warm for the season, but the season didn't seem to know what it was doing either.

"No. Tell me."

"I watched telly the other day."

She did that a lot. She also had an unfortunate habit of being more off-topic than on.

"There was this program on séances. Where they used these

witchy boards?"

"Ouija, you mean? An alphabet board?"

"Yeah. Sort of cool, isn't it? These people sat in a circle, and one was touching this arrow thingy, and it suddenly twitched and created words. The fingers never moved. It's all because of signals from the spirit world."

Her voice had risen in volume, sounding awed. Tiddles sniffed the air once and then curled up again.

"Daisy, ghosts don't exist." That might be wishful thinking, but I knew demons didn't. Dot had told me, and despite being the grandmother from hell, she'd been pretty sharp with her magical lore. Better than me, anyway.

Daisy nodded eagerly. "Yeah, the guy who moderated the program said the same. Demonstrated how you can move that arrow with tiny twists of your muscles without it ever showing. It's all a scam, he said."

I'd known it. We were going off on a tangent. "What has that got to do with Petty?"

"The questions are always phrased in such a fashion one can only ever answer yes or no. And somebody then raps the response out, usually with their knees. One rap stands for 'yes.' And two for 'no.' I wonder if that's what Petty's doing?"

I froze. Blast it, that was clever. Could Daisy be right?

My primula was no ghost. Technically, she'd risen from the dead and could at best be called a zombie, though one with a highly independent spirit. Could she be using a whacky form of Morse code? She certainly had the brains for it. If that was the right word for whatever went on in that plant.

"You know, that's a fab idea. Let's try it out, shall we?" Gingerly, I approached the table. "Uh, Petty. You're a primrose, right? *Primula vulgaris*, correct?"

*Rap.*

Daisy's eyes sparkled. "She said yes."

"Slowly, slowly, that's way too easy, I've only just started." It was hard to hide the excitement bubbling up, though.

"You're a cat."

*Rap. Rap.*

That meant no, which was correct.

"But that's a cat." I pointed at Tiddles, who raised her head, shooting us the feline take on a miffed glare.

*Rap. Swish. Rustle.*

"She said yes, Myr, she said yes."

I couldn't stand still, so I paced to the window and back again. We were on the right track, but a little more proof was needed.

"Let me try something more complex. Um, that's Aunt Eve." This time, I pointed at my cousin.

*Rap. Rap.* The pot lifted and hovered toward the top shelf that sheltered auntie's urn. There it floated, swinging gently.

"Hooray," Daisy shouted.

"Yes." I punched my fist in the air. Daisy had done it, had cracked the floral code. "Houston, we have contact."

My cousin hooted and wrapped me in a tight embrace, her powerful perfume sending an uppercut into my lungs. Giddy with bliss—or perfume—I hugged her back, and we pirouetted through the living room. Petty hovered next to our heads, bobbing up and down as if buffeted by a strong wind. Showers of sparks rained on us, and I needed no translation app to know the primula was cheering.

We had a familiar who could go invisible and communicate. A giant leap for the Magical Misfits. Not to forget myself.

"Mow." Tiddles rose and padded away in a huff, her tail curled into a question mark. I struggled with an armful of cousin who was squeezing the air out of me.

"Petty talks. I mean, really talks," Daisy said, out of breath.

"Yes, she does. And that'll make things a lot easier."

Gently, I pushed my cousin aside. "Petty, are you ill?"

*Rap. Rap.*

"She isn't ill, she's fine," Daisy said, quite unnecessarily. Once more, she danced through the room, followed by the airborne plant. "Everything's hunky-dory."

I, however, remained rooted to the spot. Something dark and smelly welled up and pushed aside my good mood. If Petty wasn't ill, why the odd behavior? Why that alien scent?

The curse?

Later, when I shared my qualms with my cousin over a bottle of bubbly and a super-sized plate of sushi delivered by Pufferfish House, Daisy pooh-poohed my fears away.

"You always overthink things, Myr, and you're such a pessimist. Most likely she was frustrated because we didn't understand her and wanted us to check the hidden pages for the instructions. I mean, if the situation really were dire, Petty wouldn't be so relaxed, would you, sweetie?" With a burp and a giggle, Daisy poured a sip of champers into Petty's pot.

That made sense, so I allowed the bubbles to fizz over my worries. With the bottle empty, we staggered up the stairs, giggly like teenagers, and blew air kisses at each other before closing the doors to our rooms.

Once I was on my own, my personal black cloud returned. If only Chris was around. But he was at his apartment, coding, which meant I would have the duvet all to myself, but I also would be alone with things like curses and the crazy stuff going on in the village.

"Myrtle, you always want what you can't have," I said into the quiet of my room. Then I let my head sink into the pillow.

That night, I had the second dream.

Just like last time, I was ambling through an emerald sea of grass, ruffled by balmy breezes. The sky was blue, the mood benign. My bare feet swishing through the dewy grass released the buzzing green scent of things alive. Just like last time, I knew I was dreaming but didn't wake up. And once more I was getting nowhere, until suddenly my mind parted from my body and floated upward, cheerful and weightless. Happy with the world, I floated along, while my body on the ground turned translucent—and suddenly was no more.

The next moment I was sitting upright in my bed, wide awake, a rosy dawn washing over my curtains.

I had slept through the night. So, why did I feel so jaded? Yesterday I had been full of beans. Today, I was full of gas. A belch bubbled up, and distress signals from my bladder forced me into the bathroom. Too much champers, most likely.

I scowled at my pale face in the mirror, shadows under my eyes that hadn't been there before. Memories of a nameless fear wormed through my gut, and I gripped the rim of the washbasin. This was getting ridiculous. I forced myself to breathe in deeply and release the air as slowly as possible. The exercise helped ease the anxiety, and a strong patchouli-scented shower boosted my mood. When I emerged from the bathroom, the aroma of freshly brewed coffee teased my nostrils.

Just what the doctor ordered.

I padded to my wardrobe; the floorboards warm under my toes. Apparently, summer was about to grace us with its presence, so I chose a fake jeans dress made of washable silk whose color made my eyes appear bluer than they were. My new rusty mohair cardigan would protect my body against early morning drafts. Paired with leather moccasins in the same tawny red, the outfit would be complete. Searching for the shoes, my gaze dropped to the space underneath the bed.

More rose petals in pale pink, just like the ones I found yesterday. Some of them even lay scattered over the duvet. Another panicky rush washed over me. No matter what Daisy or Rosie might say, something was seriously wrong, something to do with my magic.

*No, you're not being pessimistic or overthinking things. And ignoring reality won't work either.*

But it was too early to call Jochen.

—

Downstairs, everything was peaceful for once. The Simpkins sisters were busy preparing breakfast until Cecily stuck her permed head over the saloon-style swing doors.

"Morning, Myrtle. Mind fetching the papers? Those cooks are already moving about, and we better get cracking. Oh, would you like coffee or tea? We'll have ourselves a cuppa."

"Sure. And a coffee, please."

She withdrew her head, and I went outside. The sun was up, birds enjoyed a chittering contest in the hedges, and two gray squirrels were chasing each other up the fir tree next to Mrs. Mornings' house. The same moment I reached the cookery club's dew-speckled vehicles, a metallic, fruity scent hit my nostrils that made me think of pizza.

Sometimes, my cravings were beyond weird.

I strode past the row of cars and fished the newspapers from our super-sized mailbox. Another dose of the funny whiff sneaked up my nose. The wheelie bins were out since it was rubbish collection day, but both were closed. Even a quick sniff at the lids yielded none of the odd odor.

My hands full of newspaper, I turned around.

When a ray of sunshine hit the windscreens of the cars, I stopped. My sluggish brain took ages to process the scene, but once it succeeded, my stomach contracted into a bristly ball.

A sinister red goo had splattered all over the front of the guests' vehicles, like in a scene from a B-movie. Who or what had died? Or rather: how many, for such a copious amount of blood couldn't come from only one person.

Not that I was an expert in such matters.

*This can't be real.*

I blinked at the scene. It didn't change. Once more, the odor hit my nostrils.

That wasn't blood. Actually, the gunk now sliding off one side mirror reminded me of something I'd seen and recently too. And I'd breathed in exactly the same odor not so long ago.

Still light-headed, my heart banging away in my chest, I approached the cars. The fruity aroma got stronger, and finally, my synapses clicked.

Tomato sauce.

Fury rose in my gorge and replaced the panic.

Violin cases for Linda's guests, tomatoes for mine. Some practical joker was on the bloody rampage. And since parts of the goo had already crusted over, the attack must have happened earlier this morning. Not satisfied with stealing, shooting people, and causing dangerous accidents, the resident poltergeist had now added childish pranks to its repertoire.

I whipped out my phone and thumbed a number.

"Crystal Dawn B&B, Linda speaking?" She sounded harassed.

"Myrtle here, Dawn—I mean, Linda do you—"

"I was just about to call you. Can you imagine?"

"Let me guess. Tomato sauce?"

"Uh, what? No. Packs of spaghetti shoved up the exhaust pipes. One of the girls wanted to get herself a newspaper. That's how she noticed. What do you mean by tomato sauce?"

"Smeared all over the windscreens."

"Nasty. The coppers will love us."

"Not sure telling them makes any odds since no one's hurt. But insurance might cover the car wash and, for that, we need to involve the officials."

"My lot will definitely call this in, believe me."

Sarah's words rang in my ears. Things were about to get worse. Oh yes, they had, even if smearing cars with tomato sauce wasn't quite in the same league as undermining tons of rock.

My brain, finally awake, whirred along. Someone must have a serious beef with the culinary mobsters. Alternatively, my original hunch had been right, and this was about the coven. Was someone targeting Linda and me through our guests?

No, that didn't sit quite right. Unlike the horrid rock incident, the tomato and spaghetti prank and the theft of the cases was spiteful rather than dangerous.

Spiteful? Now there was an idea—Anna.

While waiting for Jochen's call, I might as well sort out the woman once and for all. But for that, I'd need help.

# 10

## CHURCH BELLS RINGING

Not much later, Chris and I set out on the footpath that ran along the river Kennet. The air was crisp but pleasant, filled with the earthy scent of green things growing. If it weren't for my sanded eyelids and heavy limbs, I would have enjoyed the walk even more. Chris fared no better, hiding cavernous yawns behind his hand.

"What time did you go to bed last night?" I asked.

"This morning. At four."

"Ack. Why didn't you lie in?"

"I tried. Can't remember what came first, the rubbish collection or the delivery truck for the café. Both made a monstrous racket, and I couldn't go back to sleep."

Should I offer him a room? Would that not come across as brash? Relationships are tricky, especially at the start.

"So, forgive me if my brain isn't up to scratch," Chris said. "You're trying to achieve what exactly?"

"Constable Cameron suggested there might be more than one idiot at large. This morning's tomato massacre just isn't in the same league as the standing stone incident. Or even the shooting. I've this hunch Anna might be behind the massacre and the theft of the violin cases, and I want her to stop sniping."

Chris growled under his breath. "If you're wrong and that wretched woman undermined a standing stone, she's bloody dangerous. Though I can't work out how she'd know when your chefs would show up."

"Easy-peasy. Right now, groups must register a day in advance. The villain checked this schedule and loosened the stone accordingly. How does that sound?"

"Wild. How could your villain be sure the chefs would touch the stone?"

"True. Hmm, but I do think Sarah should know about the schedule and since I haven't an inkling where it's kept, I might as well ask Anna."

Chris muttered something under his breath.

We reached the bridge over the Kennet, where the footpath joined Broad Street. Picture-perfect, the spot offered a magnificent view of the river's silver band burbling through the fields. Dragonflies zipped past our heads, dipping and diving for the water weeds that swayed in the current like graceful dancers.

"Pretty isn't it?"

"Very." He wrapped his fingers around my hand and we stood, cocooned in warmth and sunshine—until the curse popped up in my mind.

I shuddered and let go of his hand.

"Are you cold?"

"Nah, don't worry."

*Tell him.*

Chris deserved to know we were in danger. Yet I hated crying wolf, especially when I didn't have the full picture. In the meantime, I'd continue my sleuthing, and that was that.

The banks on both sides of the river were covered in shrubs and wildflowers, crisscrossed in places by narrow trails left behind by the hikers. We climbed one track back up to the road and followed Broad Street to the churchyard.

Avebury's burial place presented a neat front to the world, the grass mowed, the headstones all lined up; even the compost heap was as clean as a whistle; not one wilting wreath spoiled the view. As we passed under the lychgate, I caught sight of the head gardener and the intern, pruning the beech hedge into shape.

"Cal, *will* you stop your endless blather?" the old man asked. "I know you know your stuff. I know your friends aren't happy. I agree the situation's shite. But what can we do, eh?"

"Pip said he'd take action. So far, he's done zilch. Who's blathering now?" A world of woe lived in the young man's words.

"He said that? Seriously?"

"Yeppers. But if you think he loosened that stone, you're wrong. For one thing, he'd never ever pick up a spade. Poor Nina, though. I wish I could help—"

"You and your Robin Hood complex. I want nothing to do with this. Let's finish this job, and then we'll have a nice cuppa in the shed, eh?"

"Oho, Sarah'll like this," I whispered.

Chris nodded. "Indeed. You better tell her. What are these two doing, anyway? Prepping for a churchyard of the month competition?"

"I bet Anna's behind it. With her, everything is organized to the nth degree—weeds need not apply. At least the front of the church is. The cheap seats at the back are a lot more unkempt."

Chris patted my shoulder. "Look at the bright side. Like that, your ancestor's grave is safe."

So true.

———

We entered the church through the south door, a rounded portal in the wall, framed by thick pillars and a decorative border zigzagging over the top. Once arrived at the other end of the nave, my gaze hitched at some sort of old stone basin large enough to hide a human body.

"Ah, been wanting to come here for ages." Chris traced the carvings on the thing. "This is amazing."

"Seriously?"

"It's a Norman tub font. Designed for total immersion. There aren't that many left in the UK."

He looked inside, and my heart missed a beat. However, he neither freaked nor swore, so the thing must be empty.

"Why don't you treat yourself to a tour while I try to flush out Anna? As long as you don't go outside, I should be safe enough."

He frowned. "You wanted a bodyguard, now you've got one."

With Chris trailing behind, I made my way to the vestry. Its door stood half-open. I raised my hand to knock—and my gaze fell on an object, just about discernible in the crack between the door and jamb.

A violin case.

I dropped my hand and let my gaze search the bit of room visible from the entrance.

Five violin cases in total had been shoved into a corner of the vestry, half-hidden behind plastic bags bulging with fabric or clothes, only the one I had spotted first peeping out far enough to catch my attention.

My hunch concerning Anna had been spot on.

Inside the vestry, everything seemed to be quiet, though the rushing of my blood in my ears didn't help the acoustics. I pushed the door open a few more inches, half-expecting it to creak.

It didn't.

Instead, I now had a full view of an open wardrobe filled with sheets and folded strips of brocade, which I assumed to be altar decorations.

That wasn't what sucked in my gaze and amped up the rush in my ears to an angry pounding.

On the floor in front of the wardrobe lay a large plastic toy gun. Super-soakers they were called. I knew, because Jenna's kids had two.

Its tank and nozzle were caked with a reddish-brown residue that could only be tomato sauce, and the fruity, tangy odor teasing my nose confirmed my suspicions.

*Crunch.*

Someone was in the vestry.

I jumped backward, pressed myself against the cold stone of the church wall, and held my breath.

More rustling and crunching, followed by a determined footfall.

"Is that door ever going to be fixed?"

I recognized the voice—Anna. Her comment was chased by the sound of the vestry door slamming shut.

"Chris? Quick, come with me."

Thankfully, he didn't ask questions. We pelted back to the entrance and stopped at the old font.

"I saw them."

"Saw what?"

"The stolen violin cases. And one of these water gun thingies. Only it was covered in tomato sauce. I told you Anna's our poltergeist. That's at least one point ticked off on Sarah's case list."

"I'm not sure there's much of a case unless being a general nuisance is a criminal offense. Okay, the theft might stick. What on earth is the woman trying to achieve with those stunts?"

"Chri-is. We discussed this already, remember? She's madly against non-locals marrying here. So, she's trying to spook them."

"Put like that ...Fine, what's the battle plan?"

A valid question. If I turned up, Chris in tow, and put Anna on the spot, she might simply deny everything and throw us out of her church.

"The schedule has priority. Once I accuse her of committing the tomato attack, that's it. She'll clam up."

"And then what? That's assuming you get her to talk."

"It's tricky. If I expose Anna, she'll lose face. And in such a tiny village, that'd be a big deal. I really don't need more enemies." Especially not someone who knew so much about the local history she might expose the coven.

"Looks like you want to have your cake and eat it. Not sure how that's going to work."

"I can tell Anna I know what she's done and suggest she makes up for it. Discreetly, of course. Like that, no one would know that she's a bit, well …"

Storm clouds had gathered on Chris's forehead. "Prejudiced? Vindictive? Dangerous? What if she's gone beyond theft and petty misdemeanor?"

"If she acts up, all bets are off."

He crossed his arms in front of his chest. "Call Sarah now. That's your safest bet."

"Then this blows wide, and Anna will most likely lawyer up. And I'm the whistleblower who upset the balance. Not a good idea, not here, not with me being a newcomer. Let me at least try."

"I thought she hated your guts."

"She'll hate me even more if this goes all over the village, believe me."

Chris shook his head. "You're incorrigible. Fine, have it your way. But I'll be right behind you, and if she utters as much as one menacing syllable, that's it."

I stroked his cheek. "Thank you for humoring me."

He grinned. "Got no choice, do I?"

The sight of Chris's black-bottomed backside scarpering behind the altar triggered a quick giggle, but it fizzled out in an instant.

Heart beating in my throat, I raised my hand and knocked.

—

The door to the vestry popped open, and a flustered face peeped through the gap. Anna couldn't be much older than me. My money was on her being in her mid-thirties. Her mousy blonde hair was pulled back into a scrunchy, from where strands had escaped, framing features that would have been pleasant if it hadn't been for her eyes. Set unfortunately close to her sharp nose, they seemed to be headed for an imminent collision. Somehow, she reminded me of a mistrustful rodent.

"Oh, I hope you weren't looking for me. I'm rather busy," she said.

She would be if she were trying to hide the evidence.

I slapped on what I trusted to be a disarming smile. "It won't take long, promised. It's about the hassle we keep having here. First that skeleton, then the shooting, yesterday the standing stone—we really don't need the coppers to turn the place upside down all over again, do we?"

Hidden behind my guileless mien, I searched Anna's face for a reaction. Not much luck there.

"Perhaps we can pre-empt the law?

She looked at her watch. "Huh? How?"

I lowered my voice. "Don't tell anyone, but it looks like the collapse of the standing stone might indeed have been engineered. Since it nearly hit one of my guests, I'm wondering whether someone has it in for them."

Anna snorted. "Hah, heard that theory over the grapevine already. You're not very lucky with your customers, are you? Keep having a brush with death, don't they? But what has that got to do with me?"

The notion it was my fault if my guests had run-ins with the grim reaper wasn't new, but I still had a hard time keeping up the friendly façade. Channeling Daisy's acting skills, I threw what might pass as a furtive glance into the chancery. "You coordinate the visitor schedule for the henge, correct?"

"So what? Told you I'm busy here, so either come to the point, or leave me alone."

The woman was such a total bundle of joy. And our chat wasn't quite moving in the right direction. I should have read up on *Interrogations for Dummies*, or something along those lines. Now, it was too late.

"I'm trying to, okay?" *Eek.* That had come out sharper than intended. "As far as I'm aware, you're the one planning the visits. Who's at the henge when, who needs an audio tour, that sort of thing."

"And?"

"What if someone got hold of the schedule and worked out when my visitors would be on the henge? Like that, they knew when to drop a great big stone on them."

There were holes in my theory the size of a barn, and Chris had pointed them out. Anna, however, didn't seem to find anything amiss. A frown appeared on her forehead and she tapped her lips. "It's possible."

"Do you, by any chance, recall yesterday's schedule?"

She tossed her head like a shying horse. More hair escaped from the scrunchie. "People always expect me to remember every stupid detail. If you're that keen, go to the office and have a look for yourself. We're not Fort Knox. What I don't get— what's the whole point?"

*Gotcha.* The schedule was publicly available, which took care of one problem. Now to the harder part.

"This isn't the first time something rotten happens to my guests. And not only mine, Linda has the same problem. The police don't know yet. Things only clicked for me this morning."

The line of Anna's mouth hardened. I wiped my sweaty hands on my dress. The next part would be crucial. Either I could reel her in, or I'd lose her completely.

"Somebody sprayed tomato sauce over the cars parked in my front yard. Not only that, yesterday, some violin cases were stolen from the Crystal Dawn."

By now, I had lowered my voice to a murmur and Anna leaned in, wanting to hear. "Really? How bizarre," she said, in an amused tone.

"Yes. Makes me wonder whether the person responsible might also be behind the stolen skeleton—and the standing stone. Especially the standing stone. Which would mean somebody has it in for the culinary mobsters, uh …my guests. Thanks for telling me about the schedule, that's all I needed to know. My friend in the CID will love this." I nodded in my best wise woman impersonation.

Anna's eyes widened. She took a step backward. "How …oh, no, that would be murder." Her voice had risen in pitch.

"Quite so. Isobel nearly died. This has got to stop."

Anna shook her head with such vehemence the scrunchy dropped off and her wispy hair drooped to her shoulders. "No way. You're wrong. It's the rain. It loosened the stone. The thing has been wonky for ages. Everything's Jedd's fault. He should've blocked it off a long time ago."

Finally, we were getting somewhere. Unless her acting was a lot better than mine, attempted murder wasn't in her script, but if I'd truly believed that, I wouldn't be here, Chris or no Chris.

I slipped Anna a furtive glance. Yup, if I needed proof the woman was guilty of something, this was it. Her gaze darted from left to right, as if searching for the emergency exit, and she was tugging at the strands of hair dangling over her shoulder. Then she shook herself. The door opened further. "You better come in."

*Uh-oh.* But she'd smell a rat if I didn't play along.

Anna ushered me into the vestry and closed the door behind us with a determined click. "How convenient for you to have a friend in the police."

"Yes, isn't it?" I used the broadest smile in my repertoire. "She'll be glad to hear what you told me about the schedule being so accessible. Sarah's a brilliant detective. She'll nail her culprit, believe me. She's done it before."

With a little help from her friend.

Anna licked her lips. "Sure. But I just remembered something. The situation isn't as straightforward as you might think."

Of course not. "Oh?"

"It just came back to me. Your guests weren't even booked for a visit. They showed up without checking in beforehand. These people think they can jerk us yokels around. Let me show you what I mean."

She marched to a battered wooden school bench on top of which sat her handbag. Some rummaging yielded a tablet computer, which she powered up.

"In the office we only keep a printout. This is the master plan. At the moment, we're offering three different self-guided tours. You can either get the pamphlets for free or pay for the audio guides. 'Village Experience' focuses on the manor and gardens, followed by the church and the village center. The second tour takes them around the stone circle. The third one starts at the circle but afterward goes through West Kennet Avenue toward the Sanctuary."

Funny how coercion had worked wonders for her memory. "Sounds fascinating. I really must try them one day. So, the cookery club members weren't booked for any of these tours?"

"Oh yes, they were. For the one on the henge." Anna stabbed at her tablet. "But today, not yesterday. And with audio, not pamphlets. Anyway, it means the accident's got nothing to do with them. See for yourself."

The tablet got thrust close to my face, and I took an involuntary step backward, straight into the door handle.

*Ouch.* I massaged my back and then took the tablet. The facts on the screen supported Anna's story.

Something moved against my spine—the handle. It shifted ever so slightly before it slipped back up. That had to be Chris, telling me he was still out there, looking after me. Fortunately, Anna never noticed.

"How many people know of this schedule? And how accessible is it, really?"

"As I said, the printout's in the office, even if it might not always be totally up to date. I don't have the time for that. Everybody remotely involved in the visits goes in and out of there, all the time. If you were a little more interested in what we do here, you'd know."

*Touché*. But I wouldn't tell her that.

Anna was on a roll. "If someone truly wanted to hurt your guests, they would've planned for the stone to fall today. Everything else is nothing but conjecture. Which means either the whole thing was an accident, or somebody decided to indulge in some random havoc. No need for your buddy in the police to get involved." Anna snapped her mouth shut and straightened, eyes flashing in triumph.

"But that's not what we want, right? We want this to stop."

Anna huffed. "I guess so. We can't have the visitors dying. Not again."

"When you talk about the people involved, who are they?"

"Heavens, I just told you. Anyone working for the society or dealing with the tours. The director, the volunteers, the part-time assistant, the guides, the intern in the tourist info. Everyone."

"All the interns?"

Anna sniffed. "Mostly the chap manning the info. The other two don't come around much. They're busy. Well, that gardening intern is. I'm not so sure about the fashionista in the museum."

At least Anna was talking. The longer she did that, the better my chances of learning something meaty for Sarah to follow up on.

"Fair enough," I said. "But I won't buy the accident theory. I was at the henge yesterday when the stone dropped. A tourist noticed signs of recent digging. The cops are only waiting for their specialists to confirm things."

Anna shrugged. "Well, fine, then it isn't an accident. Most likely, somebody wants to cause trouble for Jedd. Doesn't surprise me in the slightest. That man is so pigheaded. Have you talked to him yet?"

"No, only heard about him. Nothing good, really."

"There you go. Tell the cops to lock him up, and that'll put an end to this rubbish." Relief brightened her face. "Is that it? I've still got plenty of sorting to do."

So did I.

I had Chris on tap, or rather on the handle, which was a definite plus. It would be nice if I could use my magical skylles to make her confess, but I didn't feel either stressed or angry. Only bewildered and sad. And tired. Very tired.

Alternatively, I could share my suspicions with Sarah in private and let Anna find out the hard way. But that was … sneaky. As sneaky as Anna had been.

My gaze fell on the plastic bags piled up in the space where I had earlier spotted the violin cases. They had to be still in the vestry. She simply didn't have enough time to shift things before I turned up.

"Why did you do it?" I asked in a conversational tone.

"Sorry?" Confusion clouded Anna's face. It segued to anger. "How dare you—"

"Not the falling rock. That wasn't you. I'm talking about the stolen violin cases and the tomato and spaghetti business this morning." My voice had a slightly squeaky tone to it; I could only hope Anna would be too upset to notice.

"What are you on about?"

"Anna, I think you know very well what I mean. I don't get it. Disappearing the cases is nasty at best, theft at worst. Squirting sauce all over the place is …childish." Sudden inspiration struck. "You were trying to implicate the interns."

Anna twitched as if zapped by an electric current. "How did you work that out …Eh, I mean …"

Bingo. A shot into the blue, but it had hit home. "I bet the toy gun and the cases are still here in the vestry. Perhaps I should call my friend to have the place searched."

I fished for my phone and held it up, but not once let her out of sight.

Anna's shoulders slumped. Slowly, she sank onto the old school bench. I almost felt sorry for her. Almost. What she had done was more moronic than evil, but her acts had been fueled by dark thoughts.

She looked up, an echo of her anger back in her eyes. "Those people don't belong here," she said. "They show no respect to the village. Vicar should never have allowed their wedding, never."

"But he did, and it's his decision, really."

"He's almost seventy, close to retirement. Gone doddery, doesn't know what he's doing." There was a stubborn set to her jaw.

"So, you were taking matters into your own hands by trying to frighten the wedding party away."

No response.

"Anna, you've caused plenty of unnecessary grief. Fine, my guests might've got their dates about the tour confused, but I reassure you they didn't do it deliberately. And they're not going to call off the marriage either."

"Hah," she said, but the venom had left her words.

"Shame on you for trying to push the blame on the interns. They aren't exactly happy as it is."

She shrugged. "They can always go away if they don't like it here."

"Most likely the work placement is part of their studies, so I can't see it being that easy."

At first, she didn't respond. The room was heavy with silence, and the handle still digging into my back moved again. I pressed my body against it. The movement stopped.

Anna traced carvings on the bench with a finger, not once meeting my eye. "What else was I supposed to do? These people kept ringing and ringing, never gave up. I'm not proud of what I did, but I couldn't stomach talking to them. I just couldn't. It's all so wrong. They should get married where they live and leave us in peace. This town has suffered enough upheaval. We don't need more."

My heart clenched. Anna was right. But she'd been the one to stir up trouble.

She looked up, pain in her eyes. "And you're now going to tell your cop friend about me."

Was I? I couldn't just let this go. But as I had told Chris this morning, I didn't want to turn the woman into an enemy.

*You already have.*

I called the inner saboteur to order and told Anna what I wanted her to do. She didn't like it. No big surprise.

"And what if they still want to finger me to the coppers later?" Her tone was bitter, her face hard.

I said nothing.

"Oh, if you insist. Fine, I'll make sure they get their stupid violin cases back. As to the cars, surely they have insurance. That'll cover the costs for the cleaning. Though they're all rich, they can afford it."

That argument was at the origin of many an insurance swindle and sent the premiums into a spiral for the rest of us. "They'll leave you alone. I'll ensure that. I don't want any fuss either. I'll tell the cops this problem's sorted, and they can focus on the stone incident. They might have to check the up-to-date plan, though."

"Someone will work it out, and I'll look like the resident idiot."

*Well, duh.* Why couldn't that blasted woman understand that I was trying to help her?

"I'll leave you to it, then." When I got no response, I slipped into the chancery.

Behind me, the door snicked shut.

# 11

### JINXED

Chris, leaning against the nearest pillar, observed me with a bemused expression on his face.

"Mission Mafia successfully concluded?"

The stale smell of must and old incense crept up on me, making me sneeze. That didn't ease the heaviness in my chest. Instead, the walls of the church were pressing in on me.

"I need fresh air."

We headed for the back of the churchyard, where old headstones leaned at wild angles, weeds had conquered the grass, and the sparrows chirped in defiance from the bushes.

Chris pulled me against his beating heart. "Care to share?"

I did. Once I had finished, I lifted my head and searched his eyes. "Sometimes I wonder why I bother."

"Because you are who you are, a force of nature. Tell Sarah what you think she needs to know, and let's hope you won't live to regret it."

*Splat.* Something wet and white landed in my cleavage. I jumped backward, pawing at the disgusting gunk and only succeeding in smearing it all over my bust. "Eek, that's bird poo.

And you stop laughing."

He didn't. His eyes were streaming, and he was leaning on the nearest headstone for support. "Oh Myrtle, you're a hoot and a half."

Still grinning, Chris pushed himself off the stone, dug in his pockets and withdrew his keys, the smartphone, and a packet of chewing gum. He then rummaged in his other pocket and fished out a wet-wipe in a foil pack. When we ate mussels the other day, we'd been given these things to clean our fingers.

"Take this."

With the help of the wipe, I rid myself of the spatter.

Chris looked at his spaceship of a watch. "I hate to say this, but I need to make a move. There's projects, including yours, waiting for me."

I looked for a rubbish bin, saw none, and shoved the wadded wipe into a side pocket of my buttpack. "Will you be around this evening?"

Chris wriggled his brows. "Will I ever."

"I could come to your place if you prefer that."

"Nah, bed's too small."

"Chris, that wasn't what I meant."

"What a shame. I'll call you when I'm done."

We said goodbye to each other, which took some time. Once his broad back had disappeared from view, I leaned against the rough surface of the headstone Chris used as a prop before, lapped up the feeble sun, and looked at nothing in particular. Until the matted briars swam into view. The sun had moved and a stray ray pierced the gloom, lighting up parts of the headstone at the front—the one that guarded the remains of Martyn Cowslip while Rosalynd Asher and Mary Anne Coldron were still lost among the dense thicket of bristly plants.

What sort of people might they have been? Tolerant, or as knuckle-headed as Anna? Would they have known the unnamed man buried under the dovecote whose remains I found? If only bones could talk.

"But they do, Myrtle, they do."

Crows cawed and exploded from the bushes in a rushing of wings, and my heart skipped a beat. *Stop having conversations with yourself. It frightens the wildlife.*

Unless one of those birds was behind the splat attack. Then we'd be even.

The opening strains of Beethoven's Fifth Symphony burst from my smartphone. A quick check of the number pushed my heartbeat into the stratosphere.

"Hello, Jochen. Great to hear from you."

"Yes, yes, same here. Though I'm afraid you might not like what I have to say." When pronouncing the v, he flirted with an f, and his th was dodgy—clear signs of distress.

"Your message to Damian must've arrived rather quickly."

"He hasn't got it yet. We discovered a second source. No need for further verification. Sadly, it's all too clear."

For a moment, we both fell silent. Unable to stand still, I prowled from the nearest headstone to a rusty fence and back again. Blasted security protocol. How was one supposed to have a meaningful conversation when one mustn't give anything away?

"Clear as in ...?"

"Tell me, how good is your sleep recently?"

Huh? "I thought we were talking about...paranormal challenges."

"Yes. Humor me for a moment."

"Apart from today, I slept reasonably well in the past few days."

"No strange dreams? You don't feel washed out or anything?"

*Uh-oh.* A lump of ice materialized where my stomach used to be.

"Dreams ...Yes, the same one twice in a row. But then my dreams are always strange. Today I feel knackered, but yesterday I was fine."

"In your dreams, do you fly? Or rather, not you, only a part of you. And the rest is still on the ground? Walking, fading?"

*Double uh-oh.* The icy lump grew. "Eh, yes. Though flying is perhaps not the right word. There's grass and a vast space, and I'm sort of floating away."

"Zat is not good. You are probably the first, but then you are the strongest."

For Jochen to drop his th completely and ignore contractions, the outlook had to be grim.

"Is this for real? What's your source, anyway?"

"The warning popped up as part of a historical record we were researching for your database. A comment referring to a Benedictine nun's diary, written in the early seventeen hundreds. The diary itself is lost, but the manuscript quotes parts of the text, talking about a 'kindred spirit'. The author was a history professor living in Weimar in 1831. We had a hard time tracing his works, but yesterday evening we finally found the treatise where this quote appears."

A subversive nun? Well, why not? A cloister might well have turned into much-needed shelter for a woman compromised by magic. Brave of her to record her knowledge when it could cost her life.

"Ah. And what exactly did the good sister write about?"

"She calls it the lost curse of the skylled, and by that she doesn't mean only those that got left behind."

He was referring to our people, the Reds, the lesser-gifted witches, left behind when the magical pop stars, the Whites, vanished through the Avebury stone circle.

We were both in severe breach of the safety protocol, but who cared? Certainly not my inner iceberg, growing inch by chilly inch.

"She cites the symptoms. That's how we know about the dreams. Unfortunately, there's nothing about the cure. Even the info on the curse itself is pretty sketchy, so I can't tell you exactly what's going to happen and how bad it is."

"Great. Just peachy."

"Yeah. Oh, I forgot two things. First of all, the curse seems to be linked to the summer solstice."

"We've passed it."

"Yes, I know. I talked this through with Damian, and he suggests the healing ritual should most likely have taken place on or around the longest day."

Not only was that unfair, it was downright rotten. Concerned about possible side effects of the solstice, we had sent most of the coven away. When absolutely zilch happened, they returned, bitching and moaning about the inconvenience and the expense, blaming all and sundry, but mostly Elmsworth, who had organized the evacuation, and me.

And now it appeared we had been right all along. Only the timing had been off.

Was it already too late?

"You mentioned two things."

"Yes, but the second bit doesn't help us, because the text isn't complete. It mentions mirrors, but then it breaks off."

A memory rose, an echo of words spoken only recently. Mirrors, something to do with mirrors.

The memory slipped from my grasp.

"If it weren't so scary, the whole thing might well be a trashy horror story."

"Very trashy," Jochen said.

"Nobody's done any rituals for the past four hundred years. I don't see why this suddenly should be an issue." While I was speaking, the answer flashed in my head, and Jochen put it into words.

"We're together again, with you at the henge. That must make a difference. Though it can't be totally disastrous, otherwise we'd have noticed something, right? Maybe, our skylles are too feeble for the curse to get a proper grip."

"We disbanded for the solstice. Perhaps that'll save our bacon."

"There's no point in speculating. We need facts."

"I'll see what I can do."

"*Ja, aber mach bitte schnell.*"

The comment came straight from the heart, so I promised a fast delivery, unsure if I could keep my promise, and finished.

With unseeing eyes, I shoved the phone into my buttpack. In the space of one call, my world had gone from tolerably weird to something utterly surreal.

Cursed, we were cursed, might be doomed.

*Get a grip on yourself.*

I snapped out of my trance. The sun had moved on, and more rays now penetrated the brambles, highlighting the dark shape of the second headstone, the one belonging to Rosalynd Asher.

"Did you die of a curse?"

I shivered; my limbs caught in the grip of the same leaden tiredness that had plagued me all morning. A tiredness that might well be something more sinister than the result of a broken night. My thoughts tumbled around in my mind, none of them meaningful, all of them wild. I should be proud of myself for solving one of the mysteries plaguing the village. Instead, Fate had just upped the ante.

I had to get moving. Had to find a solution.

"Wish me luck," I said to the silent trio among the brambles.

Someone coughed.

Panic fluttering in my throat, I whirled around.

A slender woman with a shock of auburn hair leaned against a headstone, smiling widely.

"Jenna!"

My friend rushed at me and we hugged.

"I'm so glad to be home," Jenna said.

"And I'm glad you've returned. Even if you spooked the socks off me just now." I gave her hand a gentle squeeze. It might have belonged to a child; it was that small. "How did you ever find me?"

Jenna's laugh tinkled into the sunny afternoon. She couldn't fool me. Shadows bruised her eyes, and her elfin face was pasty.

"Oh, in his last call Marty mentioned your visit, and Sweet Earth did he make me feel guilty. I shouldn't have dashed off without telling you. I'm so, so sorry."

"Jen, please. It's okay."

"No, it isn't. Anyway, it was time to return so we left early this morning. I called as soon as I'd sorted my bits and bobs. You can't imagine the amount of stuff you have to transport when you travel with kids." She winked at me. "Alma and Cecily thought you might be somewhere in the village, so I arranged with Mel that she'd show my boys around the manor—they love playing hide and seek in the house—and zoomed over. Then I lucked out and ran into Chris."

"And the kids?"

*Creak* went the churchyard gate.

"Auntie Myrtle, Auntie Myrtle." The twins raced up, each carrying a shoe carton covered in wonky sketches of fish.

"We brought you presents." Robbie pushed a carton at me.

At least I was pretty sure it was him. Not having seen the twins in the last few days made it difficult to tell them apart— same ginger hair, freckled faces, and bright, keen eyes.

His mother tutted. "How often did I tell you not to butt in when adults are talking?"

"Mu-um," the twins chorused.

"How sweet of you to think of me. Let's see what you have there, shall we?"

Robbie and Johnnie nudged each other. Two small faces beamed with glee as I fished their gifts from the box: three gull feathers, a barnacled stone, and gazillions of broken shells in a can.

"If you jiggle that, you can hear the sea," Robbie said.

"Thank you, I'll do that." I hugged them, breathed in their unique kiddie scent and, for a heartbeat, was at peace with the world.

"Now, off you run, you two. Mel's waiting for her present

and we've things to discuss," Jenna said.

The boys darted away as if catapulted.

"Rascals, both of them. Myrtle, I hear you're sleuthing again. Makes sense. I mean, hello, standing stones falling over and people getting shot? And what's this curse business?" The laughter died in Jenna's eyes.

Crikey. She wasted no time.

"Ah, the curse. I only just got the details. Tell me something. Do you suffer from odd dreams?"

She sighed. "Plenty. Most of them related to Gran." She bit her lips and gazed at the brambles.

I gave her hand another squeeze, and her fingers curled around mine as if they were a lifeline. "Jen, if you don't want to talk about her, don't. But if you need to, you know where to find me."

"Thanks, Myr. That's another reason for returning. I'm lost without someone to ground me, and you and Marty are as rock-solid as they come." She sniffed, and I rummaged for a hankie.

Rock-solid, hah. "So, you're not dreaming about grasslands and floating?"

Jenna dabbed at her eyes. "No. Should I?"

Nobody should do anything of the sort, but since she and I now made up the coven's paranormal finest, her not having the dream seemed odd. She'd been away, though. Perhaps we all had better run for the hills? Somehow, I couldn't convince myself the solution would be that easy.

"Did Dot ...does the laundry list mention a curse? Sorry, but I have to ask."

Jenna's eyes grew enormous and dark. "I ...uh, not sure."

"Actually, I suspect Bob Ignatius might be sitting on the counter curse and is stirring up trouble to put me under pressure. He called me, you know?"

She said nothing.

"To tell you the truth, Chris isn't convinced his uncle is the culprit. Anna didn't help by muddling things up with her sabotage. If you spoke to the Simpkinses, you'll know what I mean. We had a bugger of a time calming down our guests."

Jen nodded.

"But she denies responsibility for anything other than the stunt this morning and the theft of the violin cases. I'm inclined to believe her."

My friend's face was a pale oval against the dark tangle of creepers. "How can you be so ...so rational. If there really is a curse, we might all be lost. Just think of my boys." Her voice hitched at the last word. A tear coursed down her cheek, which she thumbed away.

The comment stung. "Believe me, I'm not rational at all. I have to keep a lid on it, otherwise ..."

"Sorry. "

The silence between us stretched and strained until I could bear it no longer. "I guess you also heard about the skeleton?"

Jenna cleared her throat. She nodded eagerly. "Yes. Yes, I did."

"Hagbottom-Smythe seems to think it might've belonged to a witch. Of course, he doesn't believe in magic. He mentioned a group of what he called early environmentalists, called earth ...earth somethings. They were buried in unhallowed ground, under the dovecote."

"Earth Wardens," Jenna said. "Gran ...Well, she thought that's what our ancestors labeled themselves. Actually, I would've expected her to complain about sacrilege when the archaeologists dug up the bones, which she never did."

"Maybe she thought it wiser to keep quiet. Let's assume we're talking witch. What does that mean for us?"

Jen contemplated the nearest headstone. "I wonder if the person who nicked the remains knew what ...who they took for a walk. The skeleton caper is totally cray-cray. So's the shooting. Somehow, they don't fit the standing stone thing. That's so unbelievably nasty." She heaved a deep sigh. "No matter what, I can't see how either links to the curse."

"And the curse is our biggest problem."

"Oh, yes. Myr, don't hate me, but this time you'd better leave the sleuthing to the cops. The coven needs you."

"I only got involved because last time I didn't react until it was almost too late."

*Ouch.* Last time, Jenna and Marty's grandmother had been the villain.

"Sure," Jenna said, her calm voice belied by the pain in her eyes.

Childish laughter drifted across from the manor.

"Jen, it'll be all right," I said. "We'll find a cure." Pep talk 101. I didn't even know where to begin.

Jenna raised her chin. "We will because we have to. I'll consult the laundry list, though I'm not optimistic. Your job is more difficult, I fear. You can't even see what you're supposed to be reading."

An invisible fist punched my stomach.

"Where are my brains these days? Petty wanted me to check the empty pages. She tried Daisy as well. At first, we thought she might be ill, and the cure hidden in the book. But she claims she's fine. And since she's calmed down, Daise and I thought it might've been related to our communication issues. But it isn't. Oh blast, why didn't she tell me?"

Jenna tilted her head. "Tell you? Oh, you mean that Morse thing. Daisy mentioned something. I'd so love to watch."

"You will."

"But that means your recipe book *does* have the info we need. How did you choose last time which page to unhex?"

"Sadly, the page chose me."

"You'll do it. I have every faith in you. Petty's your familiar, she knows how to save you. And us. If she tells you to search the blank pages, then you better do that and sharpish." The smile had returned to her face.

"Jen, I have no clue how to fix these blasted pages. Unless it's the murders boosting my skylles—oh, I'm so sorry."

Jenna twirled a maroon lock about her finger and regarded me closely. "That would be totally against our nature. Our skylles are there to nurture and protect, and not to kill."

"Jen—"

She waved me off. "I'll have to face up to reality, don't I? Gran said it was all about emotions and really wanting something. Well, the curse is pretty scary, and it needs sorting. Maybe Daisy can help. She deciphered Petty's morse code, after all."

"I'll ask her."

"If the Coldron sisters"—she hooked quotation marks in the air—"can't unhex the empty pages, then I'll join you."

"Ah, Shakespeare. 'When shall we three meet again'? A threesome isn't a bad idea, you know?"

Her smile turned wicked. "Sure. Try on your own, but if you need me, I'll be there."

A grammar school teacher gone landlady, an ex-barmaid gone shopkeeper, a young mother who was also the world's greatest hobby chef, and a zombie primula—not your average X-force.

But it was the only force we had.

# 12

## BICYCLE RACE

Back at the Witch's Retreat, I headed for my parlor to have a little "chat" with Petty. The moment I strode past the kitchen, Cecily leaned over the saloon-style swing doors.

"Hey, wait a moment, Alma's got something for you." Cecily moved aside for her sister.

I stopped. A tic sprang up in the corner of my eye. "Cripes, don't tell me we need more tomatoes."

Alma's homey features lit up in a brief smile. Behind her, Cecily loomed, teapot in hand.

"No, thanks to you. There's plenty," Alma said. "And those guests of ours are actually decent folk. They use their towels more than once, no need for a laundry run."

"'Tisn't good for Irene if we don't wash the towels every day," Cecily said, her tone as lugubrious as it could get.

"It might not be ideal hygiene, but it's certainly better for the environment."

Alma nodded. "That's why we leave them be. Next visit to the cleaners isn't due until we do the sheets. Oh, before I forget it, your accountant rang. He needs you to send over the latest bills. ASAP, he said."

Sheets, bills, climate change, what nice, normal problems to have. "Thanks, I'll have a go at them later. Was that it?"

Alma pulled a white envelope from the pocket in her frock. "This came."

"It's an ominous letter, addressed to you," Cecily said. "Somebody left it on the mat."

Ominous was a fitting word, though that wasn't what she meant. "Anonymous?"

Alma nodded. "There's no address on it, for sure."

My tic got more pronounced. "What's it about?"

"It's for you," Alma said, in a flat voice. "It wasn't closed, but I promise we didn't read it."

Open mouth, insert foot. The sisters might be prone to gossip, but they wouldn't touch private mail, no matter what form it took, and the sender must have known that. Why else would they leave the envelope unsealed?

"Of course you wouldn't. Sorry, wasn't thinking. May I?" I held out my hand.

With a curt nod, Alma handed across the message.

I unfolded the paper waiting inside and studied the computer-generated message.

*Tell your guests to get their cars washed at Mulam's Superclean in Swindon, and I'll cover the costs. The violin cases have been returned with an apology. I have no idea what came over me. Recently, I've been very stressed, but that's not an excuse, I know. If your and Linda's guests wish to press charges, I won't blame them, though I would prefer if they didn't. Can you arrange things with them? I'll talked to the vicar as well. If need be, I'll swear on a stack of Bibles I'm not involved with any of the other incidents. Thank you for your kindness.*

No name, but then none was needed. Ready tears sprang

into my eyes. I might be one sucky witch, but occasionally I did some good.

When I looked up, the Simpkins sisters appeared rather blurry. I wiped my eyes.

"What does it say?" Cecily asked, her tone deceptively casual.

They wouldn't sneak a peek, but of course, they were as curious as ever. To be fair, their honesty deserved a reward, payable in juicy news. Which was tricky, since I mustn't expose Anna.

"You'll like this." I read out the text—minus the parts about the vicar and the oath.

"You know that person," Alma said, her tone brooking no argument.

Cecily pushed through the doors and joined her sister.

"Yes. Please, ladies, I promised I wouldn't tell if they sorted this out."

"Promises must be kept," Alma said. Doubt vibrated in her voice, most likely about the wisdom of me making such a pledge in the first place.

"'Tisn't right, though, what they did," Cecily said.

"No, of course not. But they apologized, they'll pay for the damage, and I'm certain they won't do this again. Everybody makes mistakes."

Alma's and Cecily's agreement was lukewarm; they were staunch supporters of a tit for tat response to misbehavior. We discussed whatever other domestic challenges required my immediate attention, and then, finally, I was free to consult my familiar.

———

With the new lines of communication established, it didn't take long to work out that Petty had indeed been trying to warn Daisy and me about the curse. Knowing we finally understood each other seemed to have eased some of the urgency, but she would have continued her warnings if needed. She approved the idea of roping in my cousin, but for some odd reason, Jenna didn't feature on her magical roll call.

"Because she's no Coldron?"

The pot landed on the coffee table with a single energetic knock. Tiddles, who had been asleep on the settee, jerked up her head, her tongue blipping between her teeth.

"It's fine, sweetie podge, we're just chatting." I scratched the cat's ears, poised like furry receivers, and she responded to the petting with a throaty purr.

"Right, then it's down to Daisy and me. Uh, another thing. I discovered the hidden image after midnight. Does timing actually matter?"

Once more, the pot smacked the table in an emphatic yes.

My mood plummeted, and all the strength seeped from my limbs. I couldn't do this. Not tonight. Not when I felt so jaded. Hexing sucked the juice out of me even when I was fit.

"Uh, can't we try earlier? I feel pretty washed out as it is. It might not work."

The pot waggled. Then, the primula rapped out a timid yes.

"Okay, okay, I've got the message. Midnight it is. I'll talk to Daisy, not that she makes other plans, and I'll try to catch a nap at some point. Maybe that'll help."

This time, the knock rang out loud and clear.

One more question remained to be asked, even if I dreaded the answer. "At least, this time nobody's died. We don't need that, correct?"

When Petty stilled, my innards clenched. Then she sprang into action. Her leaves rustled; the blossoms turned in all directions, as if waiting for a transmission from an invisible library. After half of eternity had passed, she knocked out a quiet no.

My legs had turned somewhat wonky, so I sat next to the cat.

"Mrrow." Tiddles wouldn't have it. Shame on me for disturbing her slumber twice in a row. She plopped to the floor and stalked into the den, a picture of feline indignation. The knitting basket creaked as she arranged herself inside.

The tic back in my eye, I slumped on the sofa. Fur therapy would have been nice, but cats are cats. Even without Tiddles' warm pelt vibrating under my hands, I must have dozed off, because the next thing I remember was the phone on the table bursting into song, jolting me wide awake.

I checked the number on the display. Sarah.

"Oh, hullo there." I suppressed a yawn.

"Ground Control to Major Myrtle. Everything's gone suspiciously quiet at your place. No distress calls for nearly a day. Are you lot still alive?"

"No, you're talking to my ghost. Can it take a message?"

"Har, har, very funny. Honestly, I was expecting to hear from you a little earlier."

"Really?"

"I know you. But since I'm a nice person, I'll share anyway. Something earth-shattering has happened."

"Diloff is leaving?"

"Not that earth-shattering. Listen to this. Our specialists have delivered ahead of time, and it appears someone has indeed tampered with your fallen standing stone. Which makes the incident malicious intent."

"You can continue your investigation."

"Yup. So far, I interrogated the boxers off both Mr. Hagbottom-Smythe and Mr. Jedd, but all I got for my troubles was more finger-pointing. One implicates the other, and when they don't do that, they blame the interns. The poor guys seem to be the source of everything that goes wrong in the world."

"Actually, you might want to talk to them. The blond one, Pip, uttered some threats. His mate Cal seems to think he's more bark than bite, but one never knows."

"Oh, they're on my list, believe me. Did you talk to the churchwarden? For if you haven't, I can take over." That throwaway comment made it clear Sarah wanted me away from her investigation. Most likely, she was regretting ever letting me in.

"I did. She's definitely not your culprit. I might not be a pro, but I understand how people tick."

Sarah said nothing.

"Here's something interesting for you. Anna, that's the churchwarden, keeps a schedule of the tours on her tablet, listing who's due to show up when and where—like at the stones. More importantly, there's a copy hanging in the society's office. It's not always up to date, but close enough, and all the anointed have access."

"Only those?"

"My understanding is everyone can view it as long as they know where to find it. I haven't been over, so I couldn't tell."

"Anything I should know?" Sarah clicked her pen, the little noise aggravating my tic.

I needed to shore up the defenses around Anna, otherwise Sarah would go after her and destroy any goodwill I might have incurred. However, with the curse looming over my head, it might be wise to take Marty's advice, share the evidence, and steer clear of Sarah's investigation.

I rarely did wise, but this time it made sense. Sort of.

"Myrtle?"

"Yes, still here, sorry. At one point, I worried somebody might be targeting my guests. But Anna's tour schedule confirms they weren't even supposed to be on the henge that day. No way could one of them be the intended victim."

"Ah. Bugger. Here's another theory shot. I'll have to verify the facts with her in person, you understand that? Actually, that was the other reason I wanted to talk to you. Now there's clear evidence for sabotage, it's better if you take a step back. I certainly appreciate your willingness to help when I know you must be super busy. If you come across anything else, let me know, okay?"

Just as I had thought. No way. I wasn't on a switch my friend could turn on and off at her leisure. As long as the role played by

Chris's uncle was unclear, I couldn't bow out.

"Whoa, slowly. Yes, I'm busy, but you can't just rope me in and then shut me out at the next opportunity. At least tell me the gist of it. Like that, if I stumble over a clue, I might recognize it. You won't have a large team on standby. Am I right or am I right?"

A gusty sigh fluttered into my ear. "You're quite impossible."

"Chris used the expression 'force of nature'."

Sarah snickered. "Good one. Okay, my fault. I should've known better than to involve you in the first place, but I really didn't think this would move so quickly. Plus, you're right."

"Of course I am. What about?"

"My lack of team. Okeydokey, here's what I can give you. No doubt, you'll learn this via the jungle drums anyway. Jedd was spotted on the henge around eleven. He claims he'd been in the pub, but the bar staff won't vouch for him."

"People here hate his guts."

"Is Jedd that unpopular?"

"Take my word for it." A silver car roared in my mind, and I could swear I breathed exhaust fumes.

Another groan echoed in my ear. "Blast, I'm supposed to narrow down my suspects, not extend the lineup. We've certainly got plenty of complaints about that man's reckless driving. Otherwise, we've found a spade in Hagbottom-Smythe's open garage, encrusted with dirt which is currently being matched against soil samples from the henge."

"Whose spade would that be?"

"According to Mr. Jedd, most likely Hagbottom-Smythe's. Before you get excited, the curator's got an alibi. He was playing Bridge with a couple of cronies and they kept going into the small hours. As of midnight, a group of Druids was meditating in the circle, so the sabotage couldn't have happened any later."

"Could Jedd have planted the spade? To make life difficult for his rival?"

"With that lot, everything's possible. No fingerprints, of

course. The handle has been wiped down. Something's rotten in that village, I tell you. We'll shake things up and see what floats to the top. Your churchwarden comes next. Do me a favor—don't warn her."

I could only hope Anna had an alibi. At least Sarah hadn't asked about the theft and the vandalism—and I wouldn't be the one to remind her.

———

Despite its unsatisfactory outcome, the chat with Sarah had cleared the fog in my brain. I called Daisy at the shop, but she didn't respond. Most likely, she was busy. I had more luck with Rosie who I asked to start the call chain. If anybody was sitting on curse-related intel, we needed to know.

"We must call a coven meeting tomorrow at the latest."

"Leave it with me, dear," Rosie said. "You're going to try the recipe book?"

"Yes, tonight with Daisy. The more Coldrons, the merrier. If I can get hold of her, that is. I guess I'll cycle over to the shop. All this walking around is hard on the footwear."

"Good luck, dear. Look after yourself."

I nicked two tomatoes, a glass of orange juice, and a lump of cheddar from the fridge, zipped upstairs and snacked. Changed into shorts and a tee, I thundered back down, wheeled my aunt's orange bike from the shed, and pedaled into Long Street. Once I had spoken to my cousin, I would visit Chris. I hadn't heard from him for hours and yearned for his presence and his logical thinking.

*You need to tell him about the curse.*

Snap, the dratted inner voice was at it again. I shushed it. With drivers like Jedd on the prowl, losing myself in the maze that passed for my mind would only lead to an accident.

A lot of traffic was going against me, and the car stuck behind me kept revving its engine but was going nowhere. A quick glimpse over my shoulder revealed a dented green pickup-truck.

It belonged to a local farmer, and while the guy might be Mr. Grump Universe, he wouldn't run me over without provocation.

At the corner to Broad Street, I signaled right, and the truck accelerated away. I cycled on, the auntiemobile clacking and whirring past the outskirts of the old village, where rows of cottages poked their thatched roofs over the hedges. Farther on, the road snaked over a little hill before it curved into the stone bridge over the Kennet. I had learned to brake when coming down the hill; the curve looked harmless but wasn't. The bridge, however, I used as a booster before tackling Broad Street. Its light incline didn't show, but it wreaked havoc on my calf muscles every time—

*Brrringg.* Straight behind me.

Panic lanced my chest, and I jerked at the handlebars of my bike. As I rumpled over the grassy verge, fighting to stay upright, something blurred past me, headed for the hill. A helmeted man on a silver bike, waving a fist.

"Bloody peasants." He shot over the hilltop and vanished from view.

The auntiemobile crunched to a sudden standstill in a cluster of nettles and tilted to one side. I struggled with gravity, but lost. When I jumped clear of the bike, the nettles gleefully stung my bare legs.

*Ow.*

Somewhere close to the bridge, brakes screeched. Then the squeal broke off, and someone screamed, followed by crashing and rattling noises.

"No!"

My heartbeat jumped into my mouth. I stood beside the stranded bike and listened.

A splash. Then silence.

My legs on fire, my mouth dry, I left the auntiemobile lying in the nettles and sprinted along the road, over the hill and onto the bridge.

Apart from the stream's merry glugging, all was still. Too

still.

I peeped over the stone railing at the river bank below. "Hello? Are you down there? Are you okay?"

No response. I charged to the other side, where a telltale track of squished and flattened vegetation released a green scent into the air.

A pale, cold fear clawed at my heart. The cyclist had been going much too fast when he hit the curve, and as a result he went down the bank. He did brake, though. I heard it.

Out of breath, disaster scenarios circling in my brain, I stumbled down the trail I had taken with Chris this morning, following the mangled weeds. Other than the distant traffic sounds from the M4 and a tractor puttering across the field, all was quiet. Even the busy bees had ceased their buzzing. And the dragonflies were gone.

"Hello? Can you hear me? Help is coming."

The bike I found first. Its front wheel bent, the handlebar twisted, it lay in the shallows. On the narrow saddle sat a blue dragonfly, its iridescent wings sparkling in the sunlight. Of the cyclist, there was no trace.

"Hello? Can you hear me?"

Apparently not. My breath trapped in my chest, I returned up the incline, one cautious step after another, as the bank was damp and slippery. That must have been the reason the bike had gone all the way down. But where was the cyclist? It didn't take me long to show up, so he couldn't have walked away, surely. Back on the bridge, I viewed both sides of the river bank from above.

No cyclist.

He had to be here somewhere, so I scrambled back down, this time heading for the concrete tunnel under the street from where the stream gushed in brackish dampness.

That's when I saw the shoe.

The rush of water became a roar. This couldn't be happening. Not again. Not so soon. Not ever. My imagination was getting the better of me, turning harmless shoes into something sinister.

I risked another peep, and the shoe was still there. With a flattish, hard sole that had to be uncomfortable when walking.

Because that shoe hadn't been made for walking.

But that wasn't what caused the lightness in my head. I sucked in more breath and slowly, ever so slowly, used a branch to push aside the cluster of weeds.

Nope, I hadn't been wrong. How wished I was. The shoe was attached to a leg. A hairy leg. The other was folded over, covered in bloodied scrapes and scratches.

Neither leg moved. I let my gaze travel along the man's rump, caught among the weeds, which undulated like snakes in the water.

I swallowed. The cyclist, still wearing his helmet, was facing away from me, his neck twisted at an impossible angle—dead.

# 13

## DOWN BY THE RIVER

Law enforcement took its own sweet time, leaving me marooned on the bridge, alone with the chatty river—and a silent corpse.

Then the crow arrived. Or the rook, raven, whatever. Those buggers are impossible to tell apart. The bird landed on the weathered concrete parapet lining the bridge and cocked its head, its curiously light eye studying me in unashamed curiosity. With a flip of its tail feathers, the black menace dropped something gooey and strode along the top of the wall, clearly in possession of the scene. Until it took off in a feathery whisper of wings. Not upward, but down to the river bank. Down to where the body of the cyclist was lying half in, half out of the Kennet.

I leaned over the balustrade. The crow landed among the weeds and hopped toward the water, where my doomed rescue attempts had squashed the grass and exposed the muscled calves of the dead cyclist.

"Oi, you."

The bird gave me the evil eye. But it stopped its advance on the corpse.

I withdrew my head. The body was a job for the police; assuming they ever arrived. A quick look at my watch told me that only three minutes had passed since I last checked.

Below the bridge, the blasted bird cawed. Wings rattled.

Bugger, what was the critter up to? Once more, I poked my head over the parapet and found the crow perched on a hairy leg.

"Shoo." I flailed my arms.

The bird remained unfazed.

From the village side of the bridge came the sound of an engine, and I turned away from the parapet. A second later, Sarah's taupe police Vauxhall rolled up and stopped on the verge. All four doors sprang open, but DC Cameron, wearing a white boiler suit, was the first to get out. Sarah came next, still in her civilian clothes, and two uniformed officers, a man, and a woman, who had been sitting in the back. A white van parked behind and disgorged two scenes of crime officers, also kitted out in white. The whole posse, their faces grim, headed purposefully for the scene of the lethal accident, stopping in front of me the same moment a dark Audi joined the official convoy.

"I'm so sorry this keeps happening."

Sarah sighed. "Not your fault, Myr. I'm pissed off with myself. Because I saw this coming and didn't manage to prevent it. Where's the victim?"

I pointed a quivering finger at the riverbank. "Down there, halfway in the Kennet. Just follow the trail."

Sarah inclined her head at her team. "Off you go. One of you needs to block the road. The rest see what there is to see."

Off they went as instructed while the male officer tromped across the bridge and strung a blue and white police band across the street. Sarah, who had been examining the trail of squashed vegetation, looked up, a wintry smile on her face. "When I agreed you could cast an eye on things, I had evidence in mind, not another body."

The comment sounded more like her normal self; it helped to ease the tension still fisting my heart. "I appreciate your effort at lightening the mood."

"Dark humor is an occupational hazard in law enforcement. It's either that or pills, booze, and depression. Take your pick."

"Give me humor anytime. To be honest, I wasn't expecting this. I was cycling into the village when he shot past me like a lunatic."

"Hold on a sec, I need to take your statement." Sarah fished a tablet from a business-like black purse.

"Oh, my," someone said behind me. "Don't tell me this lady found more bones."

A thickset man in yet another white boiler suit plonked his metal briefcase onto the balustrade and gave the riverbank a cursory glance. He looked vaguely familiar.

My brain took a couple of seconds before it came up with a match. The pathologist.

Behind him, on the other side of the police barrier, a small group of villagers seemed to have materialized from nowhere. More were striding along Broad Street as if the smell of violent death was traveling on the air and drawing the flies.

A wave of nausea welled up. Flies were the last thing I needed.

"Vic's down by the river," Sarah said.

The pathologist leaned over the railing and sucked his teeth. "Are you sure, my dear Sergeant Widdlethorpe, this is a police matter and not some stupid accident?"

"I wish. Based on what's been happening here and because of the identity of the victim, I fear we are in business."

"You know who he is?"

Sarah's gaze found mine and held it. "We seem to have an identification, yes."

That was bold, but then I had been reasonably certain about the man's identity.

"Oh, well, your show." With that, the pathologist made for

the path and his patient.

"Right then." Sarah tapped her tablet. "Run through this afternoon's events for me."

"All of them?"

Sarah pinched her nose. "I'll re-phrase that. Tell me how you found the victim."

That was easier, but it still took me a minute to sift through the jumble of confused memories rattling around in my mind. "I was cycling along when the guy shot past me. Yelled something rude and raced over the hill and far away."

"Can you remember the exact words?"

An echo of a now-dead voice rang in my head. "He called me a peasant. Probably because I was too slow."

"And then?"

"He screamed. Oh no, hang on, first I heard a mechanical squealing. It broke off and then he screamed. Then there was more noise and more screaming. That must have been when he went off-road."

Sarah faced the curve and the sharp incline behind it. "And then?"

"I abandoned the auntiemobile...my bike and came running. Checked from the bridge but at first didn't find him. Only his bike. I'm afraid I might've trampled down the weeds, that's why you now can see ...uh, the legs from up here. But I never touched the corpse. Or saw his face. No need to feel the pulse, not when his head ..." I swallowed.

"It's fine, Myr," Sarah said soothingly. "You did well. Come, lean against this." She steered me to the stone balustrade.

From below roared the pathologist's disembodied voice. "Hey, give me a moment to get my bearings. He's stone-cold dead, that much I can confirm. Even if he's still warm enough and the limbs are nicely pliable."

At the doctor's comment, my throat tightened.

"Cheerful sod," Sarah mumbled. "And you identified him how?"

"The silver bike. And the way he was speeding. He's no better in a car. Was, I mean. And I recognized the voice."

"So, you're convinced he's—"

"The director. Jedd."

—

The moment I finished my statement, the pathologist returned, wheezing alarmingly after his short hike up the trail. Once more, the metal briefcase got plonked onto the concrete parapet. The good doctor then snapped the yellowish rubber gloves off his fingers, wadded them, and aimed the ball at the SOCO, who was measuring something on the road.

"Catch," the pathologist said in his gruff voice. The officer ignored him, and the rubber ball came to rest on the grass.

"You really are Prince Charming, aren't you?" Sarah said.

"Am I ever. Okay, I herewith declare the corpse to be dead. Do you want some prelims or don't you?"

"Spill."

"Deceased is a male in his late thirties to mid-forties. Eh, why do I bother telling you, since you seem to know the chap?"

"Because we all love procedures?"

"Fair enough. Cause of death is a broken neck. The bloke must have been scooting around that corner like the proverbial bat out of hell." The pathologist hooked a thumb over his shoulder at the curve before the bridge.

"Sarge?" The SOCO stepped up. "There's a faint skid mark on the tarmac. I'd say the brakes worked for an instant, then failed. He laid down some rubber, but only briefly."

Sarah nodded at the man. "As I feared. Check out that bike for me, will you?"

The officer turned and made his way down to the bank of the river.

"Right," the doctor said, his voice overloud. "Dead less than an hour. Only a few of our airborne friends had arrived."

"There was a crow, but I chased it away," I said.

"I meant insects, young lady," the pathologist said.

My nausea increased.

"It's all right, Myr." Sarah patted my shoulder.

"Yeah," the doctor said. "Just don't stumble over any more human remains, okay?" He winked at me, ducked under the barrier, and pushed his way through the crowd, which had swollen to a considerable size.

He hadn't started his car when the female constable shouted from below the bridge. "Sarge, mind joining us down here?"

"Yes, but I can't get too close. I'm not kitted out." To me she said, "Will be back in a second." With that, Sarah left the bridge and joined the team on the riverbank.

I leaned against the balustrade; from up here, I could see—and hear—the cops well enough. The uniformed copper in charge of crowd control seemed to take my presence for granted and made no moves to push me off. He was busy with the gawkers now pressing in on both sides. One man was making a nuisance of himself, gesticulating and arguing.

I turned my back on the people and listened to the four officers below me.

"See this?" the second SOCO, a squat female, said. "The brake wires have been cut. Not all the way through. Looks like they nipped the line at a pressure point and then made several light cuts perpendicular to the diameter cut."

"In plain English, if you don't mind," Sarah said.

"Means the moment he pressured the brakes, they burst. Somebody knew what they were doing," the SOCO said.

"Or they went online," her colleague said. "Amazing what you can find on the Internet these days. Anyway, the lab will have another go, but we're pretty sure this is what happened."

"No accident then. Just as I feared." Sarah's voice sounded resigned. "At the very least, someone risked inflicting serious injuries. The standing stone incident all over again."

"Aye, Sarge, looks like it." Cameron sighed. "Especially, since he doesn't live far away, or so I was told. First house on

Broad Street, so he must have negotiated that curve many times before."

"Our witness confirmed our vic's direction as well. He would've been coming from home."

"Posh area, this," the male SOCO said.

"Well, yes. Cameron, I need you to check out Jedd's place. Perhaps someone has seen someone who fiddled with the bike. It's not impossible. In villages like this, someone always sees something."

"But not what we want them to observe." Cameron said.

"No, but I can always harbor foolish hopes, right? Find out how often he used his bike, where he kept it, who would have had access, that sort of thing."

"Very well, sarge," said Cameron. "Uh, how would the killer have known which way the chap would cycle?"

"Our friend here must have had a routine going. Another thing you'll have to establish. Are you two done with the bike?"

"For the moment. Body is next," the SOCOs chorused.

"We'll leave you to it, then." Sarah and Cameron tramped back up the trail. He turned left while Sarah headed my way.

Her sharp gaze drilled into mine. "You heard that."

"Sorry, couldn't help it."

She sighed. "I guess since you already suspected unnatural causes, we weren't telling you anything new. The rest is verisimilitude. However, you understand that this is now a murder investigation, which means I can no longer involve you."

"Got it."

A faint smile twitched at the corner of Sarah's mouth. "I'll believe that when I see it."

She licked her lips and threw a furtive glance at the uniform guarding the barrier on the village side, hands crossed behind his back. "Actually, there's one more bit of local insight you can help me with. Remember that little conversation we had earlier today? About the encrusted spade we found? It looks a lot as if it was indeed used to fix that standing stone. The lab rats are still running soil profiles, but the visuals alone are quite convincing. Got those straight after we'd finished our call."

"Jargon alert. You're trying to tell me the caked soil on the curator's spade and on the site of the accident appears to be the same, right? And it's important to know who's behind the rock sabotage, because this person might have escalated and tampered with the bike."

"I'm proud of you."

"But Hagbottom-Smythe has an alibi, doesn't he?"

"Unfortunately, yes. The guy also insists that a spade isn't a spade. Or rather—that this spade isn't his. Instead, he claims it belongs to our dead friend down there. Who was the one claiming the thing belonged to the director. Makes me wonder how he would've known that. I mean, do you have competitions here? Who's got the biggest pitch fork and stuff?"

"Usually, it's veg." I corrected her. "Pumpkins, carrots, and courgettes. We have the Veggie of the Year contest in autumn."

Sarah massaged her temples. "Someone in this blasted place is trying to lead me up the garden path."

My gaze found the SOCOs in their white suits, moving about on the river bank. "That might well be the case. I'll let you know once I hear something."

"Sarge?" The male constable walked up. "There's a young man what's mightily upset. Claims this young lady is his." He pointed at me. "And he worries about her something chronic."

I craned my neck at the barrier and the tall man clad all in black standing at the front, scowling like a stereotype villain.

Chris.

"Perfect," Sarah said, amusement in her voice. "Right on cue." She put a hand on my arm and steered me toward the barrier, toward Chris.

She gave my shoulder a quick squeeze. "You did very well today. Just keep the details to yourself, if you please. Go home and try to switch off. Treat yourself, do something nice for a change."

"I'll see that she does," Chris said grimly.

# 14

## TROUBLE IN SPADES

Jedd might not have been the nicest of persons, but the callous way someone had wasted his life was beyond shocking. Amid my general frustration with the world, I nearly forgot to tell Daisy I needed help with our grimoire. But nothing would happen the same evening, not while I couldn't string two coherent thoughts together. Like a bawling toddler, I poured my troubles into Chris's sympathetic ear—all of them but the curse. I couldn't cope with the bloody curse on top of everything else. He let me rant; he let me cry; he made me cocoa and ensured I went to bed early. That was the last thing I remembered. Should the dream have returned during the night, it did so without leaving a trace.

Today was different. Today, I was rested, the sun on duty, the birds out in force, and if I heard the cawing of a crow among their energetic chirping, it was my own fault.

A stray ray tickled my cheek and spotlighted Chris lying next to me, suffering from a severe case of bed head and stubbles. Not wanting to wake him, I tiptoed into the shower and let the water run over my body until the bathroom was sweaty with jasmine-scented steam. Prodded into action by the fragrant warmth and needle-fine jets massaging my skin, my brain flashed reminders and must-dos in big neon letters.

Back in the bedroom, I found Chris stretching and yawning. "Rise and shine."

"Your wish is my command." He curled a finger in a come-hither gesture.

"Nope. Not before you shaved. Can't cope with the beard-burn."

"Stubble is *très chic*."

"Doesn't make your cheeks any less scratchy."

Illogical person who I was, I then hopped onto the bed, snuggled up next to my man—and remembered the curse. Joy, great timing.

My helpful gray matter pointed out Chris still didn't know about the coven's latest predicament; didn't I wish to rectify matters? Stupid of me, I should have told him yesterday. Exhaustion was no excuse, really. I shook myself and held on to my man. Later, I would involve him later—once Daisy and I had cracked the empty pages, once I knew there was hope.

Which meant waiting until tomorrow.

"You better?" Chris's voice feathered down my neck.

"Mh, mostly."

*Tell him.*

I couldn't. He shouldered so many of my worries already, burdening him with uncertainty was totally unfair. Chris was giving me so much. He was my rock. What did I give him in return? My adorable self was the obvious answer, but until I was fully clued up on this blasted jinx, it was uncertain how much of myself would be around for him to love.

All very logical, very adult thoughts, miles removed from yesterday's meltdown, but the guilt refused to budge.

*Stop moping. It won't help you with your pickle.*

A soft weight landed on the duvet. Tiddles had jumped on the bed and was padding toward us. Unlike me, the cat was focused. She wanted food, she wanted it now, and if persistent howling wouldn't prod her humans into action, breathing fish breath into someone's face usually did the job. This time was no different.

"Erk." Chris sat up, passed me a purring feline, and flung the cover aside. "Your furry friend is worse than a drill sergeant."

As he retreated into the bathroom, his firm buttocks did double duty as a mood-booster, pushing my inner bad weather front back to the horizon.

"Will be downstairs for breakfast. See you there." I stepped onto the landing.

"Yo." The shower came on.

On a whim, I tried Daisy's door and found it closed, but not locked. It appeared she was in, which she hadn't been a lot recently. If only I didn't have to wait until midnight for our tryst with the recipe book.

*What if you're unsuccessful?* The emotional bad weather front blew back in. Careful not to make a noise, I released the doorknob and turned.

"Mrowl." Tiddles shot me an accusing look.

"Shush, on my way."

Tiddles shot off, galloping along the hallway at a speed humans of an equivalent age would find challenging. I followed down the carpeted treads, though not as fast. The patter of paws preceded me all the way into the lower corridor, where I was greeted by the welcome aroma of coffee brewing. When I peeked into the kitchen, I found only my geriatric pet guarding the fridge. The clatter of crockery from next door told me Alma and Cecily were laying the tables in the conservatory.

I filled the cat's bowl. "Okay, sweetheart, here's your goo. Dig in."

The whiff of "Luxurious Liver" on an empty stomach was too much, so I fled into the breakfast room. All the French doors stood open, and a breeze tousled the curtains. Aunt Eve had planted old English climbing roses next to the entrance, and their puffy yellow heads now bobbed and swayed in the warm wind, sending in a heady scent that traveled on plenty of sunshine. On the lawn, a bunch of bold bunnies were nibbling the grass, a tableau of bucolic tranquility too pretty to be true.

"Morning, ladies."

"Hah," Alma said by way of response. "Did you see this?" She stabbed the local newspaper with a finger whose spatula-shaped nails had never seen a manicure.

"Is it about the cyclist what's been done in?" Cecily reached for the cafetière standing on the sideboard.

"Yes, but they've got the wrong end of the stick. Says here they have no name for the man, and 'twas an accident. Utter twaddle, that."

Anxiety blipped in my chest. Sarah hadn't wanted to release the name of the victim just yet, nor the fact he had been murdered.

"How would you know? Did the cops identify the victim?"

A steaming mug of coffee was pressed into my hand. I gave Cecily a grateful smile and sipped.

"You wish," Alma said.

"I knew it. That man was a bad sort, bound for a bad end," her sister said triumphantly, pouring more coffee into mugs.

I leaned against the buffet and toyed with the rim of my mug. No breaking news would ever beat the village grapevine. "Tell me, then."

Alma's bright bird eyes blinked. "That director chappie never showed up for an important"—she hooked quote fingers into the air—"meeting. My friend Betty, who does for him, said he left for a spin and didn't return."

"He was always punctured," Cecily said.

"Punctual," Alma said. "Yes, he was. Wouldn't have missed those meetings for the life of him. No, I'm telling you. It's him, what the police have. Someone offed the man. I'm only surprised it took them so long." She blew on her coffee and drank.

"Anna was at the riverbank when they brought up the body," Cecily said. "Inna black bin bag."

"Body bag," I said.

"Yes, that. You found him, didn't you? It wasn't an accident, they say."

*Whoops.* I would have to choose my words with care, lest "they" heard things not meant for their ears and I ended up on the wrong side of Sergeant Sarah. Who needed to know ASAP the lid had blown off her secret.

"That's for the police to work out. In case you wonder, I never saw the cyclist's face. A man overtook me on his bike, and soon after, I heard the crash. Tried to help, but there was absolutely nothing I could do for the poor guy. Other than call in an emergency."

"Such a shame you didn't get to see much," Cecily said. "Doesn't matter. We know it's him. And with all those coppers puttering about, it won't have been an accident, either. Bridge's still blocked, by the way." She slurped her coffee.

Alma nodded; satisfaction written all over her plain features. If the Fates wore acrylic frocks, my two housekeepers might as well apply for the job.

From the Fates, my mind leapfrogged to spades. Sarah was keen to pinpoint the rightful owner of the fateful spade. If anybody would know, it was those two. But I had to be careful. Very careful.

"The entire village seems to have Jedd pegged as a villain, and I find that unfair. Not only doesn't he deserve to die like that—if it's him—he must've done something positive in his life."

"Like what?"

"Like supporting local activities. Give lectures for the Women's Institute, participate in garden contests, stuff like that. From what I hear, he seems ...seemed to know a lot and liked people to know that he did."

Alma raised a penciled brow. "Gardening? The coppers reckon he dug up the stone?"

*Whoa.* "You're jumping to conclusions. I find it odd no one has anything good to say about the guy. Instead, everyone seems to think him a total blackguard."

"That's because he was." Cecily delivered her judgment with a firm voice. "A really nasty sort, that one. Swarmy. The sort that smiles at you and sticks daggers in your back when you're not watching."

"Smarmy, Cec. He was that. Liked to cause trouble for people, especially our curator. That's why I think it might've been him with the stone. And he nearly rammed me with his bicycle when I wasn't crossing the street fast enough."

Yep, that sounded like Jedd, all right. However, we weren't getting any further with the spade. "You're right, gardening makes no sense. I met him only once, and he didn't strike me as someone who'd enjoy manual labor. Plus, where would he get the spade from? Can't see him crawling around in people's toolsheds."

Alma snickered. "He rented his cottage. Came equipped with everything, even a shed. Dan, the owner, let everyone sneak a peek before the chap moved in. Shiny new tools. The best. Mr. High and Mighty never let anyone borrow anything." A fanatical gleam stole into her eye. "He could've driven across to the henge and dug a hole when nobody was watching."

"You really don't like him, do you? Since he didn't cordon off the wonky stone, he was responsible if something happened. By sabotaging the stone, he would have implicated himself."

"Thought he would get away with it. His ilk always does." Cecily emptied her cup and banged it onto the sideboard.

There was no point in telling the Simpkins sisters their logic was somewhat biased. And I'd better stop before I talked myself into more knots. The nugget about Jedd having access to a spade would have to do, even though it didn't matter much, since things had changed and Jedd was dead.

"Never mind. Let's leave it to the cops. It's their job."

"Huh," Cecily said.

"Bah," Alma said.

On that merry note, I traipsed next door to start the toast.

I left a message for Sarah, telling her about the rumors and Jedd's toolshed, which was my sleuth duty done for the day. I then made my way to the living room, carrying a can of Petty's fertilizer and a fresh copy of the tabloid. About to enter my parlor, I stopped.

I'd better leave the murder well alone. I had a curse to lift. But somewhere deep inside, a warning voice insisted I mustn't let go, whispered about a connection existing between the recent series of odd incidents, Jedd's death, and the curse. For one mystery, I had found a culprit—Anna. Others, like the skeleton, the shooting, the stone, and now the director's untimely demise, seemed unrelated. They might well be, but what if they weren't?

My throat tightened. What about Ignatius? Somehow, he had dropped off my radar completely.

Silly me. Chris's uncle had absolutely no reason to kill the director. Hagbottom-Smythe, however did. And with his experience in excavations, he would have known how to weaken the stone. But the curator had an alibi ...

*Give it a rest. Seriously, this isn't your biggest problem.* I slammed the door on the swarm of thoughts and entered my living room.

—

Petty was sitting in her usual place in front of the window, absorbing the sunlight. Once I entered, she bounced up and danced through the air on a level with my face, showering her environment with sparks and her citrusy, happy scent.

A man had most likely been killed, and I failed to study the grimoire yesterday. Not exactly a reason to party.

"Daisy and I will have a go at the recipe book tonight, okay?"

My familiar whooshed past me and knocked on the coffee table. Twice. Then she landed on the table's surface, radiating expectation.

*Huh?* "What do you mean by 'no'?"

Petty remained silent.

I placed the tabloid and the water can on the table and sank into the settee. "Right, let's start at the beginning. Does your good mood have something to do with the curse?"

The pot banged on the coffee table once, the knock echoing into the room.

A yes. That sounded promising.

The spark of hope was snuffed in an instant. In its stead, dread crawled over my skin. Compared to yesterday, only one thing had changed. "You're telling me Jedd's death makes a difference, and I can have a go at the recipe book now?"

*Rap.*

There, I'd known it. I was no witch; I was some weird emotional vampire who thrived on murder. I felt like storming from the room, out of my life. But my life these days involved Chris, Petty, and a lot of other beings I didn't want to lose, so I placed my hand on my abdomen and practiced diaphragm breathing instead. When that failed to calm me down, I rose, pulled the grimoire from the bookshelf, and paced into the den and back again, flipping pages while muttering swearwords under my breath.

No big surprise, the empty pages remained blank. And there wasn't the remotest trace of the mowed-grass scent and the buzz of things growing that seemed to accompany my hexing outbursts. Most importantly, I hadn't seen a single red rose petal—the so-called essence of my magic.

*What about those pale pink ones you found in your bedroom?*

I elbowed the thought aside. Too much information. "What the heck does it take to make this crap work?"

Petty joined me under the archway. Her scent, stronger than ever, increased to the point it was dizzying.

Hang on, potent scent. "My cousin?"

The pot banged once against the wall.

*Duh. Should've thought of that myself.*

Petty bounced around, sparks shooting from the blossoms,

which confirmed we were on the same page.

My familiar stopped her manic airborne acrobatics and zipped to the door. The next instant, somebody knocked. The panel swung open, and Daisy peeped in.

Telepathy? Or just coincidence?

"Hullo, Myr, the Simpkins sisters said you'd be here. Mind if I join you? They prepared breakfast. Said you'd need something more substantial than bird food."

Not waiting for my response, she entered carrying a tray laden with goodies. Somehow, my cousin looked sexy even when wearing nothing but a short terry-cloth house dress in a deep plum blue, color-coordinated fluffy mules, and artfully disheveled auburn curls that would make a hair-stylist weep with envy.

"Oh, you're reading the recipe book over breakfast. Mum did that a lot. Toast with orange marmalade or honey?"

"Did she? Marmalade, if you please. And no, I never take lemon in my tea."

The citrus slice that had dangled precariously over the cup was placed aside, and milk was poured instead. I watched Daisy load two toasts with marmalade. I wasn't hungry, but if I wanted to do magic, I needed calories.

"I drove over yesterday evening, in case you felt like consulting the grimoire after all." Daisy nibbled her toast.

A sudden warmth flushed my heart. "You're a darling, you really are. But I couldn't. Not after what happened with the cyclist."

"Ugh, I don't blame you. The poor man. It's Jedd, isn't it?"

"Mh. The Simpkins sisters certainly seem to think so."

Daisy's eyes were enormous, brown, and moist—she was the first person to show some compassion over Jedd's death. Petty was sweet, but she didn't seem to care two hoots about anyone not part of the magical circle, with the exception of Chris, perhaps. Jedd's death for her was a boon, not a tragedy. I could never blame her. Petty was who she was, sworn to protect me and, by default, the coven. Anything that helped us in her world was great news.

It still saddened me.

With an artful eye roll, Daisy sipped at her tea, all lady-like, with one finger spread aside. "Do you feel better? I mean, shall we try tonight?"

The primula floated past and banged her pot on the table twice, so hard, the cups rattled in their saucers and a spoon clattered to the floor.

Daisy's spaniel eyes widened. "Hey, take it easy. What's wrong with you?"

"Nothing. Looks like we don't have to wait until tonight. Because of Jedd's death."

A whole fusillade of sparks shot from the leaves and Petty knocked out a staccato on the table.

Inappropriate though it was, I couldn't help grinning at my cousin. She grinned back.

"Let's get cracking," I said.

# 15

## BLAST FROM THE PAST

An imaginary moth fluttered in my stomach. Was I keen on perform to an audience comprising my cousin, my magical plant, and my geriatric cat who had just sauntered in through the door Daisy left open? Not really, but dithering would get us nowhere.

"Can you lock that door for me? And pull the curtains. Don't want to spook the Simpkinses. Or the guests."

"Sure."

The magical laboratory secured, I pressed the recipe book to my bosom, while Daisy sat on the sofa, eyes scrunched shut, her hands balled into fists.

"What *are* you doing?"

"Trying to, like, give you a magical boost? I mean, we both knew I'm a bit of a ditz when it comes to hexing, but perhaps this helps a bit."

Given my cousin's magical insecurities, her offer was thoughtful and generous. I smiled at her. "Thanks."

"Ready?" she asked.

"No, but never mind. Petty, last time I prowled the room,

with the book pressed to my chest, so I'll do that again, okay?"

Petty fired a spark, which I took as assent.

For the second time this morning, I stalked back and forth between the den and the parlor, a gazillion worries crowding my mind. How did I manage to conjure up the hidden image? Back then, I'd come more or less fresh from the young Wiccan's death, and the horrid scene kept running in an endless loop. Perhaps I should recall the weeds, the mangled bicycle, the hairy legs, the head.

It was no good; my fickle gray matter shied away from the memory. Instead, a vision of the chubby curator rose in my imagination, instantly joined by Ignatius's impeccably groomed figure.

"Grrr."

"You done?"

"One sec." I slapped the grimoire on the table and turned my back on it. Last time I did that, the book started reading itself. When I couldn't stand it any longer and glimpsed over my shoulder, no miracle had happened; the pages were as empty as always.

"Rats."

Daisy opened her eyes and jumped off the sofa. "Must admit I expected something more spectacular."

"Spectacular isn't on the cards. I'll settle for things simply happening." Even to my own ears, my voice sounded churlish. As if that wasn't bad enough, my inner eye projected the grim figure of Professor Snape, towering above me and dishing out minus points for magical underperformance.

To my left, Petty did that "duh" drooping of leaves thing again. She lifted the pot and floated my way. Gently, she prodded my arm before drifting across to Daisy and nudging her hand with the pot.

"Oh, look, isn't she cute," Daisy squealed.

The primula now hovered in the airspace right above the grimoire, which—be it by coincidence or by design—lay halfway on an imaginary line between Daisy and me. On my cousin's side, the angle was a bit off; she was hampered by the armchair with the snoozing cat.

Angle. Angles were important. If only I knew what for.

Petty drifted first to the right, then pirouetted to the left, still halfway between us, but now forming the tip of a wonky triangle—

"That's it. Angles. Triangles. For triangle, read pyramid. They're supposed to have magical powers."

"Now you've lost me."

"One moment. Petty, stay where you are."

The pot dipped once in acknowledgment of my request and stopped in midair, swaying gently. Interesting that the primula should leave the initiative to me. She seemed to wait for bright ideas on my side to run a reality check, using whatever knowledge base she had access to.

"We're now arranged in pyramid formation. You and I form its base, and Petty's at the top."

Daisy scratched her head. "You reckon that'll help?"

"How am I supposed to know? Can you reach the book from where you're standing?"

"If I bend over like this, yes. And now?"

"Now comes the harder part where things actually happen. The last time, I touched a page and hey presto—image. Oh, I've forgotten something."

Daisy raised a skeptical brow.

"Last time I hit upon a random page. I reckon we better tell the thing what we want. Put your hand on it, please. And don't move," I said hastily, as Daisy did just that.

"Oh, snap," Once more, she hunched up and held on to the front panel of the closed book.

"Super. Now, watch this."

I reached across and tapped my index finger on the front panel, feeling supremely moronic. "Hello, recipe book. We need some information. On the curse. You know, the one threatening the coven. Pretty please? With sugar on top?"

The room fell silent, filled only by the ticking of the clock, and the distant whine of a lawn-trimmer. And the eye-watering pong from one of Tiddles's thankfully now infrequent farts.

Daisy gave the tome the stink eye. "This is lame." She straightened and massaged her back.

Petty's leaves drooped, and she shot toward the den, came back again, and hovered expectantly in front of my face. A pirouette followed, whereafter she addressed Daisy.

"You reckon we should walk around with the book. Together? But then, we're no longer forming a triangle."

*Rap.*

As knocks went, that wasn't a solid one. It came across as being rather hesitant.

"Petty, be honest. You're making this up." Daisy hopped around like a toddler on a sugar rush. Well, hey, at least one of us was having fun.

The leaves and petals flopped. Perhaps Petty's magical resource wasn't as true and tested as I would have liked it to be.

"She's trying to help. I'm not sure it was the pacing that did the trick. Perhaps it was more because I hugged it to my chest?"

Daisy's eyes lit up. "What if we do that together? With Petty hovering close by. Something like that, anyway."

"Last Tango in Avebury?"

"Har, har. What I mean is, like, we stay close and somehow keep the grimoire between us? How's that for a start?"

Daisy's cheeks were flushed, and her terry-cloth robe had fallen open to reveal a substantial amount of cleavage framed by frothy lace. If that five-star bosom didn't tease the grimoire into revealing its secrets, nothing would.

The downside was that I had to get rather close to my cousin and her perfume. Oh well, it was all for the greater good. We stuffed the helpless recipe book between our chests, embraced, and started our parlor-shuffle. Presumably, I was supposed to think magical thoughts, but not only did I have no clue what those might be, but also the cloying mix of synthetic musk and violets drifting from my cousin's cleavage didn't help with the focus. To add insult to injury, the old tome poked its hard corners into my chest, and Petty cavorting around us further spoiled the paranormal ambiance.

"Are you done?" Daisy breezed into my ear.

"No idea." I broke contact. The bulky tome would have dropped and smooshed my foot had I not caught it at the last moment. I placed the darn thing on the coffee table and drew a deep breath.

This was pointless. Even if we engaged the whole coven in a group-huddle—the blasted grimoire wouldn't ever—

*Slap.*

The essence of a forest, moist wood paired with distant flowers, washed through the parlor. Under my feet, the ground seemed to pulse with life. A soughing noise of trees swaying in the wind filled my ear. An odd taste, bitter yet not unpleasant, coated my tongue.

And amid a blizzard of luscious red petals, the front panel of the recipe book flew open.

The first folios featuring my aunt's and my grandmother's handwriting fluttered by as if an unseen hand was rifling through them at speed.

"Wow," said Daisy. "Look at that." Her gaze darted between the book and the petals, now covering the table like a silky cloth. More of them materialized in midair, but the flurry seemed to be thinning.

Somehow, the words needed for a response stuck in my throat. I could only sit there, lost in the greenness filling the room. None of this happened when I conjured up the hidden image.

By the time the phenomena faded, the recipe book had reached the first empty page. There, it stopped as suddenly as it had started, the next leaf quivering ever so slightly in barely suppressed anticipation.

"Quick, it wants you to do something." Daisy was bobbing up and down. So was Petty. Only she did it in the air.

Gingerly, I brushed aside a handful of ruby petals and prodded the vibrating page, which promptly shifted across to reveal—an empty double spread. Again, the quiver, the tiny crackling noises of paper rubbing on paper.

"Cripes, how the heck should I know where it's supposed to stop?"

"It doesn't know where to look, the poor thing. We forgot to tell it before we started. Curse. We need information on the curse. The one that threatens the Avebury coven." Daisy yelled at the book while trying to adjust her robe, which had fallen open on a rather risqué nightie.

"Great. Shout it to the world while you're at it, will you?"

"Just doing my bit. Oh, look." The latter was addressed at the grimoire, which was once more reading itself, flipping page after page. Until it stopped and stilled on the last double spread, right before great-aunt Petunia's script began.

Daisy clapped her hands. "Good book. Fine book. Well done. Now, we're only missing some text."

Ah, I'd forgotten something. Slowly, I extended my digit and tapped the stained surface once.

That did the trick.

—

From the edges, words washed over the page. Pale at first, they soon became clearer until a script presented itself to the eye, sepia brown and featuring whimsical little squiggles and moldy splotches. No image this time, only a disaster area of a text. The handwriting looked ancient, and the date at the bottom of the document confirmed my suspicion.

1647.

The numbers were in full body tackle with a word that might have been October, but with the calligraphy squirming across the page as if dragged along by a drunken spider, it was hard to tell.

"What does it say?" Daisy's locks tickled my ear, and her scent tortured my nostrils. Petty on the other side was rustling and sparking like there was no tomorrow, with me caught between the two loonies. At least Tiddles hadn't done more than flick the tip of her tail. Good to see someone in this place kept their act together.

"Why don't you check for yourself?"

"Can't read that stuff. It looks all funny. But this here might be a name. What do you think?" Daisy's index finger hovered over another bunch of scribbles next to the date.

I squinted. My cousin was right. The squiggles came in two short parts, the first one clearly ending on a Y while the second started with a daring C before disintegrating. Not much luck there. "Any suggestions?"

Her lips parted, the tongue poking from between them, Daisy's finger traced the rising and falling curlicues. "Let's see. Now that's a Y at the end. Got to be. And the beginning is most likely an L. This funny squiggle here could be an E or an I. But don't ask me what that other letter would be. Another L or a T, perhaps?"

She was doing amazingly well. "Lity? Lety or Lely? Or, hang on, what about Lily? Could also be Letty, but this really doesn't look like a double T to me."

"Lily sounds good. Let me try the second part." With her tongue still caught between her lips, Daisy continued tackling the outlandish squiggles. "Okay, it starts with a capital C. And then it has two funny circles which look alike. The first one must be an O, so the other one's got to be the same. And if I'm right about that funny slash being an L, then we have it here in third position." Daisy faced me, her eyes shining. "This is like in these game shows, you see? Where they're given letters and must guess the words. I saw one recently and they—"

"You're doing great, Daise. Carry on doing it. I agree with you. We're just missing three more letters. Could that one at the end be an N, for example?" Suddenly, the letters came together. My breath hitched. "That's it. Lily Coldron, October 1647."

"That's, like, a long time ago?"

A bucket of imagined ice water washed down my spine. "The magical doodle I found? Lily drew it. She even signed it. With a doodled lily of the valley and the name Coldron beside it. It's the same person, I could swear. And, perhaps, there's more. She must've been the one to hex all these pages. Daisy, she must've been an absolute badass witch to do so. And we've got her notes."

I peered up and caught Daisy's awestruck gaze.

"Oh, wow," she said, quite unnecessarily.

Like an electric shock, realization zapped through me. The last time the image had disappeared almost as quickly as I had conjured it up. So far, the text hadn't tried to escape, but we couldn't take any risks.

"Quick, take a photo." I fumbled around with my phone and finally captured the magical text.

Daisy, who had joined my conservationist efforts, only faster, pocketed her phone and had another stab at deciphering the script. The speed with which her pen flew across the notepad she had fetched from the den showed she was fast getting to grips with the crabby handwriting. There still was the odd question mark in between, but overall, we seemed to have ourselves a text. Which hadn't vanished either. Progress on all fronts.

"Okay, Daise, give. What have we got?"

"Uh, it sounds rather weird. Must be my transcription. At least I hope it is."

"Daisy—"

"Sure, sure. But don't say I didn't warn you."

On that cheerful note, she drew a deep breath and started reading aloud.

The first, larger part, wasn't a big surprise. It stated there was a curse on the people with skylles, mentioned the fact it manifested through dreams and needed to be addressed "at the Tyme when the Days are at theyre longest, latest three Sennights thereafter."

Or words to that effect.

That much we knew. Well, we hadn't known the period of grace was three weeks, but now we did, which meant we didn't have much time left before ...something happened. I'd do the arithmetic later. My mouth suddenly bone-dry, I swallowed and concentrated on Daisy's transcription.

The text was clear and to the point. Devastatingly so, for here, finally, the curse's consequences were spelled out. And here, finally, the cure was listed.

Only, it appeared we lacked the ingredients.

"Read the full interpretation for me, will you?" I said.

"When the Moone stands over the Stones at nighttime," Daisy intoned, "a coven comprising at least three Wardens shall gather within the Cyrcle, close to the stone shaped like a Horse Heade. There, you shall lyfte the mirror and in the mirror see key." Daisy scratched her ear. "That last word is mega hard to read, the quill spattered badly. But I think it says key. Uh, how's that supposed to work? The mirror shows us a key? Or is seeing the key enough? What mirror? And what key?"

My brain flashed back to the cellars of the museum. The curator's voice rang in my ears, lecturing about grave gifts—and mirrors. Nothing about keys, though.

"Maybe we misread something. Could that be a double E at the end instead of a Y?"

She squinted at the text. "It might. No, not really. Uh, back then, their spelling was all over the place, right? No idea what else this would mean."

"Carry on. We can always run this past an expert later."

"Then, you shall thrive for another Yeare. Fail and you shall fade away, in Body and Soulle, and be no more. Only should there be less than three fully skilled Wardens, be they Red or Whyte, together at the stones during the solstice, shall you be spared."

She turned toward me; her face pale. "Uh, please, Myrtle,

tell me I made a mistake. I don't wish to fade away. Perhaps this text isn't about us. It says Wardens, not witches, right?"

It did. But somehow, I couldn't imagine we'd wriggle off the hook so easily.

"When Hagbottom-Smythe told me about the missing skeleton, he mentioned a group of what he called 'early environmentalists' settling at the henge. They called themselves Earth Wardens. He said they thought they could do magic. Jen confirmed that. We're descended from those people."

Daisy didn't respond. She went more pale instead.

Unfortunately, there was more.

"The Reds are the lesser witches. Us. The ones that got left behind and disbanded. Among those staying in the village, only the Wytchetts commanded real skylles. Until Dot and Aunt Eve called the last coven back to the henge. Now, we're getting stronger. Wardens or witches, I fear Lily means us. Crap, Daisy, we're in trouble."

"Myrtle, I'm scared," Daisy said in a small voice. "I don't want to die." A fat tear welled in her eye and rolled down her cheek.

My legs wobbled, and I dropped onto the sofa. "To be honest, can't say I'm thrilled myself. Especially as I have a horrid feeling I know where one of those mirrors was until recently."

"Why's that a problem?" She sniffed.

"Because it's there no longer. Remember the skeleton I found? The Earth Warden Hagbottom-Smythe was talking about?"

Daisy nodded.

My gaze found the cat. Cats are supposed to help lower the blood pressure, and right now I needed that more than ever. "Well, according to him, some implements had been buried with the body. A mirror and some clay tablets. He showed me a sample when I was in the museum, but that mirror was mangled. The one that had been buried with the skeleton was in much better shape, he said. If I'm to believe Mistress Coldron here, we ought to see the keys reflected in a mirror for the spell to work. Which means we need a functional magical mirror."

"Oh," Daisy said, looking as miserable as I felt. "But what's with the key?"

"I have a hunch, and it really isn't much more."

"Yes?"

"Aunt Eve's clay tablets. The magical plaques of the witches."

She leaned in. "What about them?"

"Chris's family believes they serve a double purpose as keys to the underworld. At the time I thought they had mixed up their prejudices. But what if these clay tablets are our keys? That's why there were so well-guarded. The skeleton was buried with plaques as well as a special mirror. So, there's a connection. Which means we need that mirror. The one buried with the skeleton."

She licked her lips. "You don't think any odd mirror would do?"

"We'll try, of course. Back then, mirrors were rare, so we might get lucky."

"You don't believe that, do you? Would be way too easy."

"Let's try to be positive, Daise. Even if it's hard. Trouble is, the stolen mirror could be anywhere. "

"Means you must find the bone thief."

When I refocused on Daisy, I beheld big brown puppy eyes. My cousin had this wonderful way of making complex things sound simple. Her trust was touching, but she wanted the impossible. Wanted me to do a full turn, go behind Sarah's back, and search for the person responsible for the theft of Hagbottom-Smythe's precious specimens. Wanted me to hunt someone who might or might not be a murderer.

An icy hand traced my spine.

If I didn't do this and, worse, if I didn't succeed, the entire coven would fizzle out like an aspirin tablet in a glass of water.

# 16

## MISDIRECTIONS

Brake lights flared on the hatchback in front of me, and I ground the minivan to a halt. A pile-up on the motorway had spilled the westbound traffic into the countryside, where it now crawled past the village like a multi-colored caterpillar reeking of exhaust fumes. Daisy and I were caught right in it.

"Why didn't you take Long Street?" my cousin asked.

"The bridge is still blocked off, remember?"

"Ah, true."

"Want to get out and walk to the gift shop?"

She sagged in her seat. "Nah. Doesn't matter if I open a few minutes later."

"In that case, could you check for me if the Colonel has responded?"

Daisy searched her pink bucket bag for her phone.

"Yep, he says they'll wait for you. Who's coming to that emergency meeting, anyway?"

"Apart from Elmsworth? Only Damian, Rosie, and Jenna. Maybe Mel if she can make it. Not sure about Linda. Why don't you come along?"

The queue moved again, and I took my foot off the brake.

"That's kind of you," Daisy said with a tremor in her voice. When I threw her a glance, her lips quivered.

Oh heavens, what had I done now? "Something the matter, cuz?"

"It's not you. It's me. That was pretty awesome this morning, wasn't it? I mean, what we did. Together. I'm a proper witch after all, not some fluffy dud."

I reached across and clasped her hand. "Of course you are. Without you, the stunt with the recipe book wouldn't have worked. Now we know what we're up against."

Silence fell, broken by the sound of revving engines and cussing drivers. Only a hundred meters or so to the turnoff.

"I wish I didn't," Daisy said in a small voice.

"Same here. Unfortunately, we can't play ostrich, we need to act. Thanks to you, we at least stand a chance." The spunk in my voice was all fake, drawn from my teacher's basic survival kit, but my cousin wasn't aware of such fine details. Nor was she aware of the wailing black void of fear threatening to tear me apart whenever I allowed myself to drift too close to the truth.

Either the coven stopped the curse, or it would stop us. In less than a week.

I would lose Chris.

The knuckles of my hands went white as I squeezed the life out of the steering wheel. We would make it. Any other thought was unbearable.

"Why didn't the text disappear again?" Daisy asked. "Okay, it might be gone when we return, but somehow I don't think so."

"Me neither. We knew what we wanted, and we made it happen. Last time, I just triggered a page at random. That's why it must've faded."

"Odd of this Lily person to write her instructions in our recipe book and then jinx the text. I mean, without Petty, we wouldn't ever have found it."

"Precautions, most likely. In those times, the hunters were

still active. But now we've sussed how things work. If we need more information, we'll find that as well."

"Ooh, way cool," Daisy said.

Understatement of the year. With Dot gone, Lily's records made all the difference. If we lived to use them.

"I still think we should ask one more time about the keys and mirrors," Daisy said.

"What's the point? The grimoire searched itself twice already. You saw it. Most likely it found nothing because nothing's there. I bet those gadgets were pretty common back then. Lily might've assumed we'd know what she was referring to."

"Such a shame."

"You can say that."

The queue lurched ahead, leaving me with just enough space to maneuver the van away from the Swindon Road and into Main Street. As we rolled along, a sudden gust of wind flung spray at the windscreen, and I got the wipers going. Not the best day for my orange sundress. At least I had remembered to bring a fleece. The mundane thought, which yesterday wouldn't have even registered, today stung my eyes with tears. I wiped them away. The path that led to the car park behind the gift shop was narrow. One wrong move and I would scratch the van.

Another mundane thought. To heck with it all.

My luck was in, and I found a parking space, but neither Daisy nor I stirred. We sat in the van, staring at the drizzle on the windscreen until it exploded with sudden brightness. The sun was back.

Daisy sighed. "I guess I'd better make a move."

"Yeah, same here." I removed the seatbelt and opened the door. "Are you sure you don't want to come?"

Daisy nodded, the movement sending her auburn braid into a bounce. "I prefer not to be involved in the planning side of things. Always makes me feel inferior. You sort it out. You're like Mum, you'll find a solution. And if you need me, just holler."

She gave me a quick peck on the cheek, bounced from the

car and sprinted away until only the heavy scent of her perfume was left.

So much trust. So much heartbreak. It had been easier when we disliked each other.

With a sigh, I headed for Ouagadougou Cottage.

———

The honeysuckle dripping from the covered porch swung in the draft as the Colonel opened the door, green and shiny to match the window frames set deep into the stone wall. From the house's interior drifted hazy veils of ambergris together with the sad sound of whales under water.

"Ah, Mel's here," I said.

The Colonel twiddled his mustache. "Rather odd music, eh? And that scent isn't quite the thing for a crusty old soldier like me. But she claims it's soothing, and I reckon we might need that. Seems to sell tons of the stuff at the Purple Emporium."

We walked along a corridor lined with bookshelves on both sides, into a living room where more shelves crammed with books warred with the heavy wood paneling and the chocolate-brown leather furniture. The ceiling to the next floor had been removed, and the parlor was open to the gabled roof of the cottage. Two latticed oak beam frames jutted from the walls and supported the structure. For me, the best feature was the indirect lights mounted behind the top shelves, from where a golden glow washed over the ceiling. On a summer's day, no artificial lighting should have been needed, but while the fir trees threw a pleasant shade, they also blocked the sun.

"Yoo-hoo," Jenna put aside the vinyl LP she had been examining and blew me a kiss.

Next to her on the settee sat Rosie, reading glasses on her nose, papers on her lap, and a washboard of furrows on her forehead. Damian was nowhere in sight.

Mel toned down the whales. "You okay with the joss sticks?"

She pointed at a clay vase the Colonel must have brought

back from Africa. From its opening, fragrant smoke curled into the room. The vase sat on the flat back of a wooden elephant, no doubt also hailing from Africa.

"Let's say I like them in small doses. Don't worry, I'll be fine."

The glass door to the terrace stood open, and I dropped onto the slick hard surface of the leather settee placed right next to the exit. The sofa's knobs and tasseled armrests were as quaintly British as they came.

Whales wailed from the loudspeakers. Joss sticks sent smoke signals to India.

Rosie looked up from her papers and grimaced. "I've gone through all the stuff that's been handed in. These are copies, of course. Forget it. Not a single reference to the curse."

Elmsworth placed a cup of Earl Grey tea on the side table.

"Keep trying anyway," I said.

"Damian's doing that with Jochen as we speak," Rosie said. "Not sure they will be fast enough."

A sharp pain stabbed into my temples. "Don't say things like that. It only reminds me how screwed we are."

"We're not," Mel said at the same instant Jenna jumped up and joined me on the sofa. She grabbed my hand.

"Listen, Myr. I get that you're shocked and exhausted. Sweet Earth, this witching business sucks the stuffing out of you, and the news *is* rather scary. But when the message came through on the call chain, I had an inspiration."

As the coven's soothsayer and medical expert, her brainwaves carried a lot of oomph. It was also good to see she'd regained her equilibrium.

"And?"

"I'm one hundred percent convinced we'll do it. Don't ask me how, but we will. If we don't give in to despair. Especially you. We need you."

She stroked my arm and the iron band around my head eased a little. A pep talk, true, but it worked. Jenna was good at such things.

"Once I heard the news, I did a few Tarot readings," Mel said. "In every question, the Fool came up."

"And that's good news because? Sorry, I'm not really into Tarot," I said.

"It's a truly powerful card. Stands for a new beginning as well as the means to an end of something old. Represents change and risk at the same time. Totally unusual for it to appear in every single reading. And the readings weren't bad either. It won't be easy. But we'll get there, girl."

The remaining pressure on my cranium seeped away. My fellow witches were right. As long as we stood a fighting chance, we would bloody well fight.

I straightened. "Thanks for the moral support. Looks like we'd better find ourselves a lost mirror, then."

"We should try modern ones as well. Just in case," Elmsworth said.

"Sure," I said. "Curse busting take one will use a modern mirror. But in the meantime, we better search for alternatives."

"Start with Smithey," Jenna said. "He might've more of the things hanging around."

"The one he showed me was broken."

"Do it." Rosie nibbled at the earpieces of her glasses. "Won't cause any harm. That's assuming he hasn't been arrested."

"No," Mel said. "He's helping the cops with their inquiries. But they haven't locked him up. Nor did they arrest Anna. She can be a pest sometimes, but she's no murderer."

No, she wasn't. Of that I was certain, but I couldn't tell them why.

"One never knows. You'll need backup when you visit the curator," Elmsworth said sharply.

"I'll come along," said Mel. "I know him. He's not a bad sort. Do you want me to call him?"

"No. Let's surprise the man. If he's got something to hide, he might scuttle off in a hurry."

Jenna rubbed her hands. "Why don't we prepare a little script for you?"

The inspiration, when it came, wasn't accompanied by fanfares and fireworks. It just sort of crept into my brain and lay there, like a slimy pool.

"There's one more person we can ask. But I'm not convinced we should. I'm talking about Bob Ignatius."

Four pairs of eyes stared at me with varying expressions of perplexity, confusion, and disgust.

"Are you serious?" asked the Colonel. His face was the most neutral. "What does he have to offer, and how would you even get hold of the guy?"

"When we talked the other day, he wanted to send me a phone number where I could call. No idea if he did. I never checked."

Rosie's reading glasses had slipped on her nose. "Oh, I'd rather not have him involved. He's so much worse than the director, and that's saying a lot. Okay, I shouldn't speak ill of the dead. But ..."

"Then let's hope he isn't pulling strings behind the scenes," Mel said. "If Ignatius has the grave gifts now, we're royally screwed."

The Colonel's brows were doing the caterpillar thing again. "Myrtle, when he called you, what exactly did he want?"

"He wants to exploit our skylles for his business. He wasn't ...oh, not quite threatening me. But something about our well-being or words to that effect. I should be worried about it. He denied responsibility for the shooting, but he was a lot more vague about that skeleton. Chris keeps saying it would be unlike his uncle to act like that. He thinks the man would first threaten a couple of times before striking."

The people in the room were silent. The whales wailed on. The fugue caused by the joss sticks thickened, despite the open door. Sweat covered my forehead.

"I've got to call him. Before we do anything else."

"I agree with you," Elmsworth said. "See if you can find that number. But call him from my landline, not your phone. Otherwise, he thinks he's got you on tap."

I checked my mail, hoping the message had got lost in the spam. It hadn't.

The mail said nothing helpful either, only contained a mobile number and five words.

*Call me when you're ready.*

I wasn't, but I called him anyway.

———

"Ah, Ms. Coldron, what a pleasant surprise. How are you on this fine day?" The voice dripped treacle and venom in equal measures.

"Mr. Ignatius, I'm not contacting you to make polite conversation."

When he laughed, he sounded a lot like Chris. "No, of course not. I reckon, by now, you've worked out your tribe is in danger?" His tone was as calm and unconcerned as if he was reading out the bus timetable. He knew. The bastard knew.

Despite Jenna's hand on my thigh and Rosie's closeness, my heartbeat was gathering speed, thumping away into my head.

"We're on top of that, don't you worry. Causing us grief won't change a thing."

"In what respect? And, shouldn't we rather be talking about our deal?"

"There won't be any deal."

"Why not?" He sounded amused.

"How can you be sure we won't put a spell on you?" I had lowered my voice, channeling Anjelica Huston in an ancient, ancient film. But witching was an ancient skill.

At first, he remained silent. "Are you threatening me?"

"I could ask you the same question, Mr. Ignatius."

"I don't threaten. I deliver." The voice was sharper, less slippery. I must have rattled his cage.

Heavy breathing on the other end of the line. "At least, you're more rational than your aunt. She flipped whenever my name was mentioned."

"I won't flip. But I might curse you yet." Delivered in the same cultured, deadpan voice he was using, the words coming from my mouth, spawned by my imagination, made me shiver.

"Did you call to tell me that? You'd be surprised, but I'd like to see you around quite a while longer."

*To better have us hex for him. Yeah, right.*

"Then why did you take the skeleton? And the mirrors and keys?"

For a moment, Ignatius fell quiet. There was a low-level buzzing in the background. Did I smell something green? I checked my hands. No rose petals, but this might well be some weird form of underhand hexing. I had a purpose, and I was emotionally charged up, so there.

"You have bones on your mind. I'm not sure that's going to help you with the curse. From what you're saying, you must've discovered the antidote. How annoying. I was hoping to deal based on a nice little text on the subject that happens to sit in my vaults."

"Not interested."

"I suppose you won't believe me when I tell you I haven't done anything to that skeleton you keep harping on about?"

"That's not what you implied the first time round."

A snicker teased my ear. "I so enjoy riling people. Unfortunately, I don't possess the implements you need to fix the curse or have the faintest clue where to find them. I'm afraid you're on your own there. And while we're at it, I'm not behind your latest ...accidents either."

My stomach did a little flip. The green buzzing faded away. The smarmy git had nothing to trade. What would I have done if he did?

"That's all I needed to know."

"You believe me?"

"I do."

"Interesting. Well, if that's the case, there's probably not much sense in continuing this conversation. But the deal still stands. Never forget that."

With that, Ignatius cut the connection. He had proven to be a dead end. Hopefully, we'd have more luck with Hagbottom-Smythe.

# 17

## NOT HAPPY EVER AFTER

Whenever Mel was on the move, everything fluttered—the filmy layers over her generous body, her hands, even her wavy blonde mane which she pinned back with Hello Kitty barrettes. She was sensitive, sensible, and solid, and I was very glad she was there for the meeting with Hagbottom-Smythe. We had rounded the corner of the building housing the Magic Mushroom, headed for the museum, when Mel came to a sudden stop, a bit like a sailing ship grounded by a reef.

Her face scrunched with concern. "Are you sure you want to go ahead? You already did the hexing this morning. And you sparred with that Ignatius git. Enough for one day, I'd say."

"Aw, Mel, you're the kindest. I'm okay, actually. I'm doing something constructive, which helps. As does Jenna's script."

She laughed. "She's wasting her talents, isn't she? She should join the Dramatic Society."

"Quite so. Let's hope our acting is up to par."

She nodded, and her hair danced over her shoulders. "Yours certainly is. You did great with Chris's uncle."

Some of that might be owed to my skylles, though I doubted

I'd be able to do a repeat performance for the curator. He simply didn't irk me enough.

Arrived at the museum, we found the cannonball at the entrance gone, and the door shut. I yanked it open. "After you."

The place rang with the yells and giggles of what had to be at least two primary school classes. Goggle-eyed, they clustered around the presentation box which contained a child's bones, not listening to their teacher's lecture.

"Oh dear," Mel said. "So not good. Smithey hates kids."

As if to prove her right, the tubby figure stomping around in the glass-fronted office was red in the face and gesticulated wildly. He shouted at someone out of sight.

Mel pursed her lips. "Ack, he's having another go at Nina, the poor thing. Because she was the only female in the trio, she got saddled with the secretarial duties. It's sexist, that's what it is."

The door to the office banged against the wall, and the miniskirted young woman barged outside. "I didn't, I didn't. You'll regret that, you retarded old hippo." She raced for the entrance, and we jumped out of her way.

Nina zoomed past and stormed from the museum. Mel looked at me. "Maybe we should try another time," she said.

Hagbottom-Smythe appeared at the door to his office, mopping his brow with a handkerchief that could double up as a bedsheet.

"Oh, it's you again," he said. Given the puce tinge to his face, the voice was remarkably steady.

Shrill laughter drilled into my ears, and I winced.

The curator turned even redder in the face. "Are you coming or what? This noise is absolutely diabolical." He retreated into his office, slamming the door shut behind him so hard, I expected the glass to burst from its frame. The door, apparently used to this treatment, held.

"Oopsie," Mel said. "We'd better leave him alone. Unfortunately, his foul moods can last for days," Mel said.

"We don't have days. You go first, though. You he likes. Ready?"

She nodded and entered with a flutter of dimpled fingers. "Hullo, John."

Some of the beetroot faded from the curator's face. "Always a pleasure to see you. And you, Ms. Coldron."

The scowl he shot in my general direction belied his words. Well, he couldn't do worse than throw me out. "I wanted to reassure myself the cops returned your skeleton."

The curator mopped his brow. "They did. Decent of you to sort that out, though I would've preferred not to receive my specimen in a pink washing basket. And I would appreciate it even more if you could tell those coppers to leave me alone. This snotty female sergeant treats me like a suspect."

Unfortunately, that was exactly what he was.

Hagbottom-Smythe sank into the nearest chair, a comfortable, padded affair. Its backrest tilted at an alarming angle. With a bellow that evoked visions of enraged hippos, he launched himself forward and landed on his feet.

"That was her. She's messed with my seat."

"Oh dear," said Mel. "How annoying."

To hide the snigger tickling my nose, I slapped a suitably bland expression onto my face. "You mean your intern? She charged outside as if pursued by a demon."

He sat down again, this time avoiding the backrest. "Only by me. Caught her sniffing around where she didn't belong. Down in the cellar. I knew there and then she stole my skeleton. That's why I fired her. I've had enough of her sly little remarks. Not to mention her astounding inefficiency. This chair got fixed the other day. She's messed with it, I tell you." He pursed his mouth, channeling a carp chasing after a water insect.

"How can you be certain it was her?"

Mel bounced me a warning glance.

Hagbottom-Smythe growled. "I know her type. No use to anybody, as snarky as they come, and all she wants to do is hang around with those two young men. Hah. When I was young, we worked our fingers to the bone."

"Oh dear," Mel said. "So annoying. Why don't you sit down? I've brought some lovely Kusmi tea. The best for relaxation."

Hagbottom-Smythe slumped into his chair. Sighed. "Thank you, Mel. I'd love one."

Mel winked, sashayed into the corner, and busied herself with the kettle.

To me, he said in an apologetic tone, "She always messes with things." He glared at the piles on his desk that must have grown mold before Nina, the intern, was born.

His face might be less florid, but there was still a crabby quiver in his voice, warning me to be careful. "Look at the bright side. At least your exhibit's where it belongs. Actually, I'd like your opinion on something."

Mel gave me an encouraging nod from over the teapot. We were back on script.

"Ancient remains?" Hagbottom-Smythe's voice had mellowed further. He leaned forward. The chair creaked ominously.

"Not quite," Mel said, her voice sweeter than toffee apples. "Myrtle owns two Neolithic clay tablets, like the grave gifts you found with the skeleton."

"There's plenty of them around hereabouts. What do you have in mind?"

I was trying to save the coven, including myself, from extinction. However, it was unlikely the curator would take kindly to such an explanation, even if it was the truth.

"My aunt was an investigative journalist, and she researched the witch hunts. I wanted to share her findings with the community. My family used to be local, you see? In fact, I'm planning to start with a presentation at the Women's Institute, and I thought I might liven things up with a few choice relics from the past." The bit with the WI was vital. We'd gathered the curator was more likely to give us what we wanted if there was only a small audience and, most importantly, no outsiders involved.

"Your family, young lady, hasn't been local for over four hundred years."

"Sure, but now we're back, and I want to do my bit for the village." My support, so far, comprised tripping up villains, but that wasn't on his must-know list either. Especially not if the man fidgeting in front of me was one of them. "Until you told me the other day, I hadn't known about these tablets being used as grave gifts."

"Mph," said Hagbottom-Smythe. "Fine, fine, I'm always game for supporting the local ladies. They do much good for the community. "

"How simply marvelous," I gushed. To me it sounded over the top, but I could see Hagbottom-Smythe was lapping it up while Mel was making strangled noises. "It would be nice to be able to show a mirror with my clay tablets."

He wrinkled his nose. "Are you so sure they ever were grave gifts? And I can't let precious artifacts out of my hands. But you know what? I happen to own some professional photos which you can use during your presentation. Just tell the ladies that I'll arrange a special tour for them another day to see the actual objects. How does that sound?"

Mel sobered in an instant. "Uh, I think my fellow WI members would much prefer a genuine mirror. Photos don't quite cut ice."

The curator waggled a pudgy finger. "No, sorry, I can't let my exhibits out of sight, not even for you, and certainly not after what happened. The skeleton might be back, but the grave gifts are still gone. And that mirror was superb. In pristine condition. You could even see your reflection." He ran a hand over his shiny pate, chasing imaginary hairs.

*Great, just ram the message home. We need that mirror.*

Hagbottom-Smythe jumped up from his chair. "Let me show you."

He banged open doors in a filing cabinet at the back and rummaged around. A pile of paper slipped and cascaded to the floor.

"Bloody bureaucracy," he said. He stepped over the paper flurry and extricated two large photos from a brown envelope.

The first one he placed on the desk. Mel and I craned our necks. One discolored and misshapen object I only recognized because I had seen the original.

"Uh, what's that when it's at home?" Mel asked.

"A bronze mirror," I said.

"Quite right." The curator's tone was approving, and an odd sense of pride swept over me. Foolish, all considered.

"The others more or less resemble this one. Now, look at this. It's the one buried with our missing skeleton. Well, this fellow's no longer missing, but his gifts are. They were truly superb."

I stared at the photo Hagbottom-Smythe was dangling in my face. He was right. While the mirror was speckled and dull, it still clearly was a mirror. With a bit of TLC, we might fix it. Only, where was the blasted thing?

"Here." The curator slid his photos back into their envelope and handed them over. "Use this for your presentation. I'd like them returned, though. Tell me when the ladies want their tour. And in the meantime, get law enforcement off my back."

"I'll arrange it with the WI." Mel's look was mildly murderous. The women from the Institute would probably give her an earful for being forced to endure the curator's lectures.

When I placed the photos in my purse, Hagbottom-Smythe looked so wistful, guilt came knocking. Here was somebody who genuinely cared about the items under his protection. No way could that man be a murderer, a subversive schemer who crept through the night to destabilize historical monuments and cut brake lines on bicycles. Provoked, he might have knocked out the director with a clay tablet or a file. Or a spade, if need be. But this merciless malice?

Highly unlikely.

—

Outside the museum, Mel drew a deep breath. I braced myself for a tirade, but what I got was a lot worse than griping from my witchy friend. A tall, black-clad man marched across the courtyard; his swarthy face flushed with fury.

Chris. He knew. Crap, crap, crap. His bloody uncle must have spilled the beans.

I swallowed since my mouth had gone drier than the curator's records. "Ugh, I guess I should've told him about the curse."

Mel tilted her head. "You didn't?"

"No, I wanted the facts first. It's all happening so fast, and I didn't want to ...bother him." The last two words came out on a sob when I didn't mean them to.

"Oh dear."

"You can say that."

Chris crunched to a halt. He said nothing. Not a word. Like a wall, the silence stood between us, grew and spread until there was nothing left but the dryness in my mouth and a limp wonkiness where my legs were supposed to be.

"I guess, I better leave you. See you, Myrtle." Mel fluttered her fingers, and, with a nod at Chris, sailed off.

Behind me, the glass doors slammed open and the kids burst into the courtyard. A screaming and yodeling flood, they rushed past us. Chris looked at me. I stared back. Even if the hardness hadn't completely melted from his face, the corners of his mouth twitched. Three cheers for those kids.

"What have you been up to?"

"I'll tell you the complete story, but not here. And I'd murder for a coffee."

"Then, let's go to my place."

—

Chris might have replaced the rickety deckchairs on his balcony with new ones, but the scowl remained on his face. The scowl was better than his earlier fury, was something I could deal with. Not so his icy good manners. The more polite the man became, the more impossible he was to handle. He withdrew into himself and might as well dwell somewhere on the rims of a remote galaxy where no friendly spaceships dared to boldly go.

For the moment, I was content to sip my coffee and ignore the human iceberg in the other chair. It was Chris who broke first.

"Talk to me."

I put down my mug. "Once I find the right words. First, let me apologize. I should've told you."

"Yes."

"I didn't know until very recently."

"When?"

"After we'd flushed out Anna. Jochen called me. Even then, we didn't have the full story. It might've been a false alert."

He steepled his long fingers. "It isn't. My uncle called me. You gave him a license to gloat."

"Believe me, he needs no license for that."

"What if he'd tricked you? He's very good at that."

I swallowed down an angry retort that would've only made things worse. "You seem to think me a pushover."

"I don't. But by asking, you gave him the upper hand."

A fiery wave rolled through my veins and something green flickered in my peripheral vision. I thrust my face close to his. "I'm trying to save thirty-seven witches plus the kids. No way can I ignore a potential lifeline, even if it means contacting your tosser of an uncle."

"You could've asked me first. Don't you trust me anymore?"

"This isn't about trust. This is about time, a commodity we're short of. Plus, I didn't want to bother you with more rubbish."

"Bother me anytime. Just don't cut me out. You made me look like an idiot and, boy, did he enjoy that."

My cheeks burned. Chris was right, but that didn't make things any better.

"Sorry, but can't you get it into your thick head? I couldn't upset you over something that might've been nothing but stupid rumor." By now, the world had gone rather blurry, so I pretended to sip the dregs of my coffee.

"Something was upsetting you. I knew it. Next time, tell me. Please." Chris raked his hand through his hair. "If it affects you, I want to know. It's bad enough when my asshat of an uncle rings me up to crow about his victory."

"Victory? Because I contacted him? Jeez, that guy really has an ego problem."

"Didn't you agree to cooperate?"

"I wish to point out I did no such thing. Is the guy deaf or what?"

"Ah." Chris's expression brightened. "Oh, okay. Must admit that had me worried. As to being deaf—in a way, he is."

"His problem. But I had to ask him, don't you see?" I fished out a crumpled hankie and blew my nose.

"Guess so. Next time, you better consult your recipe book. Now you know how it ticks. Which I also would've appreciated to hear about."

Anger washed through my body, hot and fast. I jumped from my seat. "Chris, we only worked it out this morning. You're the one who's being unreasonable."

The fury in Chris's dark eyes flared once and died. "Noted. Now we've got this settled like civilized people. Let's focus on the curse. What the blazes is going on? And sit down, will you?"

I sat. "Didn't your uncle explain?"

"No, he just said the coven was jinxed, but he fully expected you to get to grips with things. I had to pretend to be in the picture, otherwise, he would've been even fuller of himself." Chris's jaw muscles bunched.

"How kind of him." I brought Chris up to speed. "To succeed with this ritual, we need a special mirror and a key. Or keys plural, need to check once more. Whereby, I don't think we're talking actual keys. I'm thinking more in terms of clay tablets. Unfortunately, we can't be sure."

He massaged his temples. "Why do you think the tablets are the key?"

"Eh, weren't you the one to say those Neolithic chunks of clay I've got in the safe are some sort of key to the underworld? Plus, the curator claims our—the witch skeleton we found came with those items and some other contemporary burials did too. That's why I'm convinced we're talking figurative keys rather than real ones. Especially since they were also buried with mirrors. Too much of a coincidence."

"Fair enough. So, you have the keys, but not the mirrors? That's assuming it has to be a special mirror."

"Correct. Mel and I went to see the curator, to see if we could borrow one of his."

"And?"

"The mirrors he has are useless. The one halfway acceptable specimen came with the stolen skeleton and has disappeared."

A whole caravan of emotions slowly moved across Chris's face. He reached across and caressed my cheek. " That's ...not good."

"No, but time's running out. We need to establish who's responsible for the skelly-napping and do so fast, otherwise the entire coven might be a goner. Okay, maybe those who haven't done magic are safe. No idea. But the thief has the magical items we need. At the very least they know where they are. And yes, you don't need to tell me. I'm fully aware it means I might be going after a killer, which is why I would like to enlist your help. If you want to, that is."

Chris made an impatient gesture with his hand and swiped his mug off the table. It rolled across the balcony, spilling coffee along the way.

He jumped up. "Blast it all. Don't give me that rubbish." He stalked the balcony. "I was mostly upset because of my uncle. Of course, I'll help you."

The warmth was back in the air, and the birds were singing. Not a crow among them. We had survived our first row. With a bit of luck, it might not be our last.

I pulled the curator's photos from my backpack. "Look at this."

Chris looked. He tapped the photo of the semi-functional mirror with one long index finger. "You're telling me this is what you need? And this is what you have." He flapped the photo with the discolored mess.

"Not I, the curator has it. He doesn't want to hand it over, but it's gone beyond repair, I'd say."

Chris scrutinized the image of the stolen mirror. "That'll take work, but okay."

"Unfortunately, I have no idea where to look. And before you tell me to try a modern mirror, rest assured we will. But I'm not getting my hopes up."

"Better not. It's the graves, then."

"Graves?"

A mischievous gleam stole into his eyes. "Don't tell me that hasn't occurred to anyone yet. The three graves of your ancestors at the back of the churchyard. If one witch skeleton had mirrors as grave gifts, those surely do as well."

I stared at Chris. The man was a genuine miracle.

But I wouldn't tell him. It would only go to his head.

# 18

## REFLECTIONS

"Team Graveyard, are you clear on your instructions?" Colonel Elmsworth glanced over the rims of his half-moon glasses and shuffled his paperwork. Behind his back, an apple wood bonfire sizzled and billowed fragrant smoke into the Wytchett's orchard, providing much-needed warmth after a short but determined downpour around lunchtime. The coven sat scattered on picnic blankets (the proper, British variety insulated at the bottom), folding chairs, and moldy beanbags the men had dragged from the farm's cellar. Daisy being Daisy, she'd scored a place on the Hollywood swing.

Chris sharing a chair with me was even better than the swing. If the curse had one positive side effect, my man's acceptance by the coven, as grudging as it might be, was it.

"Hang on a sec," Damian placed a smartphone on the garden table, now out on the lawn. "Jochen and his gang want to listen in. With that, we're complete."

Elmsworth rustled a bunch of papers "Right. No more interruptions, please. We've got an awful lot to plow through."

*Yeah, awful being the operative word here.*

"Okay, Team Graveyard. Who's on it again?" Pen poised, Elmsworth scanned the crowd.

"Me," Marty said.

"Me too," Hugh, a tattooed and pierced young man with a blond crewcut said. Apparently, he was our pest control specialist.

"And me," Chris said.

"You've got archaeological expertise, correct?" Elmsworth asked.

Chris waggled his hand. "So, so. I'm really a historian by design, focus on the Neolithic Period. But I've been on digs, yes."

He must have been one busy history student. The most exciting thing I did at university was coordinate cramming sessions on English and German grammar. Not much help with our hexing troubles.

"Okay, Chris, you're in charge. Liaise with your fellow diggers. You'll need shovels, tarps, and stuff. Come and see me after the meeting. What we also need is plenty of people standing guard. We must not, I repeat, must not be disturbed. Those of you interested in helping with that can also talk to me later."

What a harebrained scheme. Dark figures wielding shovels by lantern light flitted through my gray matter. The next vision was even more disturbing: the grave robbers getting disrupted during their dirty deed.

"Let's hope this won't be necessary." Linda flipped her long black hair over her shoulder. "I'm actually confident the modern mirrors will do the trick."

Her comment drew murmured assent.

"Team Graveyard is a contingency," Colonel Elmsworth said. "Right, so Team Mirror's next. Who's on that?"

"All the ones who ever hexed something," Mrs. Mornings said. She sounded mortally offended not to be one of the chosen few.

"So, Myrtle, Daisy, Jenna, and Rosie, right?"

"What about you, Colonel?" Mrs. Bingham asked. "You

scried in your shower, after all."

Elmsworth stroked his mustache, trying hard not to look pleased. "Ehem, I'm running mission command, so I'd rather not get personally involved unless it's necessary. Let's see. We need people to collect mirrors. Can I entrust you with that, Emma?"

"Pfff," said Mrs. Bingham. "Actually—"

"Great, thanks, Emma. I knew I could rely on you." Elmsworth winked at me. Buster, who'd been lying under the table, clambered out and yawned.

"Weather conditions are clear. I verified that already." The Colonel unfolded a large sheet of paper, covered in arrows and diagrams.

"Is a clear sky actually a requirement?" Linda asked. "I mean, what happens if a bad weather front moves in after the solstice? It can happen, right?"

The rough surface of the wall behind me was unpleasantly chill, and the armrest of the chair I shared with Chris was digging into my posterior, so I shifted, careful not to upset our balance. "Lily only wrote about the moon standing over the stones at night, which to me excludes a new moon, nothing else."

"Ah," Linda said. "Convenient."

"Yup. Actually, my biggest worry is the plaques." No matter how much I fidgeted around, the numbness in my bum was spreading. "Watch out, Chris, I'm getting up."

We rose together.

"I was coming to them," Elmsworth said. "They're my biggest worry as well. We need written authorization from you, Myrtle, and volunteers to fetch them, since you and Daisy are needed here. Plus, we need security, in case Ignatius makes our life even more impossible. I don't need to tell you how vulnerable the clay tablets are once they leave the vault."

A chorus of catcalls and seriously naughty comments concerning Mr. Ignatius's character defects echoed through the orchard. It took a while for the din to die down, but at the end of the turmoil, the Colonel had his volunteers.

"Once they're out, they'll have to be guarded at all times," Elmsworth said. "Strategically, the best approach would be to turn up at the bank en masse. Once we have them, we need, let's say, at least three groups of two cars minimum each that take different routes back to the village." He rustled the papers, his face shining with excitement. The Colonel would plan his attacks the old-fashioned way, but if anybody could keep the magical plaques of the witches safe, it was him.

"And what do I do? Car's at the garage, I can't dig, and I haven't hexed anything yet." Mel's diaphanous robes fluttered in distress.

"You and Linda better come with us," Daisy said. "At the very least, we'll need someone to chase off the tourists."

The spark of hope in my chest flared. We might make it yet.

———

I returned to my kitchen for a mug of tea—sans Chris, since he was busy organizing his voluntary grave robbers. I was greeted by the clock on the wall, ticking away precious seconds. Our campaign was under way, but it was no good. The wits I would need later had gone on strike.

What did Jen or Mel say? Oh yes, hexing took the stuffing out of people. If I was to coax cures from a mirror, I had better recharge a body battery as weak as the tea I never noticed I'd drunk. Daisy had been in slumber land for over an hour when I dragged myself up the stairs and into my bed, where I then lay wide awake, listening to a snoring cat and the continued ticking of an imagined clock in my head.

At some point, I must have sunk into an exhausted sleep, for here was the dreamy green valley again, the grass ocean undulating gently in a draft that never seemed to reach my bare arms. Warm and content, well-being fizzed through my body, as if I had just spent an extended session in the spa.

This time, I didn't walk the grass, or sensed the dew on my

feet. This time, I was an observer, floating higher and higher, alone in the sky above the sea of green, rejuvenated, unspoilt by human presence. Funnily enough, the sky was green too, and something bright and sparkly fizzed all around me, filling my nostrils with the earthy aroma of moist flora.

This time, there was no figure below my floaty feet, no translucent image of Myrtle as she plodded along the ground. The world was empty of humans, just as it should be, and my spirit now lifting, constantly rising, was filled with an eerie calm. So many had gone before, had become one with the essence of this place called Earth. All I had to do was follow. So easy to do—

A wrecking ball collided with my stomach. Air exploded from my mouth in a strangled gasp.

I shot upright in the bed, clutched my midriff, and struggled with the acid threatening to erupt. Measured breaths helped to claw back control, and after sucking in plenty of air, the pain and nausea eased somewhat.

I cleared my streaming eyes and beheld the root of all evil. Petty squatted close to me on the mattress, flooding my nose with the peppery scent of her anger. Pale pink rose petals drifted through the air like lost snowflakes until they came to settle on the plant.

"Are you out of your mind? What was that in aid of?"

*Rap. Rap.*

"No? What's that supposed to mean?"

The primula launched into the air and swayed above me, like the bell of doom. She then dipped her pot and rose again. Dipped and rose once more.

By now, my brain had unfogged enough for me to realize I would have nearly succumbed to the blasted curse had she not given me the botanical version of a Heimlich rescue maneuver.

"Oh, crap. Petty, how did you know? Forget it. You did. That's all that matters. Thank you." I sank back into the pillows and massaged my stomach, still sending up "not-happy" signals.

The pepper aroma was replaced by Petty's lemon scent as

she returned to the mattress. A pink petal landed on my nose and I swiped it away.

Happy I wasn't. But strangely enough, I wasn't tired either. Befuddled, true, but no longer exhausted, which caused a stray thought to wander into my mind. Perhaps there was more to this curse than just the threat. Perhaps it also boosted physical and magical strength. If the coven survived, we might end up more competent than before.

*Yeah, right.*

I placed my feet on the runner, grabbed a half-empty glass of water from the nightstand, and greedily downed the tepid fluid. When I ran my hands through my tousled hair, I hit upon more pale petals and sent them tumbling to the floor.

I should have made the connection; I really should have. The curse was affecting my skylles, calling them during the dream and bleaching the petals, the manifestation of my magic. Since I produced red petals this morning, the phenomenon hopefully wouldn't be permanent.

Outside, the light was already mellowing. Evening was on its way.

"Why does that effing curse not stick to the schedule? It's much too early."

With a soft plop, Petty landed on the covers next to me. Her blossoms were turned my way. She shook herself, then fluttered her leaves in indecision.

"Well, perhaps I'm just leading the way. I was the first to hex, after all." Apart from Aunt Eve and Dot, both dead now.

Petty's blossoms dipped and bobbed as if to nod their worried assent. A curled brown leaf dropped from a stem and sailed to the floor. A spiky ball lodged in my throat. I'd never noticed brown leaves on my familiar apart from the one time I rejected her in Jen's cellar and sent her to die.

"You okay?"

Yes, she knocked. I could only hope she knew what she was on about.

A quick glance at my watch revealed I had plenty of time before Daisy and I were due for curse busting, so I used up all my cranberry shower gel and then slapped on a pair of jeans to go with a beautiful moss-green mohair cardigan my aunt had once knitted for me. It was old but much beloved. Tonight, I would take all the armor I could find, even if it came in baby soft wool. A rustle reminded me that Petty was still there, even if Tiddles, the little traitor, had wandered off in search of food.

The curtain outside the landing clinked and footsteps creaked across the floorboards.

"Myrtle?" My cousin.

"I'm almost ready. Come in."

Daisy slipped into the room, grinning. "Had some pleasant dreams? You were out for the count when I checked. You looked so happy. You were smiling. There was still time and I couldn't bring it over me to disturb you. Uh, is something the matter?"

"It's fine." It was now.

"Petty was hovering, obviously wanting to get in. That's why I opened the door for her. Wasn't sure whether she could read the clock, but I thought she would wake you up when needed. You know, instinct and that." Daisy tilted her head. "Was that wrong?"

I wrapped her in a fierce embrace. "You're a lifesaver."

—

Waiting for the moon to come out took nail-biting eons, but eventually daylight released its grip on the world. The contours of the apple orchard blurred into indigo until the leafy branches created a monochrome backdrop to the drama that was about to unfold. That was the signal for Team Mirror to make their way to the henge, where the magical keys were waiting for us. The gravestone caper was apparently prepped and ready to go ahead if needed.

We knew we wouldn't be alone among the standing stones. Someone always was out there, worshipping, meditating under the stars or whatever it was people did in a stone circle at night when they weren't curse busting. A bunch of women waving mirrors and Neolithic relics at the moon would fit right in.

Just as Lily had decreed, the waxing moon stood high above the stone circle. Beefed up by wax candles in glass jars, its hazy veils helped to see enough of the trail we were on, but occasionally clouds popped up, causing us to trip over roots and slip on the sodden grass.

"Should've brought Maglites," Jenna said. "Or smartphones."

"They weren't in Lily's instructions," Daisy said. For the life of me, I couldn't work out whether she was being sarcastic or not.

"Candles are more authentic and their flames reveal the truth," Linda said. "For what we are planning, artificial light is just—wrong."

Neither Rosie nor Mel raised any objections to that statement, so we stumbled on, guided by the candles' feeble flicker and surrounded by a restless gloom. Kindly enough, the clouds eventually shifted their fluffy selves and revealed the standing stones, flooded with the moon's silvery beams and casting longish shadows onto the ground. Trees and bushes melted into the night, and above it stretched a sky pricked with stars that wouldn't have looked very different when Lily was walking the Earth.

If I hadn't been wound tight with anxiety, I might have enjoyed the view. Like glowy embers, fireplaces flickered in the distance and voices floated across, but in our corner of the henge, we were alone in a damp darkness that smelled of earthworms, soggy vegetation, and even soggier sheep.

"Myrtle?" Daisy whispered.

I slipped on a root. Once I had regained my balance, I whispered back. "Yes?"

"Are you sure there's only one horse head standing stone?"

"Yes," Linda said with determination. "Not another one like it. Better even, there was only the one four hundred years ago.

We're here anyway. Look."

She pointed at a mass ahead of us, darker than the shadows of the night. I'd seen it many times by daylight and it indeed resembled the arched head of a horse, rising from a chunk of gray-beige stone. There even was something that, from the right angle, could pass for an eye. Behind the horse head stone, the shadows shifted.

"We're here," somebody whispered. "We have the keys. I mean, the magical plaques."

That was reassuring to hear, and there was absolutely no reason for my heart to beat into my throat.

Jenna started the show by waggling a clay tablet toward the mirror held by Daisy. When nothing earth-shattering happened, they changed positions. Then it was my turn to hold up a tablet to be reflected in the mirror. I used only one, since Lily had most likely written key singular, not keys. We checked that once more before setting out. The woman's handwriting truly was atrocious.

We then swapped the tablets and used a different mirror, Mrs. Bingham having gone all out and collecting a grand total of twenty of them, one dating back to the last century, which we used first. When it didn't perform, we ran through all permutations we could think of, even using both keys and two mirrors at one point.

Zilch.

We raised the mirrors at the moon; we turned them the other way. We had me and Daisy waving the keys at three mirrors.

Nothing happened, apart from Mrs. Mornings slipping on the grass and twisting her ankle. No doubt that would become my fault later.

By now, the moonlight was so bright that, with a bit of squinting, the funny scratches on the tablets stood out. But if I had hoped the moon revealed a secret code, I was disappointed. The scratches, funny chevrons, and wriggles were still only that: scratches and wriggles and their reflections in the mirrors.

No sparks, no mysterious revelations, nothing. Apart from a sensation of dread. We were missing something vital.

An owl was on duty and hooted its derision into the darkness. The other coven members lurking behind the stones—those that weren't on the graveyard shift, stirred. Time to accept defeat.

"It hasn't worked." Rosie leaned against the horse head stone. Then, she jumped aside as if she expected the thing to fall over.

"Big surprise." Linda said. "Things are never that easy. Looks like we need the original mirrors."

"Could the keys be something else? Not the clay tablets, but proper keys instead?" Damian stepped up from nowhere.

"Hagbottom-Smythe only showed me the mangled bronze mirror and those clay tablets. He never mentioned keys of any sort. Actually, we'd be royally screwed, because I wouldn't know the right key from Adam. Maybe it's only the mirror part of the equation we got wrong. That was my fear all along. As Linda says, we need the originals."

The Colonel harrumphed from somewhere behind the nearest standing stone. "That means Team Graveyard is next. I'll give Lentulus a call. His lot is on standby. The rest of you, please move into position." He sounded remarkably chipper, even seemed to look forward to the part I dreaded the most.

The owl hooted its mockery one final time as the coven members hurried to the churchyard in small, hopefully inconspicuous clusters.

"And now?" Daisy asked.

"Now we join them. Come on, ladies." With that, Jenna led the way.

She was more than welcome to the pole position.

# 19

## IN A COUNTRY CHURCHYARD

The path snaking along the back of the Whacky Bramble was empty and the pub itself closed. Greg allowed himself one day off per week; he worked hard enough for it. The closure of the village watering hole was another reason for trying our illegal excavations tonight. No pub meant less risk of patrons staggering about. Only the pub sign, a cross-eyed cartoon blackberry, was illuminated and creaked gently in the rising wind. Headlights glared in the distance, but we had crossed the street before the car they belonged to braked into the s-curve that led through Avebury and then roared away.

So close to the village, there was more ambient light, and we reached the farmhouse buildings that housed the Magic Mushroom Café and the museum without further slip-ups. Streetlights sprayed sulfurous orange light over the car park, but between and behind them, the darkness had come alive. Coven members swarmed the place, and despite being fully aware of their presence, I jumped every time I heard a scuffle or an urgent whisper drifting from the gloom. We had snuffed the candles; it took only one insomniac to sound the alarm.

Between them, the moon and the lamps did a decent enough job. That didn't stop me from stubbing my toe on a root.

"Blast" I stooped to massage my bruised foot.

"What's up?" Rosie asked.

"Ignore me. I stumbled."

As if to distract her attention, a double bong sounded from the church tower. Half-past midnight. Witching hour yet again.

A nervous giggle rose in my throat. I didn't have enough saliva to swallow it down, so it took revenge and turned into a hiccup.

"Myrtle, stop that," Linda said.

"Ho—hic—how?"

"Swallow seven times, for heaven's sake."

"What with?" Another hiccup burst in my throat and Daisy pressed a bottle into my hand. I downed the sweetish drink in one go.

"Hic. Nope, didn't work."

"Password?" A sharp whisper hissed from a dusky gap between two streetlights.

"You must be joking," Rosie snapped. "Who are you, anyway?"

The gate to the churchyard creaked open, and a large shape peeled from the night. A familiar shape. Relief bubbled up and pushed out my hiccup.

"Chris, stop that nonsense." Rather inconsequentially, I then threw myself into his arms. The man shook with suppressed laughter. Stupid jokes always helped him release tension, but his special brand of gallows' humor on top of all this adrenaline was too much. Still, he was warm, he was real, and whatever horrors lay in store for us faded into the distance for a short, but blessed moment.

Chris released me gently. "We've started."

"Do I have to watch?"

"It'll be pretty dark. You don't need to worry so much." I couldn't see Chris's face, but he was talking in the oh-soreasonable tone he used when dealing with morons and small children. And me in my funkier moods. "They're going to dig up your ancestor, Myrtle."

"Guess what? That's exactly the reason I'm so jittery. This is personal. Plus, the whole scheme is crazy. If we're discovered—"

"I understand. However, it'd be better if you could hang around for a bit. Just in case you need to ...explain things."

"Explain what to whom?"

"The cops, for example," he said.

"How? Oh hello, dear copper, no worries. I experienced this yearning to meet Mary Anne face to skull, so I asked a few friends to knock on her headstone? That won't wash with the boys and girls in blue. And I still don't get why it has to be her."

"Because Mary Anne is right at the back, her marker is less crumbly, and it's the only place where more than one person can dig at the same time. We can always try the others later," he said in a tone that was probably meant to be soothing.

"We don't have all night to plow the graveyard," Linda said.

"No, that would take too long. One grave is bad enough."

Chris's tone was so upbeat I gave him a light punch in the solar plexus.

"Oof."

A faint scraping carried from the churchyard that made me shiver in my thermal socks.

"Let's at least not stand here where everybody can see us." Linda pushed through the gate and we followed.

The solid body of the church blocked not only the street lights but also the moon, wrapping the scene in darkness. We slalomed our way around headstones, guided by the light from a lantern placed in the shrubbery, where the diggers were struggling with the sodden earth, more than once getting their shovels entangled in the rampant brambles.

*Crunch.*

"Rats, Marty said. "Bloody wall."

"Shhh." That could have been Rosie, but it was hard to

identify a person by their hissing.

Fortunately, there were no houses on this side of the church, the only accommodation being Chris's flat over the café. Still, uneasiness quickened my innards into a bubbly mess. What if a stray tourist had followed us from the henge? What if one of them felt the urge to commune with the dead in the dark? The muffled, but persistent, noises would draw them like moths.

"Myrtle, where are you?" Daisy had already reached the blackberry thicket, her elegant curves outlined against the soft glow coming from within the hedge.

"Here." I ditched my worries, at least for the moment, grabbed Chris's hand, and together we circumnavigated the half-submerged *memento mori*.

Another owl hooted, this time from the front of the church.

Frantic scrabbling was the response. Chris's hand jerked in mine; he pulled me behind the square block of a fenced family grave.

"What the—"

"Shhh."

Silence fell over the churchyard, penetrated by the distant growl of the M4.

I strained into the darkness but heard nothing at first. When my ears finally picked up a sound, it was the unmistakable slapping of shoes on wet grass. Someone was creeping closer, one step at a time, until the intruder too stood still. Suddenly, what had been a rather chilly night exploded into a stifling heat that made me run a finger under the collar of my tee. Sweat trickled down my chest. A giant hoover had sucked in all the air, forcing me to take short, shallow breaths that sent little sparks dancing in front of my eyes.

The owl hooted twice, sounding a lot closer. The footfall crunched on, this time without any pretensions of creeping.

"Sorry, false alarm," said the Colonel.

It took a little while before I could muster civilized discourse. "What's with the owl?"

"That was me," the Colonel explained. "I'm good with bird sounds, so we agreed to use an owl's cry as intruder warning."

"Why did you hoot at the henge? Did someone notice us?"

"I didn't hoot at the henge. Might've been a real owl."

Elmsworth swung around and addressed the black mass of brambles. "Carry on, nothing to worry about. A light went on in the house opposite the church, but it's all dark again."

"Aye," Marty said, followed by scurrying noises, while Elmsworth beat an orderly retreat toward the front.

The lantern lit up once more, the digging continued, and for a long while, all we heard was scraping and shoveling.

"Can you join, Chris? I'd like to swap. Back's killing me," Marty said from the thicket.

"Sure, mate." He released my hand and disappeared into the prickly shrubbery. "How far have you got?"

"We're not quite two feet down, I reckon. I can only hope you're right about these early burials not being so deep."

"Yup, they only started the six-feet-under business after the London plague in 1665. I'll slow down, though. Just in case Mary Anne's in a really shallow grave."

"Let's hope we find her at all. We couldn't go for a body-sized hole. There's not enough space for all that earth, and it's hard to shift. The ground is sodden from the rain at the top and still caked from the heatwave below, but it's getting better. Dustier, anyway."

The last thing I needed to discuss in the small hours was the soil quality in country churchyards.

The digging continued, but less vigorously. Suddenly, an owl's hoot broke into the scraping.

"Blast," Chris said. The light winked out again, and the coven did a repeat performance of playing hide and seek among the brambles and gravestones.

We listened into a night that, even without our shenanigans, was anything from truly quiet. Like before, motoring noises from the M4 were carried along by a wind that wriggled the branches, sending icy fingers across my sweaty brow and coaxing an earthy smell from the ground. Not an unpleasant odor, just disturbing, given our location.

The owl hooted again, twice this time, and the light came back on in the bramble thicket.

"Is it safe?" I hissed my words.

"Yes," the hedge hissed back. "Double hoot means the danger is over," Hugh, the pest control specialist, said.

As if to confirm Marty's comment, the Colonel's heavy footsteps approached. "Sorry, same house that caused trouble before. Some idiot even opened the window and leaned out. Didn't seem to spot anything amiss and now the lights are out again. I suggest you speed up, just in case that person decides to investigate. Any progress?"

"Yes, we've got ourselves a great big hole," Hugh growled. "Another foot or so, and we're in business."

"Have a bit more respect for the dead, will you?" Rosie said.

"They should have a bit of respect for us and not play hard to get." With that, the scrunching continued.

"I better check on that annoying insomniac," the Colonel said and turned around. "Damian isn't all that good with the hooting. He sounds like a crow with bronchitis."

He marched off, but this time a grave must have got in the way. "Of all the cursed ..."

*Pling*. The latter-day resurrection men ceased their shoveling.

"Ah," Chris said. "Slowly, be careful there."

"What?" Linda, Daisy, and Rosie asked simultaneously. I said nothing, I was too busy mopping sweat off my brow.

"Give me a moment." Chris's voice buzzed with excitement. "No, put that shovel away, Marty. I need a brush."

Nothing much happened for way too long until Marty called out. "Myrtle, could you come? I think Chris has found something."

I sucked in whatever oxygen remained in the thin air and

bent under a thorny creeper Hugh was holding up for me. Chris and Marty were staring into a shallow trench, sketchily illuminated by the lantern the latter was holding. There really wasn't enough air for us all. And I really didn't feel like checking out that hole.

"It's all right," Chris said. "It's not scary. Just ..."

"What?"

"See for yourself."

I took my courage into my shivering hands, peeked at the trench at my feet, and saw what he had seen.

—

Despite having been buried for hundreds of years, wrapped in something that now was in tatters, the saucer-sized mirror flickered dully in the lantern light. But the glass was cracked and stained, its decorative frame blackened and bent. Delicate hand bones stood out against the soil, as if Mary Anne were proffering her gadget. To one side lay a corroded piece of metal. It must have been placed on top, and the noise we heard had been the shovel hitting it.

"Oh, double blast." Jenna's voice rang out so close to my ear, I would have jumped had a thorny creeper not been in my way. "Doesn't look good."

"Nope. Still, we must have that mirror," I said.

"It's an odd arrangement," Chris said. "I wasn't expecting to find anything so ...high up. As if she wanted to share it. Looks almost as if she was buried with her arm extended."

An ocean roared in my ears, like long-forgotten voices, calling to me. When Jenna put her arm around my shoulders, they dimmed somewhat. But they didn't go away.

"They wanted to help, I'm sure of that," she said.

"The intention might've been good, but the results aren't," Chris said. "I suspect, though, they hexed the grave. Otherwise, this canvas,"—he pointed at the rags—"would be long gone."

With Jen by my side, I stepped to the edge of the hole in the ground. "Mirror's still there. It's what we came for." I wasn't half as chipper as I made myself sound.

The ocean's wild roar swelled in my ears, the voices calling out to me, urging me to accept Mary Anne's gift. I could only hope she didn't die to hand over her magical implement. That would really be the pits. Perhaps the old witches always got buried that way. Just in case a rookie lost their mirror.

The thoughts dropped away as the ground wobbled under my feet. The hole blurred and a skeletonized hand seemed to wave at me. I reached out for support, but there was nothing to hold on to, only prickly creepers covered in small pinkish flowers. Until my flailing hands hit upon a fleecy chest.

"Whoa, steady there," Chris said. He pulled me aside and propped me up. "Careful, you nearly stumbled into the hole."

"It's nothing. I'm a bit hexed out. I guess this is where I pick up the mirror?" When I sneaked a peek at the grave, the bones were still in the same position they'd been before my fit of the wobbles.

"Better if I do it." Jenna pushed her way past the men. "I'll need a container."

Container? My idiotic brain dished up images of coffins.

Wordlessly, Rosie passed a Tupperware box over my shoulder. I peeled off the lid and returned to the grave, trying hard to ignore my ancestor's graceful bones and the gift she was bearing.

Her mirror might be beyond repair. Perhaps we'd taken too long to arrive. But I could have sworn her burial was unusual, and someone back then guessed—or knew one day the coven would be in trouble and ensured the mirror would be within reach.

Tears welled up, and I blinked them away. I watched a rather fuzzy Jenna bend down and, with a gloved hand, give the sad gadget an exploratory tug.

Gently, Jenna pried the long handle from what had been a hand, disturbing only two small bones that rolled aside. A knucklebone remained caked to the handle. She placed her prize in the box, looked up, and shared her sweet smile.

"I'm sure she won't mind the disturbance. And we'll put her remains back where they belong, don't you worry."

"She'll be fine," Marty said. "It's all for a good cause. "

How I wanted to believe him.

"Can somebody hold this?" He passed over the plastic container.

I grabbed it before Rosie could intervene and risked a quick peek at the contents. The lantern light was dancing wildly, driven by gusts that had found their way into the brambles. The flickering didn't help, nor did the remnants of my tears. But the sorry sight was visible enough: a discolored, cracked mirror and a human knucklebone.

"Ladies, you better leave us. Now we need to shift the soil back to where it belongs," Chris said.

"If someone comes in here, they'll spot the dig no matter what you do," Jenna said.

"There's more rain forecast, that'll spread the earth around nicely and cover our tracks. Usually, nobody bothers with these graves."

Not correct if the faint, but persistent, whiff of urine was anything to judge by.

"If someone does, we'll blame it on the resident idiot. The one who steals skeletons." Rosie was already on the move, scuttling backward like a giant crab.

Together with the other girls, I escaped from the suffocating confines of the bramble thicket into a drizzle. The wind was tugging at my hair and got under my anorak, sending shivers down my spine. How could I ever have been hot before?

Behind us, the scraping and scuffing started with renewed vigor.

"We better take the mirror home. It's almost three already," Daisy said.

A line from *Gone with the Wind* flashed into my mind.

"Tomorrow is another day." Tomorrow had already arrived. Quite a while ago. Whatever second wind had carried me had left long ago, turning my legs into a pair of macaroni. I needed shuteye. But I could only risk it with Petty present.

"Can someone take care of the thing, please? I'm not a morning person. I might drop it."

"Sure," Rosie said. For somebody her age and general condition, she sounded disgustingly fresh at this ungodly hour. "Jenna and I will have a go at it tomorrow. Uh, mean later today. Let's see if we can't fix it. That gives you time to rustle up the skeleton thief. In case we don't get this thing back together." She tapped on the lid of the box.

"Not without sleep."

And not if sleep killed me. Somehow, the thought didn't shock me anymore. I had gone numb inside.

"We should've dug up the other two graves as well," Linda said. "Their mirrors might be in better shape."

Now, that was typical. Originally, she had voiced all sorts of concerns over the digging; now she had issues with no digging. That woman really needed to make her mind up.

"If my memory serves me, we agreed to only try if nothing else works, remember?" My voice sounded sharper than I had intended, but I had no patience left for the likes of her. "Three graves in one night is pushing it a bit."

"Sorry." Linda averted her eyes. "I'm tired."

"We all are," Rosie said. "Let's go. We got lucky so far, don't tempt fate at this time of the morning."

I wasn't going to do that, so Daisy drove us home.

"I'll wait for Chris," I said once we arrived in the parlor, having fended off an exuberant Petty and a confused cat who wanted feeding.

"Are you sure?"

I wasn't, but I sent Daisy to bed, anyway. I couldn't stomach my cousin's inevitable panic had I explained I feared placing my head on a pillow, never to wake up. Better to sit in the armchair for a bit, with the plant on duty, just in case I dozed off.

—

Sunlight tickled my nose, followed by the aromas of coffee and roasting bacon. For a moment, I felt lost in space and time. Slowly, I rotated my stiff shoulders. This wasn't my bed. I turned my head the other way and beheld the shelf with its rows and rows of books and my aunt's urn sitting on top as if she'd acted as the silent guardian during my rest.

My head cleared a bit more. I must have fallen asleep on the settee. And I was still around to take stock, which was cool.

Myrtle versus curse, one-nil.

I yawned. While certainly deep, my sleep had been too short. I stretched my aching limbs and my duvet slipped off. Some kind soul must have tucked it around me and even placed a pillow under my head. The same caring person had pulled the curtains tight. Since they never closed properly, the rays of a bright new day reached through the gap and lit up the living room.

Petty, sitting on the coffee table, turned her blossoms my way. But she appeared cheerful rather than concerned, her lemony happy scent drifting across.

Not a lot of Sherlocking was needed to deduce that Chris had arrived, put me to bed ...sofa, and then presumably did the same for himself, only upstairs. The footprints on the old Turkish carpet, the mud now dried and flaking, were a dead giveaway.

I must have slept well into the morning, since the breakfast smells were already waning. Poor Linda. Without helpers, she would have had to drag herself out of bed after much too short a night to look after her guests while I was wallowing on my sofa, courtesy of the Simpkins sisters. No wonder she was so crabby. She worked her socks off, while I could swan around.

*Send the Simpkinses over.*

What a fabulous idea. And I would put my privileges to good use and have another go at finding the stolen mirror. With not even two full days left to the end of Lily's period of grace and Mary Anne's mirror in such a state, sitting on my hands was out of the question, no matter what the Tarot or Jen's vibes said.

A quick glance at my watch revealed it was after ten, which meant I had slept almost six hours without interruptions or dreams. Enough to boost the energy I needed for sleuthing.

*Talking of sleuths, what about Sarah?*

Occasionally, that little voice was useful. If my friend had caught her murderer, and that person had stolen the skeleton, there was no need for me to investigate anything, though it would be well-nigh impossible to worm my way into the clink and question a murder suspect about grave gifts.

I pushed aside the duvet and swung my legs on the floor. Nature was calling loudly, but first I needed to know how the investigation fared. I fired up the computer in the den. After what felt like ages, the local news flickered over the screen, and I skimmed the text in a hurry. No mentions of an arrest. No report of ...ah there.

*Wiltshire Police are still investigating the demise of 41-year-old Peter Jedd, Director for the Society for the Promotion of Neolithic Wiltshire. Mr. Jedd was found dead two days ago by a local woman after the brake cables of his bike had been tampered with by persons unknown. The suspicious death is one in a series of incidents the police believe to be interconnected.*

And more in the same vein. This answered my question. No, the police had not yet made an arrest. The murderer was still out there. Perhaps even plotting the next deed. Or lying low, which would be the smart thing to do.

But the killer didn't strike me as someone who'd do us the favor of cutting this crap. No, that person wanted to be seen and heard, wanted to be acknowledged for their cleverness. As did the skeleton thief. My tired mind blurred the boundaries between the two saboteurs, blended them into one. It made no odds. We had to have that mirror and fast.

"Weeds must," I could hear Cecily saying in my head.

There weren't many players left. While I couldn't discard Hagbottom-Smythe, he'd slipped to the bottom of my list. Anna had sworn she wasn't a killer, and I believed her. That Sarah hadn't arrested either of them only confirmed my ruling. Jedd had turned out to be the victim, and, amazingly enough, Bob Ignatius wasn't guilty of anything other than being a slimy tosser.

That left the interns. The three students topped my shockingly short list of suspects, with Nina right up there with the stars. She had been in the museum cellar. She had good reasons to hate both Hagbottom-Smythe and Jedd. If the curator was right and she'd tampered with his chair, she might also have sabotaged something else. Like Jedd's brake cables.

I would find out. Later. After I had my coffee and something more substantial than the obligatory yogurt. But first I needed to get upstairs undisturbed. The Fates were smiling on me, and soon I tiptoed past the bed and the motionless male form curled up in the spare blanket. Having sought and found relief, I showered. Ten minutes later, my dripping hair wrapped in a towel and the rest of me covered in my fluffy bathrobe, I emerged and found the form hadn't moved. Only the slow rising and falling of the blanket told me that Chris might well be dead to the world, but otherwise still among the living.

A fierce tenderness welled up, choking my throat. How many men would rob graves in the darkest hours to save their woman from impending doom? Not many, for sure.

*Not many women walking around with a curse hanging over their heads either.* True love came in funny shapes and sizes.

As quietly as possible, I slapped on a pair of jeans, a tee, and a fleece vest, which I could discard should the day fulfill its promise of sunshine. Then I tiptoed out again, into the kitchen, where Alma and Cecily were washing up dishes.

"Morning ladies."

"Morning Myrtle. Are you done in the living room? We still need to hoover. The corridor was in an almighty state, and we sorted that out, but we didn't want to disturb you."

Straight to the point. No questions asked why I wasn't in my bed. But the mud was an invader and would be ousted without mercy.

"Frightfully kind of you. Sorry for the inconvenience, but we were involved in some eh— outdoor activities and I guess Chris simply forgot to take his shoes off."

Worried about me, he would have dashed straight to the living room, not once considering minor things like muddy feet.

"Well, at least he remembered afterward. No dirt on the stairs, just in the corridor," Alma said, switched on the cooker, and whisked eggs for an omelet. She threw me a curious look from under her poodle perm, but if she ever heard about our nightly adventures, it wouldn't be from me. Instead, I asked if they'd consider helping Linda, which they did, delighted as always to earn extra cash no matter how well I paid them. Linda, when asked, was gushing with gratefulness, so good vibes all around. Half an hour later, I was on my way, serenaded by a hoover.

# 20

## MASQUERADES

Despite the full English and the bright light of a new day, I felt too shabby around the edges for a walk, let alone a bicycle trip, and took the van instead. Given the short distance, the car wasn't ecologically viable, but the curse counted as extenuating circumstances, right?

Of course, the Fates made me circle the village car park for futile five minutes. Fuming, I returned to Main Street and parked in the driveway of Ouagadougou Cottage behind the Colonel's vintage Rover. I left him a message under the wipers and headed for the car park—where now two spaces were free.

*A nice morning to you too.*

My money was on Sarah forbidding any of her suspects to leave, and she'd said the interns were on her list, or something along those lines. Nina being unlikely to hang around at the museum, the society's office in the old stables was my first port of call.

No interns. Instead, I was hailed by a friendly pensioner, knee-deep in that morning's mail. I had met her once or twice in Mel's New Age shop, where she bought her crystals.

"You're looking for Nina? Oh, she was ever so upset, poor little thing. Our curator can be rather crabby. He's so much better out excavating. Hasn't done that enough recently." She shoved the sleeves of her over-long pullover up her thin arms. "Though I can't imagine he'd want to use another spade any time soon after what happened at the stone circle." She tittered.

I could recognize a prompt when it jumped up and down in front of me. "Oh dear, was it now his tool someone used to loosen the stone?"

The arms of her pullover slipped, and she shoved them back up. "Haven't you heard, luv? It was Jedd's. His landlord recognized it. Looks like someone used it to dig up the stone and then put it in our curator's toolshed, wanting him to look guilty. Most likely the killer. Pretty stupid if you ask me, since Smithey has a rock-solid alibi."

"He was playing Bridge into the small hours."

"Quite so. Even the coppers seem to think he's okay. They're now after our interns. Such lovely young people. Why would they do something so horrid?"

Why would anyone do horrid things to their fellow humans? Because it floated their boat? "Baffles the mind, doesn't it? Uh, about Nina ..."

"Oh, she's around. That sharp young sergeant what's in charge has ordered all three of them not to leave the village. Just like they do in these murder series." The sleeves slipped again, and she fiddled with them. "As if Nina would hurt a fly. That other young man, the blond one, mind you—" Her bright blue eyes glittered, reminding me of the crow, or whatever that pesky bird had been.

"Pip you mean?"

"Has an odd name for sure. Forever mouthing off how he'd do 'things', whatever those might be. One wonders. And he hated our director with a vengeance. Didn't give him the fancy position he wanted, but stuck him in the tourist office. Nina, now she's a bit vain, but she'll get there eventually."

Never underestimate a senior citizen. That sounded as if I should watch my back around Pip, rather than Nina.

"Cal struck me as being a pleasant young man. He's the one working with the gardener."

"Oh, he *is*. His family owns a garden center somewhere down Bristol way and our Jack, that's the gardener, is teaching him loads. So, he's happy. Well, mostly. Sometimes, Jack dishes out tough love." She tittered. "But Cal's fine."

She leaned in, and I followed suit. "He even pleaded with Jedd on Pip's behalf, because that young chap wasn't content with being where he was. Got nowhere, of course. His Highness Jedd wouldn't budge for nobody." She clapped her hands in front of her mouth. "Oops, shouldn't talk bad of the dead. Mind you, he *really* wasn't the easiest of people. Cal was mightily upset, poor boy. Well, Pip was even more upset. Yelled at his friend for getting him into Jedd's black books. But it was kind of Cal to try, wasn't it?"

"Very much so."

"Come to think of it, Nina yelled a lot, too. At that Pip chap. I think she fancies Cal over him. Serves him right, eh?" A smile sent her wrinkles into a dance.

"Did the sergeant in charge of the case talk to you yet?"

The woman widened her sharp blue eyes. "No, do you think she will? That'd be fabulous. I love watching my murder series, I really do. Never miss one. *Death in Paradise* is my favorite."

Not only in crime series were little old ladies a lot more dangerous than they let on.

"I'll see that she does. To come back to my question, would you know where Nina is right now?"

"She's in the kitchen, helping with the costumes. Just go through there, luv."

"There" turned out to be a door at the rear of the stable building that gave access to the manor garden and its lavish display of lavender.

As I balanced over the uneven paving stones meandering

toward the entrance, voices drifted over the walled garden to my left: Cal, the intern and Jack, the head gardener.

I stopped. Listened.

"Heavens, knock it off. There's nothing more you can do. Perhaps, now Jedd's dead, we'll get somebody more competent, and then that other chap ...what's his name again?"

"Pip."

"Right. Pip can talk to them."

"He'll miss an entire year if the university doesn't accept his placement. And they won't. Handing out tourist info is no good for a business admin course."

"He's young. Surely, another year is nothing in the grand scheme of things."

"It isn't *fair*. Things shouldn't be like that. And just because he's young doesn't mean people like Jedd can waste his time. It's so rotten."

"Sure, sure. Sometimes, life can be a bitch, huh? Now, you'd better fetch the compost. High time we did some work here."

The screech from the wheelbarrow covered Cal's response.

Our very own Miss Marple was right. Cal sounded like a decent sort, someone who cared about justice and looked after his friends. While this was reassuring, it didn't help me with the precious grave gifts. Since Nina was the one I'd come for, I might as well start with her. Decision taken, I headed for the entrance of the manor.

---

The high-pitched squeals of a saxophone tortured my ears upon entry.

Costumes, the woman had said. The only costumes I knew about were displayed in the former kitchen, which was now blocked off by a sign on an easel saying "No entry." Inside, two women were discussing hems and stitches. One sounded vaguely familiar.

I hesitated only a second before knocking on the door frame.

"Sorry for disturbing you. Is Nina around?"

"She's with me. Come in."

I did, and at the same moment, the voice registered. By now, it was too late to turn back.

A tall woman rose from the floor, clad in the long skirts and mobcap of days gone past. She turned in a rustle of skirts, and I faced Anna the churchwarden.

"Good morning, Myrtle."

"Good morning, Anna."

The second person in the room stood next to a large stone sink. Nina was wearing the somewhat rumpled guise of the former French queen Marie-Antoinette, minus her wig, but plus a pair of grubby trainers peeking from under the crinoline and stylish, black-rimmed glasses. The fake queen exercised an exaggerated curtsy, which I reciprocated in kind. Her move sent across a dusty smell I couldn't immediately place. Then it came to me. Mothballs.

Anna must have interpreted my expression correctly. "The Women from the Institute have fixed the costumes. They were getting tatty. One would've hoped they'd bother to wash them."

"What do you need costumes for, if I may ask?"

"Visitors can try them on and take pictures of themselves in the period rooms." Anna's lugubrious face became even more somber. "We weren't sure if it's the right thing to do. Given that Peter …But the guests love it, you see?"

"Of course."

"The show must go on," Nina said. "And it's fun. Haven't had a lot of that lately." She fumbled around in a box and retrieved a rather bedraggled white period wig, covered with plastic roses, mauve feathers, and straggly locks.

The churchwarden might not have been my first choice as a potential bodyguard; the setting was bizarre, but here was my chance to meet Nina with another person in the room to cover my back.

I should have known better. The Fates had it in for me

today. Her body rigid as a rod, Anna forced a smile at Nina. "Would you mind leaving us alone for a minute? There's a load of costumes in the scullery you can unpack."

"Sure." The intern ducked into the room behind, presumably the scullery.

With a set jaw, Anna walked across and closed the door.

*Oops.* A confrontation hadn't featured in my plans for today. "Uh, actually, I came to talk to her."

"Later. I've got a bone to pick with you."

"Bone?" My voice sounded somewhat squeaky.

"Because of the police."

Sometimes, a frontal assault is the only way out. "I got your note, thank you very much. I never once blabbed on you, if that's what you mean. Not to the cops and not to anyone else. For what it's worth, I believed you. Still do. But I can't stop the police from investigating a murder."

"You didn't send that sergeant after me. What's her name?"

"Sarah Widdlethorpe. Yes, she's my friend. No, I haven't sicced her on you. Once Jedd died, she had to question everyone who knew him. Which you did."

Some of the rigidness went out of Anna's stance. "Oh, I see. I assumed you'd ...well ..."

"No. I swear I didn't."

"Didn't what?" Her tone had gone sharp again.

*Give it a rest, will you?* "Pass on what you confessed in confidence."

Anna pulled off her mobcap and her blonde hair rose like a halo. "The woman's like a human terrier."

I couldn't help the grin. "Yes, she's pretty thorough. But surely you managed, otherwise she'd have dragged you to the cop shop ages ago."

"She did. Before she would sort of accept I wasn't her killer, I had to confess everything. I was hoping not having to do that three times."

"Three? Oh, you mean the vicar."

"He forgave me. He's a good man, though a tick doddery."
She sighed. "The wedding will go ahead."

"Ah. That's good, I suppose."

"Mph."

Anna might have regretted her act, but she didn't appear to
have dropped a single prejudice. Her problem, not mine. "But it
means you're now off the hook for the murder. Which is good."

She tensed again. The woman really needed a holiday. But
so did I.

"You don't think I'm guilty?" Anna asked.

"Once more with feeling. No."

"No?"

*Mamma mia, who's the terrier here?* "No. You're not the
type."

"Oh. All right." Mobcap in hand, she sank onto a camping
chair. Then she looked up. "I also have a solid alibi for the bicycle
accident. I was in the church all morning, with people coming
and going all the time, including yourself. As of ten-thirty or so,
I was closeted with the vicar. He came around soon after you
left, and I confessed everything."

"No need for you to tell me," I said mildly.

"I want to. John's in the clear as well, by the way. Jedd sent
the auditors after him, and he was sweating it out with them the
whole morning until well after lunchtime."

"Ah. Looks like the cops know when exactly the brake cables
were cut."

A little voice in my head berated me that none of this was
getting me closer to the skeleton thief and the grave gifts. But
one never knew. In any case, another little voice kept egging me
on.

"Jedd was seen cycling to work in the morning without
problems, which he apparently couldn't have if the brakes had
already been in a state."

"Where was his car? He's been driving all over the place,
terrorizing people."

A quick grin flitted over Anna's unhappy rodent face. "At the garage. He got too close to someone who then scratched the paintwork with their umbrella."

"Ah, I see." I saw indeed. If Jedd had been driving his car, he might still be alive. Car brakes were more difficult to sabotage. What did the woman in the society office call it? Rough justice? No, tough love. Not the same thing at all.

"Yes, I'm sure you do. Anyway, that morning he cycled to work. When I say morning, it was around nine. By that time, I'd already been in the church for ages. People kept disturbing me, and there's no way I could've made it to Peter's place and back again. Even the sergeant accepted that. Took a while. Looks like Peter also raced home without problems and then set out for another spin during his lunch break—that man always took extended breaks and at funny times as well—and *bang*."

Bang indeed.

"I didn't get that bit from the cops, in case you wondered. But the sergeant phrased her questions in such a way that tells me she must have narrowed down the time when somebody messed with the bike. Noon or thereabouts. So, it can't have been me."

"Good."

"Yes, because first you were with me, then the vicar. He made me see the light. I dropped the message at your place and then drove to Swindon. My customers will also vouch for that. It wasn't me, I swear." Her voice rose to a screech.

She *really* needed a holiday. "For heaven's sake, I said I believed you."

The scullery door slammed open, and Nina barged out. Another woman who seemed to live in *alto* all the time, perhaps the reason those two had gravitated toward each other.

"What's up? Are you all right, Anna?"

"Yes. Yes, I suppose I am. Sorry." She rammed the mobcap back on her head. "Right, Myrtle, what is it you wanted? Otherwise, we'd better have a go at sorting these rags."

If I didn't want to leave empty-handed, I would have to feed them a story. "I'm trying to find some missing grave gifts and was hoping Nina could help."

Nina, now wearing the scruffy wig, which didn't go with her glasses, threw me a confused look. "Grave gifts?"

"Afraid so. I need them for a presentation I want to make. It's about the village history."

Outside, shoes scuffed across the flagstones. Somebody poked their head into the old kitchen.

"Sorry, this room is temporarily closed," Nina said in a chirpy tone. "Idiots," she added under her breath. The head withdrew.

"That wasn't very polite of you," Anna said.

Nina shrugged, sending the feathers on her wig into a wild wave. "They can't have heard. What was that about grave gifts? You're not talking about the skeleton the old hippo …the curator keeps harping on and on about?"

"I am, actually. It came with a rather well-preserved mirror which has been mislaid. And some clay tablets."

"Oh yes, he's harping on about those as well, especially the mirror. Accuses me of stealing his precious exhibits."

*And did you?* A competent witch, someone like Lily, would have hexed Nina into confessing. I wasn't a competent witch, so I couldn't. Shouldn't really, not with the curse warping my skylles.

"You'd never do something like that," Anna said. "John can be a real moron sometimes. I'll talk to him."

Nina opened her mouth and then closed it again. "Please," she said. She swung around to face me. "I haven't got your grave gifts. No idea what happened to them." Her gaze slipped to one side. There was something she wasn't telling me.

"Nor did I cut brake cables. Or mess with the old fart's chair. Why would I? Lardball throwing himself against the backrest all the time would break a cast-iron railing, believe me."

"Thanks. Shame about the exhibits, then."

Nina shrugged. "There's, like, tons of these tablet thingies? I don't get it."

Despite her costume and all that drama, this didn't seem to be an act. I'd learned to read body language as part of my teach-training, and I believed her when she claimed not to be a killer or a thief. She also seemed to speak the truth about the grave gifts.

So, what was she lying about?

Nina faced the window. "I never thought it would be like this. Bloody internships are such a beast to find. This wasn't what I wanted and turned out even worse than expected. How's filing silly invoices in a dusty museum going to help me with a job at Cap Gemini?"

"Every bit of experience counts," Anna said.

"Not this, no. Cal's reasonably okay. The gardener might be a crusty old sod, but he's flexible and showing him stuff. Plus, his folks own a nice, profitable business for him to inherit. Pip, now he's seriously pissed off." She swung back and pulled a face. "With Jedd dead, the intern scheme will fizzle out. Makes me wonder if we'll still get our certificates. I'll freak if we don't. All that hassle for nothing."

There had to be a clue here somewhere. Something that might serve as a bargaining chip when I next talked to Sarah. I was so not looking forward to that conversation. "Let's hope it doesn't come to that. Out of interest, how were you assigned to your jobs? And who identified them in the first place?"

"Jedd had connections to our uni," Nina said. "The positions were advertised, and we applied. We must do internships. It's part of the curriculum in business administration. There never are enough good placements to go around. So, there's a lottery, and you take pot luck. Hah, see where it got me. Accused of stealing ancient bones and bumping off management."

"If anybody will find the truth, it's the sergeant," I said. "So, Pip isn't happy with his lot, because he's not doing something that counts toward his curriculum?"

"Correct. Not enough hours, see? What I did sort of marginally qualifies, and I stuck it out long enough. But officially he isn't even part time. Cal's fine. As I said, the wrinkly involves him in everything, like the planning, the ordering, and so on. Plus, his uncle can give him a certificate any time."

"In that case, why did he bother coming here?"

Nina grinned. "Because of me, see? Fancies me rotten, and so does Pip. Hah, Pip, as if I ever …He's not my type, nor is Cal, really. That was the only good thing. Watching the two guys stumble over their tongues."

No, I didn't much like Nina, not even the tame version. She could have been a charming young woman with her heart-shaped, intelligent face if it hadn't been for the queen bee attitude and arrogance radiating from every pore.

"He's such a windbag, thinks he's God's gift to the world. Keeps banging on about it being a better place, if people accepted his superior judgment." Nina said. "He can go, like, totally ballistic about nothing. Bit like a Robin Hood complex, but seriously off the mark sometimes."

That made me even less inclined to talk to Pip, at least not on my own.

An idea took root in my mind. What if the guy, driven by his complex, thought it fit to revenge his fellow students by lashing out at their tormentors, Hagbottom-Smythe and Jedd both? Was it possible someone would steal bones, loosen standing stones, and cut brake wires because they were being ill-treated? Which they were, from what Nina had told me, no doubts there. The whole internship program had been set up for the benefits of the business owners rather than the students. Would that be motivation enough for Pip to start off with the skeleton caper and then graduate to murder, trying to muddy the waters as he went along, by planting spades where they didn't belong?

Perhaps Pip didn't mean to kill, tried to "only" cause accidents. Which was bad enough. The seed grew. I would have to tell Sarah. Blast, I had neither the time nor the nerves for this.

"Oh, crikey. What a mess," Anna said. She ripped off her cap and wrung it in her hands. "Listen, I'll make sure someone signs your certificates. You won't go without. You earned them."

From the pockets of Anna's apron shrilled old-fashioned ringtones. "Excuse me for a moment." With a swishing of skirts, she opened the back door to the kitchen and disappeared into the garden.

"Is that all?" Nina's expression had turned sullen again.

Thoughts swarmed my head like midgets. I had to plead my case one last time. "If you hear anything about the mirror, will you tell me? Here's my card."

She pocketed it. "Sure, though I doubt I'll be of much help. Odd that the bones showed up, but not the gifts."

"Very."

Her gaze turned sharp. "Why are you so keen to get hold of these stupid gimmicks?"

"Because of the presentation I'm planning. The curator refuses to part with them. He wants people to visit the museum." I gave her a conspiratorial wink. "I don't think anyone's eager to have him pontificate."

Nina's laugh bubbled up. "No. They wouldn't be. Okay, if I hear anything, I'll let you know. Promised. But I really, really didn't steal that bloody skeleton or those grave thingies. Must admit, it was funny to watch the curator running around like a headless chicken. But he got, like, totally grumpy afterward. He works himself into a state when the slightest thing goes wrong. So, there was no point in doing something stupid like that. I would only hurt myself, see?"

Oddly enough, I did. "It's fine, thanks."

She tossed me a grateful smile and ducked back into the scullery, this time leaving the door open.

Nina wasn't exactly a happy hamster, but I couldn't blame her. Instead, I now blamed Pip. Unless I had my facts upside down, Nina and Cal were out of it and Pip very much in. A possible saboteur gone killer; did he also steal the skeleton? For if he didn't, I would have taken an unnecessary risk for nothing. In any case, he was the person to see first. But not on my own, not without backup.

Who to call? Sarah? No, she'd only arrest him.

Chris would kill me if I took stupid risks. I thumbed his number.

"You've reached Lentulus IT solutions. Please leave a number after the beep, and I will call you back as soon as possible."

*Beep.*

"Chris, if you're up, could you give me a buzz? I might've an idea about the skeleton thief, but I don't want to confront the guy on my own."

I sat in the kitchen, while Nina dug through the bag of clothes, occasionally uttering squeals of delight. Anna seemed to have gone, perhaps embarrassed about her earlier outburst.

I checked my phone. No messages. The time was moving on, and Chris probably still asleep.

Who else could I rope into my harebrained schemes?

Daisy. She knew Pip. She'd help.

# 21

## TREASURE HUNT

"**U**h, Myrtle, you sure this is a good idea? Knick-Knack's will be, like, really busy soon? I can't keep the shop closed for long."

Sometimes, Daisy's priorities were seriously skewed. If we didn't lift the curse, the shop would close forever. "Pip might know where the mirror is, Daise. If he does, he might be a killer, and I'd rather not face him on my own."

"Oh, snap. Sure, I'm coming."

The souvenir shop locked, we headed for the henge and the information trailer parked close to the gated entrance from the Swindon Road. Painted a virulent shade of purple and cut open on its long side, the old caravan dutifully displayed the tourist office sign and was surrounded by displays crammed with brochures that offered trips, accommodation, food, and whatever else a visitor's heart might desire. Bashfully hidden behind stood three ComPotty portable toilets.

I did a full turn to take it all in. People were swarming the henge, almost as if the recent death had boosted business. Even better, since it meant we wouldn't be alone with a potential murderer. As I watched, more tourists pushed through the gate, quite a few of them beelining the information trailer. Fortunately, they left reasonably quickly.

We waited until business came to a lull and then stepped up. There was Pip, slouched behind his counter, a wooden board loaded with brochures reaching from one part of the trailer to the other. A three-day stubble and a five-star bored expression on his face, Pip was toying with his phone. He'd stretched out his jeans-clad long legs under the board, and it wouldn't have taken much to trip me up. To round off the general "don't bother me" message, a piece of cheesecake, a plastic fork rammed into its middle, teetered precariously on a stack of Avebury guides.

Pip looked up, his blonde fringe dangling into his eyes. He heaved a deep sigh. "May I help you?"

Daisy pushed past me. "Hey, Pip."

He sat up, suddenly a lot more alive. "Daisy. Hey." Pip bounced from his chair, lifted the flap set into the counter, and clomped down the steps, thumbs hooked into the belt loops of his low-slung jeans. He gave me a curt nod. "She with you?"

Daisy batted her eyelashes. "My cousin. She's actually the one who wants to ask you something."

"Oh-kay. Sure." He unhooked his thumbs and wiped his hands on his jeans, running through his repertoire of respectful expressions. His right hand twitched as if unsure whether he should shake mine or not.

I might as well have a sign on my forehead that said "Over thirty? Approach with caution." Seriously, Daisy wasn't that much younger than me, and no doubt even she had a couple of years on the guy. I released him from his conundrum by waggling my fingers, Mel-style.

"Hiya. Sorry to disturb you, but I'm searching for something, and I'm counting on your help."

He tossed me a vacant look. "Of course. Might need to speed up a bit. People will want brochures and ask all sorts of pointless questions."

He was right. Out of the corner of my eye, I spotted a group of hikers striding purposefully for the trailer. One, a man clad in a spanking-new windbreaker, pushed past the others and stopped beside me.

"Quick question. Path to Kennet Long Barrow?"

Pip glared at him. "Hello to you too, sir. Over there." He flapped his hand at the henge. "Marked by a green triangle, you can't miss it. And now, if you please, I was helping this lady."

The hiker re-joined his group, growling under his breath. Customer care this wasn't, but since the chap had been rude himself, the cold shoulder treatment sort of served him right.

"See, it's always like that. Not one quiet moment. Nag, nag, nag the whole time. Somebody's supposed to relieve me for breaks, but I can't rely on that. I never get to eat. And if I ...uh, nip out for a sec, there's a queue when I come back, everybody bitching and moaning. And because I only work two days per week, I'm not even getting in enough hours since officially I'm on an eight-hour shift. In reality, it's a minimum of twelve."

If his story was true, the arrangements were seriously illegal. However, we had better get back on topic, fast, before the next tourist showed up. "Sounds shocking. If I were you, I'd send an official complaint. Check with Anna. She should be able to help. Now, sorry, but I still need something from you."

He sighed. "If you insist."

The attitude was strong with this one, which meant nothing short of a double whammy would shake him out of his insouciance. "I need the grave gifts that came with the stolen skeleton. For an important presentation. I talked to the curator, but after what happened, he's digging his heels in when it comes to lending stuff."

Pip's blue eyes became enormous and round. He took a step backward, hand on his heart, his shock too overdone to be genuine. "How the blazes should I know ...What skeleton? Now you freak me out."

*Only because you know what I'm talking about.*

"The one lifted from the museum and dumped on a hiking trail. It's been returned now, but that's where all the troubles started."

Daisy burst into a giggle, and I gave her a sharp look.

"Troubles?" Pip's clouded brow cleared. "Oh, the bit with the standing stone. Downright scary. Like Jedd's death. Though, if you ask me, the bastard had it coming."

It took some effort, but I only raised a brow.

Pip launched a tirade about his woes, as lengthy as it was wordy. At its center seemed to fester a severe anxiety about not getting the certificate he needed. I had heard that one from Nina before. So far, their stories matched. He had also not answered my question.

I stepped aside for a harassed-looking young mother in need of a place to change nappies. Two bookings for guided tours, one complaint about the muddy car park, and three hungry tourists later, the trailer quietened down once more. But the next lot was already tramping in. If Pip hadn't been so obnoxious and if he hadn't been my numero uno murder suspect, I would have felt sorry for the guy. Staffing the info trailer wasn't a job for the faint-hearted.

Pip gulped a coke, his Adam's apple moving as he swallowed. "Ah, that's better. See what I have to put up with? So, where's that bunch of bones these days? Is Saggybottoms still running around in circles? That was fun to watch."

Daisy sighed. "Are you listening at all? The skeleton's been returned. We're after the mirror and Neolithic clay tablets, the grave gifts that were in the same box. Those haven't been handed in yet."

"Some grave gifts. Hey, why are you asking me? I never ..." An odd expression surfaced in Pips handsome face. He tossed his fringe aside. "Funny you should mention Neolithic tablets. I saw some recently."

"Where?" Daisy and I said as one.

"In the museum?" she added.

Super, now she was writing the script for him.

"No." His gaze slipped top left, to the sky, which told me he was most likely searching his memory, not cooking up a lie.

Progress.

"That's the odd thing about it. The ones I saw were elsewhere. And they were quite dirty. Caked with earth. Grave gifts, you said. Makes me wonder ..." His fringe once more covered his eyes, which made his expression hard to read.

I tilted my head and said nothing. Somewhere, I read silence was supposed to be a smart interrogation technique, since people felt obliged to fill the lull with words.

Pip was no exception. "Someone showed these funny stones to me. Said they'd found them and would take them home as a souvenir."

*What about the mirror?* But I kept quiet. Fortunately, Daisy did as well.

"Huh. Odd stuff, that." Pip tugged at his fringe. His eyes focused on a spot over my left shoulder as if he was searching for the truth among the racks of tourism pamphlets. He reached for his coke. Sipped pensively. Plunked the empty bottle on the counter.

He sought my gaze. "Why did you say you needed those thingies?"

I made sure not to lose the piercing regard of those blue eyes. He wasn't half as featherbrained as he was letting on. "To liven up a presentation. Once I've done that, they need to go back to the museum where they belong. Yes, I know it's slightly illegal, but like I said, the curator's guarding his exhibits like the proverbial dragon."

"Are you a teacher, then?"

"Used to be, though this isn't for a class."

Pip laughed. "Man, my teachers would never bother with such detail. Fine. He really shouldn't have done what he did. And if they belonged with the skeleton, he mustn't keep these doodahs. That's stealing."

"He?"

"I'm talking about Cal."

Something cold and hard materialized in my stomach. First Nina, then Pip, now Cal—who was the true villain on this set?

Pip bit his lip. "Do you think I should tell the sergeant? When I talked to the constable, he came across all chatty and friendly. Then he said they wanted an official statement. That means … we're suspects, right?" His voice had lowered to a whisper, and the swagger had drained from his posture.

"If there's something you know, you'd better tell the cops." Daisy shared her solar smile with the guy.

Pip nodded at no one I could see. "I hate to rat on a mate, but if you ask me Cal's got a screw loose. He nicked that thing from the museum to teach old Saggybottoms a lesson. A warning, he called it."

"A warning? You're telling me he stole the skeleton?"

Pip licked his lips. "I reckon it was about showing off to Nina. He only came here because he believed he could hit the sack with her. But she enjoys stringing people on." He tossed Daisy an inquisitive look, but she turned her back on him and fingered the Witch's Retreat brochure from the nearest stand.

A stream of thoughts raged in my head. Order, I needed some order here. "So, he nicked the skeleton to impress his inamorata and piss off her boss. He didn't happen to sabotage Saggy …the curator's chair while he was at it, did he? And does he happen to be a good shot? He certainly could tell a spade from a shovel. Seems to be quite handy with his tools, that guy." I didn't dare to mention bicycles.

The guilty look on Pip's face told me all I needed to know. Slowly, the guilt morphed to horror, and Pip froze.

"Oh, shit. You're not telling me—No, seriously. He wouldn't have fixed the bike. He's not totally off his rocker."

"Is he? Off his rocker I mean?"

"No. Not really. Well, actually …Uh, obsessing is probably a better word. Has these grand ideas about how the world should be. And how people should be shown the error of their ways if they don't do what's 'right'. Right meaning the way he does things. Bit like Robin Hood, only *noir*. And it's not about money. He's rolling in dough. Unlike me." Pip looked up. "It can't have been him. I mean, Jedd was an absolute tosser, but you can't …I mean, I wouldn't …"

I believed him, just like I had believed the others. Those I had talked to. One by one, the suspects had fallen over like dominoes. Only one was left, and if he wasn't our killer, I'd eat a whole brochure for dinner.

Cal.

Blast it. When Nina mentioned a Robin Hood complex, she'd been talking about Cal, not Pip. At the time, it didn't register, but it certainly did now. To get our mirror, I would have to confront him. Or perhaps not. Maybe there was a way of getting at the mirror without getting too close to a killer.

"Listen, when the sergeant comes—"

"In an hour or so."

"Good. When she shows up, you tell her what you told me. You must. Otherwise, this will never end. Do you understand?"

He nodded slowly. "Wasn't planning to, but crap, you're right."

"Any idea where your friend hid the tablets and the mirror he stole?" Daisy asked the question next on my list, and she did it in a tone that would have kept a whole sweet shop in business for months.

Pip chewed his cheek. "Not sure whether they're still in the same place, but the last time he had them hidden among his stuff in the garden shed. Maybe Nina knows more."

Perhaps she did. That must have been what she'd been—not exactly lying about, but hiding from me.

"He rents a room in a B&B in Calston. Found it funny because of his name, see? But it seems to be pretty basic, and the landlady is, like, super nosy?"

*Yeah, tell me all about nosy landladies.*

"I guess, if you were looking for them, now would be a good time," Pip said, suddenly the epitome of helpfulness. "That's assuming they're still there. He'd be busy the whole afternoon, he said. They're flinging dung or something. It's not that these grave thingies belong to him. Will you really return them to old Saggybottoms? Promise? I don't want to have anything to do with this."

"I will. Won't need them for long, anyway. Where would I find that shed?"

"Past the walled garden, on the other side of the manor. A good place to have a quiet beer with a friend. To think ...Oh, jeez."

Voices bubbled up around us. The footfall of many booted feet approached. A fresh wave of visitors was crowding the trailer, clearing their throats, fidgeting.

I looked up and beheld the smiling faces of the culinary mobsters.

"Oh, hello, Mrs. Coldron, there you are. Been wanting to talk to you," Isobel said.

"Sorry for making myself scarce recently." I balanced from one foot to another. They were friendly people. I should be there for them more often, but curses took precedence over my duties as a landlady.

"No worries, all is fine. The vicar contacted us and everything's going ahead as planned. He said we owe it to you, and let me just say—thank you."

"A pleasure. Happy for you it all worked out." *Can things please work out for me as well?*

"You're invited to the wedding," Isobel said. "Bring whoever you like."

I thanked them as profusely as I could, promised I would try my best, which—curse permitting—I would. Then I turned to Pip one last time.

"Okay, thanks a bunch for the information. Don't forget to tell ...you know who."

"I guess I will."

The shock was wearing off, and sunshine here was already wriggling off the hook. No way.

—

Back at the gift shop, I took my leave from Daisy. She'd asked whether she should come, and for a moment I had been tempted. There was safety in numbers. But it would look odd if two people turned up where one was already too much, and I didn't want to draw any more attention to my quest.

"Promise me you won't do anything silly," Daisy said.

"Silly like what?"

"Silly like confronting Cal."

"You heard Pip. Cal's working. It's way past his lunch break. Not to forget, he's always with the head gardener, so I'll be fine. Once I have the mirror, I'll call the police to make sure our mutual friend doesn't suffer from sudden amnesia."

"Okay, I guess. But if I don't hear from you in an hour—"

"You sound the alarm. Thanks, Daise."

Daisy's eyes were soft, brown, and earnest. "I hope you'll be safe."

"It's fine, Daise, honestly. Here, let me call Chris once more."

He wasn't in. Nor was the Colonel. I left both a message, though. Daisy was hopping around, too edgy to be of any help, so I sent her off with a promise to keep her on speed dial and ping her if I got into trouble.

I started off for the manor, but stopped again after a few steps.

Sarah would string me up with the weekly washing if Pip happened to mention my visit before I did. If I found the mirror, and if it did the job, I would want to have a friend left. A friend who was trying to solve a murder and serve justice. But then, I was trying to protect my coven from a nasty end and didn't want the mirror confiscated.

I weighed the phone in my hand. If I told her about Pip's

evidence, she would interrogate him first, which would still give me enough time to retrieve the magical mirror. She might also be too busy to answer the phone herself.

Feeling rotten about all that subterfuge, I thumbed her number. "The number you're calling is not available. Please leave your message after the tone."

Bingo. Finally, the Fates cut me some slack.

"Sarah, it's Myrtle. Don't throw a hissy fit. I haven't been deliberately sleuthing behind your back. I really needed to find something, and I've been rushed off my feet. While looking for it, I chatted up a few people, including the churchwarden, and one thing came to another. If you talk to Pip, the intern in the tourist info, he can explain what's going on. Gotta dash, I'll try again later. Good luck."

Duty done—well, sort of—I switched my phone to vibrate and headed for the manor.

—

The kind woman in the society's office was still on duty, and she even let me use the back entrance once more.

"Not sure if Nina's still around, though."

"No, I forgot something, thanks." I dashed off before she could tap me for details. In case she watched, I entered the manor but squeezed past the no entry sign, into the now-empty kitchen. I then left via a side door and followed the house's mottled gray wall to the back. Rows of mullioned windows overlooked the lawn, a patch of emerald lushness, pristine as if the heatwave never happened.

I was waiting for somebody to throw open a window and shout, "Oi, you," but that didn't happen either. At the other end of the manor, back of the walled garden, Pip had said. Well, here I stood facing beds with old English roses, but no shed, which meant I must be on the wrong side of the wall.

There were only two archways in sight. One led to the official visitor entrance, the other to the cherry orchard, and that was where I went.

No roses here, just crooked trees and wildflowers raising their heads from among the long-haired grass—corncockles, harebells, and the tall purple stalks of foxgloves, their rural perfume tinging the air. Bees and butterflies tumbled around, buzzing, dipping, and enjoying life.

And in the middle of the meadow squatted a brick shack. I swished my way through the grass and peeped through a smeared glass pane. Not much to see. A door was needed.

The wheelbarrow I found first. Empty and whiffing faintly of manure, it stood beside a white wooden door. If someone was inside the shed, the door would be standing open. It didn't, which meant that the person was either working, or—to judge by the wheelbarrow—might return to fetch more compost. And that, in turn, meant I had to shift gears. My heartbeat drumming me on, I approached the entrance.

Please, let it be unlocked, I begged nobody in particular and twisted the copper knob. Obligingly, the door creaked open, releasing a musty, earthy smell. I slipped inside, into a space set up by a neat freak.

Flower pots, precisely stacked according to size, rose toward the gabled roof. Shiny gardener's tools were lined along the walls with almost regimental precision. In the middle stood a rough wooden table, its surface disappearing among two opposing armies of seedlings in pots and stacks of plastic markers, while bags with soil and horn chips hunkered below. Behind the table, on the far side of the stone wall, I spotted rows and rows of crude shelving holding bulbs here, fertilizer there, and an array of little boxes, bottles, and pots in between.

Frustration crashed over me like a rogue wave. What had I been thinking? The place might be incredibly organized. But it was also crammed to the rafters with stuff. Spotting one small mirror among all these gardening paraphernalia was asking a lot ...too much of Fate.

# 22

## THE RACE IS ON

Was I still alone, still safe? Dread ballooning in my stomach, I shot from the shed. A trail of flattened grass indicated the gardeners must have been moving back and forth between the cherry orchard and their shack. Right now, the trail was empty. No bushes along the wall, either, where someone might hide. Reassuringly far away, the head gardener was shouting something. A saw whined in response.

It was now or never.

Back inside the shed, I discarded the flotilla of seedlings from my list of likely hiding places. Instead, I peeked underneath the table, in case something had been taped to its underbelly.

No such luck.

The sacks with soil and fertilizer would be used all the time to fill the pots with the seedlings, and the tools would also be in high demand. My best bet was the shelf on the back wall facing the entrance, which meant leaving the safety of the open door and venturing further into the shed. For an instant, I stood and listened. No footsteps, no heavy breathing, only a faint electrical hum.

What if the gardeners needed their wheelbarrow?

Lurid visions of murderous interns materialized in my mind, and I dashed back outside.

The scene was unchanged, the trail still empty, the saw whining away. Somewhere in the garden, something heavy—a branch? crashed to the ground. The garden was lush, green, and the light so bright, my eyes hurt. Insects buzzed, the sound of their flight rasping at my nerves. My heartbeat vibrated into my brainpan, and a grassy taste danced on my tongue.

*Oh, no.* My skylles were on the rise.

I was wasting precious time, so I returned to the shack and followed the dancing dust motes to its back wall. The racks I could reach without a ladder I searched first. Countless packs of seedlings, fertilizer, and bottles with an amazing variety of poison later I'd found exactly zero mirrors. My gaze fell to the top racks. For those I'd need a ladder—crap, what was that?

I did my best to ignore the hum in the shed that seemed to grow louder by the second. I must have imagined—

A stealthy footfall. Outside.

*Stupid, you didn't close the door behind you.* I must have done it subconsciously, wanting to be able to hear what was going on, not wanting to be locked in. But now the open door would betray my presence.

Time passed. Dust motes danced. No one entered. The crazy gallop of my heart slowed to a canter, while the white noise filled the shed with its insistent drone.

False alarm.

My gaze fell on a small fridge next to the entrance. Which tools would require cooling? Pip had mentioned beers. What if Cal had hidden his loot in the fridge? It was worth a try, so I pushed past the seeding table and opened the fridge door. Yup, plenty of beer, pale ale by the looks of it. No clay tablets or mirrors, though, which was a real shame.

I swung around. The crammed shelf was taunting me, but the task was hopeless. I needed help. A quick glance at my smartwatch revealed I'd only twenty minutes left before Daisy would alert the troops.

*Crunch.*

I froze. The footsteps I'd heard earlier had been for real.

Slowly, inexorably, the door creaked toward me, hiding my body in the shadows behind. My gaze found a crack in the wooden panel, and I made good use of the natural spy-hole.

The mud-encrusted blade of a shovel appeared in midair, followed by two hands gripping its handle. Male hands. Smooth yet strong, they belonged to a young man. An odd sense of detachment numbed my head as I drew these conclusions, as if my brain were floating above my body, still stuck in the recess between fridge and door, with only a thin wooden pane between me and a murderer. My feet itched with the urge to run; my fists opened and closed, feeble, useless.

And still the shovel came on, until a squat, muscular shape shifted into sight. When I spotted the mousey brown hair, now somewhat disheveled, I knew my luck had run out.

Cal was here.

He stopped and listened to the unnatural quiet that had fallen in the shed, interrupted only by the humming of the fridge.

Dust tickled my nose. Acid burned the back of my throat. A pale pink petal tumbled from my hand. Then another one.

Rats. When I needed my skylles more than ever, I couldn't trust them because of the blasted curse.

*Skylles, down.*

The shovel arced to the floor, its blade pinging against the concrete. Cal stood frozen for a moment until he dropped the tool altogether, not caring where it fell, and rushed for the shelf at the back, where he fingered the packs and bottles I had shifted but dropped back in place. It appeared I had covered my tracks well, for he grabbed the step ladder stacked with the other tools, climbed up, and reached for a roll of twine that sat right at the edge of the top shelf. Accompanied by muted swearing, Cal then fiddled with the cardboard tube the rope had been coiled around. Finally, he removed two items that might well be Neolithic clay tablets. Where was the mirror?

The tension went from his body. "Phew," he said to himself.

With his back to me, he returned the tablets to their hiding place, giving me the chance to leave—

*Creak.* Either the Fates grew bored and sent in some wind, or I'd hit the door panel. My heartbeat spiked. I bolted from my hidey hole and grabbed the shovel while Cal clattered down the ladder.

My rustic weapon raised against the man now advancing with all too obvious menace, I crab-stepped backward.

"Stay where you are." My voice sounded like Daisy's, breathless and shrill.

Amazingly, Cal obeyed. "Ah, so I was right after all. I didn't leave that door open," he said in a conversational tone.

A fresh breeze caressed my sweaty neck. The bump under the soles of my shoes told me I had reached the threshold, but I wasn't yet out of the shed away from Cal, who regarded me as if I were an oversized bug.

I might get out, but how would I keep him in? "What are you even doing here?" I asked.

He tossed his head. "You're one nosy bugger. Nina came around, told me you were asking about mirrors and stuff, but I didn't realize you'd add one and one together quite so fast. Jack's a great guy, lets me go whenever I've got private business."

I took half a step backward. The breeze on my neck grew stronger. "What are you talking about?"

I dry-swallowed. Cal wasn't an impressive male specimen, but he was at least seven years younger than me and fit from the manual labor. And I didn't like his conniving expression. But I was the one with the shovel. Plus, there was a table between us, and I was already halfway outside the shed.

Halfway wasn't half good enough.

He grinned. "You'd like to know, eh?"

I inched my way backward. I needed to keep him talking, keep him distracted from what I was doing. Assuming I didn't accuse him of murder, things might still work out.

If only that bloody shovel weren't so heavy. If only I could use my skylles.

"I'm doing a presentation," I said. "There were some grave gifts with the skeleton you took for a walk. That was you, wasn't it?" The skeleton wasn't the problem here. As long as I kept him focused on that, he was unlikely to come after me.

I took another mini shuffle backward. Now would be an excellent time to hex the guy.

*Hex him how?*

Excellent question. Unfortunately, the response was nowhere near as good. With the way the curse was going, I'd better not run any risks. And the curse was definitely hanging around. Otherwise, the petals wouldn't be pink.

Cal's eyes glowed with a fanatical pride. "Yes. Wasn't that a brilliant move? People always think they can ignore me. But I'll teach you all a lesson, oh yes."

"Ah, life can be so unfair," I said in my best toddler-soothing tones. I had to keep him talking until I was outside. A stab at the dark made me say, "Did you use the wheelbarrow for transport?"

"Yes, I scattered the bones where they'd be found. But were they? No way. Even the weather is against me." He scowled.

"So, you shot the next person who came near the bones to stir the pot." Another inch backward. Sweat coated my palms. That shovel was getting heavier by the second.

"Stroke of genius, eh? Stupid little pooch. Dogs like that aren't natural. They should be forbidden. "

I hefted the shovel.

"Heavy, eh? Shall I help you?" He moved to the side of the table.

I lifted the shovel higher. "Stop. I've got no qualms whatsoever to hit you. I'd rather not, but I will."

Disgust pulled Cal's features into a grimace. "Nosy parkers

like you shouldn't exist. There's too many of your ilk in this world."

I kept my eyes trained on his face, watching every twitch of his muscles. Any minute now, I would have to turn and run. My back tingled at the thought.

No way.

Curse or no curse, I'd have to use my skylles. Cal was bunching his muscles, ready to pounce, and my arms were quivering under the strain. Since I was acting in self-defense, I might get away with it. In any case, the adrenaline coursing through my system was enough to hex a whole landscaping team, let alone one murderous intern.

I sought his leering gaze and willed him to fall asleep. A sharp pain drilled into my temples. The sweet perfume of roses reached my nostrils. Then it was gone.

Cal blinked. Massaged his head. "Uh ...what? The mirror? Oh, you mean that broken, ugly rubbish? Shoved that into the nearest bin."

Fury shot through my system until it pooled in my belly. The little maggot had thrown away the coven's future. "Which bin?"

His grin turned nasty. "Oh, that's what you're really after. Well, tough luck. Can't remember where I put it, and hey, the bins have been emptied since then."

Unfortunately, he had a point there. And he was enjoying himself so much, he had to be speaking the truth. My fury boiled itself out. In its stead, blackness washed over me. Our survival now depended on Mary Anne's broken mirror.

Cal jerked and backed into the ladder that scraped across the concrete. "Hey what's that?."

"What's what?"

"Eh, there was a weird light in your eyes?"

*You ain't seen nothing yet, sunshine.* The humming in my skull was back, and this time it didn't come from the fridge.

Cal pouted. "I'm talking to you. Don't ignore me. Do you hear? I don't like it when people do that. How dare you think you can jerk me around? Me? Like our asshole director. I bet he was really surprised when the brakes didn't work. Kablow! Hah. I've shown him. I'll show you all."

The echo of his outburst hadn't died down when fury erupted in my chest, and the rose fragrance filled my being. The hum swelled to a roaring crescendo into which flashed hot, white lightning. I raised the shovel, now as light as a feather, over my head, pale pink petals swirling all around me.

Cal screeched like a cornered rat and backed into the shelf. "What's wrong with you?"

*Don't morph the shovel into a cactus or you'll be out for the count.*

I didn't morph the blasted thing. I threw it.

Cal swore and twisted aside.

I whisked around, slammed the door shut, and rammed the bolt home the same moment a massive body hit the panel from the other side. Cal recovered a tick too fast for my taste.

I half-staggered, half-ran across the meadow, all the time fumbling with my phone, expecting it to have run out of either juice or signal. It hadn't, but I only reached Sarah's voicemail the very moment a bellow rang out, like a verbal cannonball.

"Cal, are you in there?"

I whirled around, saw a burly figure fiddling with the bolt. The head gardener.

"Don't," I whispered. Cleared my throat and shouted. "Don't!"

Too late, Cal charged from the shed, straight into the stocky figure of his colleague.

"Oof." The head gardener staggered aside.

Phone in my hand, I dashed off.

# 23

## HIDE AND SEEK

Where had all the people gone? Someone, anyone, had to be around to save me from the angry pounding of feet behind me, getting closer all the time. The answer arrived with three sonorous bongs from the church tower. Wednesday afternoon. The grounds were closed for today, and I was on my own.

Fueled by panic, I charged through the orchard into the walled garden. Which exit was closest?

"I'm coming," trilled from beyond the wall. The little bastard was enjoying himself.

The official entrance would be locked, so I charged into the back garden, sweat dripping down my brow and into my eyes, my lungs and leg muscles burning from the strain. A cat would now race up a tree, but I was no cat. A bunny would disappear down a hole, but there weren't any.

Hole. Hidey hole. Even if the back door to the society office was still open, I'd never make it before the guy caught up with me. But there was one thing I could try.

The lawn behind the manor house was as empty as the walled garden had been. Only the topiaries watched over my breathless stampede.

There. The kitchen entrance. The door would be unlocked. It just had to be. In this village, people seldom locked their back door.

Yes! The knob yielded to my frantic yank, and I was in.

Into the corridor I dashed, foolishly hoping for voices, staff doing things they couldn't do with visitors around, but all was still.

In every thriller I ever read, the survivors didn't go up, but stayed down. But the only safe place I could think of, blinking like a beacon in my mind, was up, so I charged the stairs, two treads at a time. Arrived in the first-floor corridor, I forced my unwilling body to turn away from the nearest entrance and tiptoed as fast as I dared into the second room. The Tudor bedchamber might be closer, but it wasn't connected with the other rooms like this one was.

Cal wasn't far behind me. The second I crossed the threshold, he reached the top of the steps. My heart banged against my ribcage, searching for a way out.

"I know you're there," Cal said in a singsong voice.

He had indeed stomped into the Tudor bedroom, where he kept banging about, swearing wildly. There was plenty of furniture in that place, including some large, heavy boxes, which would give me the time I needed.

Apart from a dressmaker's doll and a yellowish daybed, the third room featured a narrow door set into the faded cream wainscoting. Not exactly hidden, but not super obvious either. Otherwise, this chamber was empty, the oaken floorboards dirty.

They creaked. Of course they would.

Every single footstep boomed through the vacant space. Godzilla couldn't have made more of a racket, but Cal in the first room was even louder.

Should I risk it? Try to return downstairs instead of hiding?

I sneaked outside, where the old servant staircase led

toward safety. Who would have thought that a rainy Sunday spent exploring the manor house with Chris a week—a lifetime ago might save my bacon? Torn by indecision, I hesitated at the top of the steps.

"I know you're up here. Don't even think you can escape."

I threw myself backward into the yellow room a split second before Cal charged into the hallway.

"You're mincemeat," he hollered. "Just like that woman. Nearly pancaked by a standing stone. Not what he wanted either, hah. Hey, wasn't that a great coincidence about her being your guest?"

His overloud boasting masked the creaks that accompanied my dash across the yellow room, where I then yanked open the interior door and slipped into the cabinet. Cal fell silent a heartbeat after I'd clicked its door shut from within.

The oblong space was narrow, forcing me to edge past a box made of red damask. Its lid stood open, revealing a chamber pot. Close to the window was yet another door, leading to some sort of cupboard just about big enough for one desperate woman. I wormed my way inside and closed the door, the knob slipping in my clammy hands.

When Chris and I had visited the manor, we laughed about the golden tassels and ornaments on the box, wondering what the purpose of the cupboard might have been. We only found it because it had been gaping open at the time. Otherwise, the panel fitted flush with the wall it was set into. When closed, the access to the cupboard was even better concealed than the entrance to the toilet, and if I was lucky, the secret cupboard might save my life.

I willed the murderer to go away. Listened to the heavy tread of booted feet in the yellow room, louder than the roaring in my head.

Did Cal see me enter? He couldn't have. He'd been too busy bragging about the standing stone. And who the heck did Cal mean by "he?"

Cal's swearing morphed into a white noise. Hope flickered in the stuffy darkness of the cabinet. Until the footsteps returned, and somebody yanked the door to the lavatory open. Panic exploded in my chest.

Outside, someone grunted. Stopped at the chamber pot.

I bit my fists to stop myself from moaning. Why didn't I brave the stairs and go down?

*Stupid, stupid, stupid.*

Wherever my skylles might lurk, they refused to come out. No smell of roses, no pain in my head. The curse, bollixing things up again?

Something rustled, then I heard the trickle of liquid close to me. Very close.

More rustling. "I'll get you, bitch. I'm a genius. You stand no chance."

He'd seen me. He knew where I was.

I recoiled, and the sharp edge of a shelf dug into my back. Pain lanced into my side, and suddenly the musty cabinet came alive with a rose fragrance and there was a fizzing in my ears.

My skylles were more unpredictable than the weather.

Cal tromped off once more. But the racket was fading, which meant he must have left. He also must have left the toilet door open since I could hear him all the way to the exit I had been so close to taking. In the corridor, he stopped and shouted something I couldn't understand. Then he ran down the servant steps.

Somewhere, probably on the ground floor of the house, something banged, followed by a breathless silence.

I forced myself to count to fifty. Slowly. When everything remained quiet, I inched open the door, halfway expecting to be confronted with Cal's leering face. But the lavatory was empty.

The chamber pot wasn't. Its bottom was covered by a copious amount of urine, filling the cabinet with its pungent reek. The disgusting swine had peed into the historical chamber pot while I was hiding right next to him.

As expected, the door stood open, so I slipped out and squeezed along the walls, which reduced the creaking, but not a lot. At the exit, I stopped and listened for ten heartbeats in eternity. When still nobody rushed me, I moved into the corridor.

It was empty.

Step by careful step, I climbed down the servant staircase, straining to notice anything that wouldn't form part of the typical sounds of an old house warming under the sun. Halfway to the ground floor, I stopped.

The manor was deadly quiet.

Panic gripped my throat, and something both icy and hot brushed along my spine. Was it premonition or sheer lunacy? Whatever it was, it made me turn around and scuttle back up to the first floor.

I could never tackle Cal on my own. I needed professional help, preferably in the form of burly constables wielding truncheons. Only a brutal force would stop that guy.

Back in the yellow room, I burrowed in the pockets of my jeans for my smartphone—to find a text message from Sarah. She'd also called at some point. Not only she; I had a few messages. Instead of turning the vibration function on, I'd switched off all notifications.

No time for that now. I read what she had written.

*Where are you?*

My fingers had never been faster; they flitted over the screen like frightened mice.

*Avebury Manor. Top floor. SOS. Cal's the killer. He's here. Don't call.*

There, I'd named him. Even if he offed me, that should be enough to cause trouble for the little bastard. If I lived, I'd make sure justice was served, and if it was the last thing I did before the curse got me.

I returned to the cabinet, tempted to close the lid on the disgusting mess, but doing so might have clued Cal up.

*Scuffle.*

Stealthy footsteps crept up from below, and fresh panic twisted my heart. I slid back into the priest hole, pulled the door shut with one hand. In the other, I held the phone.

Another message lit up.

*Hide. We're coming.*

The inside of the cabinet was bathed in the cold blue light glowing from Sarah's message, like a ray of hope in the darkness of my hidey hole.

The screen turned black, and I was once more enshrouded in gloom. A nasty thought burrowed into my mind. Did I close the toilet cabinet behind me? Would Cal even remember leaving it open? If he did, I was toast.

Yes, there was a scraping noise outside, as if somebody was creeping around, trying to be rat-quiet.

If he found me, I'd use my skylles, the curse be damned. The vibrations rolling through the ground under my feet, the fizzing and sparkling in the air reassured me I wasn't without a weapon, as flawed as it might be.

But until he attacked me, there was nothing I could do. Other than wait. And listen, hoping the drum solo in my chest wouldn't give me away.

The scraping noise became more subdued and faded away altogether, as if Cal had left the yellow room.

Nothing happened for quite a while, apart from my back being icy, while my chest radiated heat from all the stress.

Odd.

A gelid draft slithered down my spine on spider pads. Was that air current new, or had it been there before, and I simply didn't notice? My feverish imagination shifted into overdrive. Priest holes, assuming this was one, sometimes led to secret passages. I sniffed the air. Definitely fresher than the room had been, even before Cal took a leak.

I pocketed the phone and twisted and cramped my body around, careful not to bump the door open with my hip. Finally,

I faced the shelf. Then I ran my fingers over the boards, tracing their outline. Dust was the only reward for my efforts, but the air was noticeably moving back here.

"Come on, give." I whispered under my breath.

My fingers probed the wooden panels, found ridges and knots, but they were nothing but roughness in the wood. I shifted to the left, and there it was, a hole in the shelf's back panel, too smooth to be natural. As I poked my digit through, it touched a tautly strung wire. My finger hooked around the thin strip, I pulled.

With a *clack*, the whole shelf swung into a frigid absence of light.

Once more, I stopped to listen, but the yellow room still seemed to be empty or, if it wasn't, Cal was keeping his trap shut for once.

*Move.*

Gingerly, I stretched out my leg and tested the floor with my foot. It met with solid stone. I held on to the frame with one hand and fumbled around in the space behind the shelf with the other. It ripped through a gauzy, silky substance coated with dust.

Cobwebs.

My inner eye, ever so helpful, flashed visions of spiders, their mandibles opening and closing, their far too many feet ready to advance on me.

It wouldn't do. I needed to see where I was going, so I fingered my smartphone and pressed the button at its side.

The cold bluish glow from Sarah's last message reflected on the dusty curtains of webs long abandoned, or at least currently unoccupied. They dangled from the ceiling above a spiral staircase that led into the bowels of the house. One more step in the dark and I would have stumbled on the worn stones.

I stepped across the threshold, then turned around and pushed the wooden panel shut. One uneven tread after another, I climbed down, my progress illuminated only by the glow from my phone, with Sarah's message displayed on the screen like a charm of the digital age. I kept tapping the message to keep it lit up. Once, I hexed myself into a torch, but I couldn't remember how I pulled that stunt.

The light from the screen was enough to guide me down the staircase, one hand trailing along the rough-hewn stones of the wall, moldy, clammy, and reeking of saltpeter, while the other clutched the smartphone in a sweaty death grip.

Eons passed until I reached the downstairs landing, where another cobwebby veil hid a door panel. This time I worked out what I had missed upstairs—the web wasn't real, but fabric. A bit like a Halloween decoration, this one complete with plastic spiders and as dusty as the other had been.

The bolt that kept the door closed was connected to the same wire mechanism as above. I ripped through the gauzy veil and pressed my ear against the wood. Yay, voices, quite a few of them, none of them sounding like Cal. That gave me the courage to pull the wire. The latch tilted, and the door snicked open. I squeezed past and emerged into a corridor covered in wainscoting, painted in an institutional green. The ceiling featured strip lighting and old heating pipes as the only available decoration.

I emerged in the cellar just as a commotion broke out on the floor above me.

"Police. Stop!"

The sound of running feet. Lots of them.

Shouting echoed through the manor house, but it was moving away from me. Emboldened, I made for the steps leading up at the other end of the dingy hallway, ending up in the scullery, its massive stone sinks now overflowing with bags and boxes filled with billowy skirts, lacy shawls, and embroidered waistcoats. Electric light from the kitchen fell into a rectangle on the floor. And inside of it, a shadow spread, quivered—and withdrew.

But the person who'd thrown the shadow was still waiting in the other room, biding their time. It couldn't be Cal. It mustn't be him. Surely, the ruckus meant the cops were chasing his sorry backside. But what if he escaped?

The silence in the scullery hurt my ears. My invisible opponent shifted ever so slightly, fabric rubbing on fabric, chased by a tiny metallic noise.

A weapon getting readied?

Unless *in extremis*, using the skylles sizzling under my skin was risky, so I fumbled through the nearest heap of costumes, not once letting the door out of sight. My fingers hit something knotted and hairy.

A quick peek revealed Marie-Antoinette's wig. This wouldn't do. I took a step back. Then another one.

"Police, lower your weapons!" someone shouted.

My arm twitched in response and the wig sailed through the scullery until it flopped onto the floor. Sarah peeked around the corner, first at me, then at the wig, piled in an untidy heap at her feet.

The tension seeped from my legs, leaving nothing but pudding behind. I staggered toward the nearest chair and sat, hard.

"Weren't you supposed to be on the top floor?" Sarah's voice was deceptively calm.

"I was, but I discovered the emergency exit. Where's Cal?"

"Cameron wins the sprint at the annual police decathlon every time. He's caught and arrested the guy. How the heck did you manage to get that particular tiger by the tail? Especially when I told you not to meddle." Anger seethed in her voice, only barely hidden by a veneer of good manners and the remains of our friendship.

"Newsflash. I wasn't planning to confront him. He'd stolen something I needed. Sarah, I'm not mad."

"I disagree. What on earth can be so important it makes you interfere with a murder investigation?" Her voice could have cut through a glacier.

Tears pricked the inside of my eyelids. When I fantasized

about justice being served, I hadn't envisaged myself at the receiving end. "Because of what you call meddling, you'll get a confession, or something close to it. That chap was so full of himself, he kept bragging about his crimes."

"He'll claim you're lying. His word against yours. Once he's lawyered up, he'll do just that."

"Why did he pursue me?"

"You pissed him off."

"He tried to kill me."

"You're exaggerating."

I shot from my seat. "In that case, you don't need my statement, do you? Excuse me, I'm out of here." The room was swimming, and a sob stuck in my throat.

Sarah grabbed my arm. "You'll go nowhere before I know what the blazes is going on. And I'm still waiting to hear what made you face a killer." Her voice had softened, but not a lot.

I yanked my arm from her grasp. "None of your business. Told you it was important, period. Nor did I 'face' him. I called you immediately after talking to Pip, remember? Actually, I alerted tons of people—"

"Who pinged me in turn. Lentulus. Your cousin. And Colonel Elmsworth."

"See? I was careful. Or thought I was. Only things went tits-up. And I've had quite enough of this rubbish. You want my statement, then take it. Otherwise, I'm leaving."

We glared at each other over the unruly wig. Until Sarah sighed. "It's been a long day. Let's stop this before we both do or say things we might regret later. In a way, it was my fault. I let you in on the investigation."

"And I discovered quite a few things. You were wrong, you know?"

"About what?"

"Your escalation theory. He never did. It was all the same to him—stealing a skeleton, scaring a senior citizen, sabotaging the stone, the bicycle. People are just stage props for the Cal show. I wonder what triggered him. I mean, it's not as if he had any personal stakes in the matter."

"That sort of person is an accident waiting to happen, I'm afraid. One perceived slight to their ego too many and they blow." Sarah shook her head. "Enough of the psychobabble. Thanks to you, he's off the streets. I don't dare to imagine who might've ended up in his crosshairs next. I'll drive you home. Tell me your story on the way. Everything, not only the bits you deem relevant."

Everything not being on the cards, I came as close to the truth as I dared. Instead, I looked Sarah straight in the eye once I'd finished. "One day, I will explain. I promise. Trust me—I had a reason for searching the shed."

Sarah stared at the windscreen and heaved a sigh that came from deep down inside. "Fine. If you want to play it that way. But don't wait forever with sharing your truth." As if to smooth out the harshness in her tone, she reached for me and we hugged.

"You're mad," she said. "But I like you that way. Means I'm mad as well. Stay out of trouble."

*How? The mirror we have is broken.*

When she had left, I curled up in my armchair, Tiddles licking my chin, Petty hovering by my side. Our period of grace, the three "Sennights" were almost up. We had the keys, or thought we did. But the mirror I'd been seeking, the mirror for which I'd crossed the path of a murderous dung-for-brains, had been lost before I even set out.

I might have helped justice. But I had no clue how to help the coven.

# 24

## OUT OF BODY

If running from a killer classified as a marrow-chilling experience, waiting for the end of my life was worse. I fretted through the afternoon and evening. At first, I was on my own, then the others arrived. Chris, Jenna, the Ragworts, Elmsworth, Mel. Even Linda was there. Too jaded to talk, I let their worries wash over me.

Finally, the endless day neared the end, ushering in the bright light of a waxing moon that flared from the indigo skies as if to mock us.

This time, I took Petty along for the ride. My poor darling Chris was left at the fringe of the circle, in case his witch hunting genes would foul up the counter spell. Ridiculous, maybe. But we didn't know any better. When he took me in his arms, it felt like the last goodbye. It wouldn't be, not yet. But somehow, his kiss tasted of the dress rehearsal for the final parting.

Not much later, Jenna, Rosie, and I hunkered in the shadow thrown by the horse head stone. Lamps, candles, and torches flickered their unsteady light on the scene. Petty whisked past me, landed next to the horse head stone, and fired off a colorful barrage of sparks.

She too would be lost if we failed.

Rosie had carried the mirror, its blinded shards carefully cleaned by Chris's expert hands, the metal scrubbed as clean as possible. Cracks ran across the surface like a spider web, and the reflection it showed was blurred and fogged. But it was a mirror. The last magical mirror. Buried once, then resurrected and received from the gracious hands of the dead. We had a zombie primula. Why not a zombie mirror?

"Daisy, can you read out the instructions once more, in case we've missed something?"

Daisy fiddled with her phone. She cleared her throat.

"When the Moone stands over the Stones at nighttime, a coven comprising at least three Wardens shall gather within the Cyrcle, close to the stone shaped like a Horse Heade. There, you shall lyfte the Mirror and in the Mirror see key."

That was as clear as things were about to get. I licked my lips; they had suddenly lost all moisture. This was it. "Shall we?"

I reached for my primula with one hand and with the other lifted the mirror so it reflected the light of the moon. The image was dull, but it was there. Slowly, Jenna presented the plaque on her outstretched palm. She reached across until the mirror reflected what I fervently hoped was a magical key.

We waited.

Nothing happened.

I jiggled the mirror. Jenna waved the key. Petty burst into a rustling and sparking spree.

Nothing. Just—nothing.

Petty reacted first, her leaves and blossoms drooping. From the coven circling us echoed whispers, sobs, muttered swearwords. My arm with the mirror took on a leaden weight. I dropped it, fingers smarting from its scratchy grip.

"Sweet Earth, it's over," Jenna whispered.

There had to be something we could do; there had to be. We still had the time to dig in the other graves; we still had hope. Just as I opened my mouth to tell them, white-hot pain seared my skull. The people, the stones, the moon all got sucked into a blinding tunnel of light until there was nothing left but a shrilling hiss in my brain, reeking of rotting soil. Eventually, the noise faded away, leaving behind blessed darkness, stirred by a cool breeze.

I caught myself lifting, rising toward a presence that called for me.

Colors flowed into a well-known scene. My feet dangled over the same grassy expanse of green that had lived in my dreams. Weightless as a feather, I drifted upward on the currents headed for skies so green, so full of life and warmth. Faces were drifting in the brightness, and voices called from beyond the great void.

They all spoke the same word. "No."

*No?*

They were right. It wasn't fair. My three sennights hadn't ended yet. Up on the magical plane, wherever and whatever it was, someone was cheating something rotten.

My ascent stopped. For a moment I hung suspended in the air, at what would have been tree-height had there been any trees. But there were none. Only grass, the breeze blowing strange patterns into the furry green carpet.

Suddenly, the scenery imploded with a slurping noise. The same sharp pain as before lanced my brain and sent me into a dark oblivion.

—

I awoke on a hard, slippery surface. Its light strobing rhythmically into the darkness, an ambulance shot away with a wail. People were talking, but I couldn't understand a word they were saying.

My head throbbed, so I took my time sitting up. I didn't die. I was still at the henge. Petty was somewhere close; I smelled the pungent scent she gave off whenever she was angry. Why angry? It wasn't my fault I kept being ambushed by magic.

Lantern and candle lights danced in the gloom like fireflies, surfing on the wave of dizziness that threatened to overtake me. A few deep breaths took care of that, and I gave the woman crouching by my side a wan smile.

"Are you feeling better?" Jenna asked. "It's typical. We call two ambulances and get a grand total of one. Myr's still in a coma. That's why they took her away first. I'm so sorry."

*They've taken me away? But I'm right here.*

"Are you okay, Rosie? You're looking rather pale."

*Rosie?* I raised my hands in front of my eyes. Only they weren't mine. Blotchy and wrinkled, they belonged to an older woman.

I'd landed in Rosie's body.

But—if my consciousness was running Rosie, where was she?

*Rosie? Are you in here?*

No response. Instead, my magical plant popped into view and hovered in front of my ...Rosie's face. What an impossible pickle.

Revulsion rose. I wanted out, away from this idiotic magic we couldn't control.

"Rosie?" Jen put her hand on my arm.

*I'm not Rosie.*

"Leave me alone. Please ..." I staggered off, and the coven parted for me.

Rosie's body wasn't young, but it was fit. The joints might creak, and the legs be heavy, but they pounded on anyway, the heartbeat a steady rhythm in my chest. Even if it glitched once in a while, I sensed I had nothing to fear from that corner. Rosie's body seemed to know where it wanted to be, so I let it carry me all the way to the banks of the river, where streetlight painted the bridge orange. The police barrier was gone, and I went down the slippery slope that led to the water. When I finally stopped, the gurgle of the Kennet filled my ears.

Rosie once told me that water helped calm her down when stressed. Even with me in the driving seat, it seemed to work.

Well, sort of. My breathing slowed, but the worries refused to lift. I bent over the burbling stream until it reflected Rosie's waxen face, her haunted eyes.

Digging up the other mirrors wouldn't get us off the hook. I knew it. The mirrors were lost, and so was most of the ancient lore.

Something rustled behind me and the reflection of a common houseplant totally out of season appeared in the water.

"Petty? How did you get here?"

"I carried her." Daisy's voice made my heartbeat stumble before it picked up again. She had been so quiet, I didn't hear her coming. "She hovered after you, but ran out of steam pretty quickly."

She at least knew who I really was.

"What's wrong with you?" Jenna appeared on my other side.

I should tell them it was all over. But somehow, I couldn't.

"Surely, you suffering from some after-effects of ...well, whatever happened at the henge," Jenna said. "You should be in hospital like Myrtle not hanging around at the river."

*I'm not in the hospital. I'm right here with you.*

The words never left my head.

Instead I stared at the reflections of Rosie's face and my magical flower hovering next to me.

Water. Reflections in the water. Mirrors reflected faces.

I'd been beyond stupid.

"In the Mirror see key," that long-dead ancestor of mine seemed to have written. Even with her outlandish spelling, this part of the instruction jarred from the start.

I jumped up. A sharp pain shot into my back.

*Ow.* I rubbed my lower spine. To heck with stiff joints and lumbago.

"Daisy, I need the instruction we discovered in the recipe book."

"We?"

I looked her straight in the eyes. "It's me, Myrtle. Don't ask me what happened, but somehow I ended up in Rosie's body. No idea where she is."

"What?" Daisy said.

"You can't be serious." Jenna said.

"I am. We'll sort it out later. Please, can you call up the text for me?"

"Eh, sure." Daisy's finger danced over her smartphone until she found what she was looking for.

I squinted at the handwriting scrawling across the rectangle. Impossible to read the fine print in this feeble light, even without the complication of aging eyes.

"Can you make that larger? I mean, a lot larger? And can you scroll down to that bit with the keys?"

Daisy did as bid. Jenna, glancing over my shoulder, studied the text. "Sweet Earth, I never saw the original. This is absolutely amazeboggling."

"You haven't seen this text?"

"We all read Daisy's transcription, obviously. Many times, too. But I never saw this."

"I had my hands full and plain forgot," I said with feeling. "Sorry for that. Daisy, can you read out the last part of that sentence?"

"In the mirror see key?"

"It can't be."

I squinted at the text, magnified by modern magic. The last word still read as key—hang on, no it didn't.

What I'd taken to be the bottom loop of a Y might well be yet another splotch of mold. Or a dead fly. And at the beginning, the quill had splattered over what everyone, including myself and Chris, had assumed to be a K—

"Thee," Jen said. Her breath was hot on my cheek. "This doesn't say key at all, you know?"

"What doesn't?" Daisy retracted her phone and stared at its screen. "Oh that. Yes, it does. It's key, possibly written with two E. It's all splotched up."

Unlike me, Rosie was a very patient person, and her body chemistry reflected that. But even she was swamped by hot frustration. Most of it was directed at me. Some of it at Chris. He had read plenty of old texts. Why didn't he question my interpretation?

"May I?" I snatched the phone from Daisy's hand and enlarged the word to the point it disintegrated into a muddle of lines. "We might have ourselves a TH instead of a K. And two EEs at the end. Which would sort of fit Jen's theory."

My magical primula responded with a wild rustling of stalks.

"Can I have another look?" Jenna took the phone and scrolled through the text. "Okeydokey, I'd say the rest is fine, but to me this reads a lot like 'in the mirror see thee.'"

"Crap. Got it all wrong." I kicked the nettles.

A slow smile surfaced on Jenna's face. "It really is you, Myrtle. Well, if that says 'thee' and not 'key', I'd say, it changes things."

Daisy crossed her arms in front of her chest. "How?"

"If we are to see 'thee', it must mean us. As in we see ourselves and not the clay tablets." I explained.

Daisy uncrossed her arms. "Oh. Ah."

"Yes, exactly that. And I say, let's try now. Where are the others?"

"Pub's just closed, so they're waiting until the streets are clear to have another go at the graves," Jenna said. "We don't need them. There are three of us. Do you think you can make it back to the stones?"

"I guess so. Thankfully, Rosie keeps herself fit."

With the helping hands of Jenna and Daisy, I got back up to street level and from there toward the horse head stone.

Daisy tried first. She raised Mary Anne's cracked gift at the moon, now surrounded by a milky glow, a sure sign the weather was changing. She then turned the mirror until a blurred reflection of her face showed among the spiderweb of carefully glued shards. Jenna did the same. Then it was my turn to face the mirror that, with a bit of goodwill, reflected a distorted image of Rosie.

And something else. Somewhere, in the depths of her eyes, an ember flashed. Grew and turned green.

"Your eyes!" Daisy and Jenna shouted simultaneously. I ripped my gaze away from the reflection and faced them. Their eyes were also flickering green.

Petty bobbed and bounced about, sending fireworks into the balmy night. When I looked at my fellow witches once more, the light in their eyes was gone.

And so was the curse. I knew it. We were safe.

Somewhere behind the standing stones people cheered and came running.

The coven. All of them free from the curse. We had worked a miracle.

No, I corrected myself. Not quite. Lily and the old nun had been clear on that front. The curse would come back to haunt us. Next year. But then we would know what to do.

Too many misinterpretations, so many mistakes. *To err is human. To learn from your failures divine.*

Suddenly, there was a roar in my ears. Daisy's and Jenna's faces wobbled, elongated, and with a loud slurping sound they vanished into the darkness. The shrill hissing was back in my head, as I was tumbling and flailing about, falling, falling ...

—

"Myrtle? Myrtle? Oh, thank the resident deities, nurse, come quick, she's waking up."

Chris's voice and the sharp odor of disinfectant hit my senses at the same time. Pain howled through every fiber of my being. I nearly let go, wanted to be sucked back into that void, away from the agony.

*You mustn't.* I struggled; I gritted my teeth against the heat in my head and rallied the pockets of strength still hiding in my body ...my body, not Rosie's.

That gave me the much-needed push, and I opened my eyes to smile at my beloved witch hunter.

# 25

## CELEBRATIONS

"Will you take this woman to be your wedded wife, to live together in marriage? Do you promise to love her, comfort her, honor and keep her, for better or worse, in sickness and health?"

"And do you promise to only serve homemade pasta?" Isobel mumbled the words under her breath, but I gave her a thumbs up, to signal I'd noticed.

As did my other guests. Giggles and snorts popped from the members of the Mafia Cookery Club, decked out in all colors of the rainbow, not just the reds and blacks of their logo. The couple, one woman wearing a slim white robe, the other an elegant ivory tuxedo, never took note. They were too busy swapping rings.

Anna might not have liked the chefs in "her" church, but that didn't stop her from going all out. Garlands of white roses, pink carnations, and ferns filled the nave with a subtle scent. The basket at the entrance contained biodegradable confetti, and every single cushion on the pews had been arranged with mathematical precision. Pachelbel's Canon rose and swelled, and my thoughts did likewise, slipping back to the last few days.

Rosie had returned to her body. She remembered suffering from a sudden headache and then the world dropped away. When she came to, she found herself on a stretcher, being loaded into an ambulance. Today, she was sitting in a pew to my right, wearing her best suit. Her hands clasped Damian's. Their eyes shone, no doubt with memories of their special day.

Many of the villagers seemed to do the same, to judge by the sniffles and surreptitiously wiped eyes.

The Neolithic clay tablets, the magical plaques of the witches, were safely back in the bank vault in Swindon, joined by Mary Anne's mirror. Once we had sorted ourselves out, we would investigate if there was a way of spelling a replica. Jochen's researchers were already scouring old records for intel.

As to the true purpose of our magical plaques, we'd simply have to wait. At least they were protected once more from Ignatius.

Chris wasn't around, had fallen behind on his coding, nor did he dig weddings, he said. My heart fluttered like the wings of a small bird. We would see. Our relationship was still young.

The Colonel had traveled to Germany to pick up more historical information Jochen's intrepid teams had dug up; another reason Chris needed to kick the database into shape. Last I'd heard, Elmsworth was enjoying the beer, while Buster nipped ankles and chased Alsatians.

Applause broke out in the church and, escorted by Handel's Water Music, the newlyweds made for the exit. The vicar pretended not to notice the vermicelli shower that hit the moment the couple stepped into the soggy churchyard—and a cloudburst.

The rain came down so hard, it caused mini-explosions in the puddles. I opened auntie's bright green golf umbrella and squelched outside. If any traces had been left of our illicit digging, they would have been washed away. Mary Anne's skeleton was complete again, her delicate knucklebone returned where it belonged. We had argued whether to clean and straighten the stones, but that would have drawn attention to them. Instead, we scattered wildflowers on the three graves.

Our ancestors might be gone, but they would never be forgotten. And one day, we would find out what really happened back then. Without selling our souls to Ignatius.

And the murderer? Cal surprised us all when he confessed, confirming every part of the official statement I'd made at the cop shop. He seemed to believe his trial would be all over the media, with him as the righteous and much-wronged star to be acquitted to further glory.

Fat chance.

Sarah had called last night, giving me the news and apologizing afterward. I had done the same. We were friends again. She didn't even ask why I did what I did, though I knew her too well. For the moment, my misdeeds might be filed with the cold cases, but one day those would get opened. I could only hope that day didn't come so soon.

No more sleuthing, I swore to myself. Yes, I had been faster than law enforcement. But at what price? On the other hand, had I connected the dots earlier, I might have found a second, better mirror, now buried under tons of rubbish.

"Cal claims there was some sort of snowstorm in the shed," Sarah said right at the end of the call. "And he saw a weird light in your eyes."

Oopsie. So he hadn't forgotten. "How's that possible?"

She laughed. "Illegal substances, no doubt. Don't worry about it. Thought it might amuse you."

Hardly likely.

"A word, Ms. Coldron?" Hagbottom-Smythe stepped up, holding a black umbrella.

"Don't tell me another skeleton has disappeared."

"No, no. All present and accounted for, I can assure you. No, it's ...that young rotter."

"Cal?"

The curator winced. "Oh dear. I fear I might be to blame for some of his actions. I'm in two minds whether I should tell the police. But that wouldn't change things now, would it?"

Despite my promises, curiosity tickled my restless brain. "What do you mean?"

Hagbottom-Smythe threw a nervous glance over his shoulder. "You seem to be a young woman with a superior intellect. And you're acquainted with that police officer. Can we perhaps ..." He gestured at the path that led to the vestry, and I went along.

He stopped under a fir tree. "About that standing stone accident...See, I wasn't quite honest about that business with the skeleton. I knew it was gone since I'd overheard a conversation between the two male students. Our...eh, murderer seemed to think the loss of the old remains made me look bad in his... Peter's eyes and that would make him ...the young man look good in that female's eyes. I didn't know what to do, so I kept quiet."

The curator fell silent. Rain plopped on our umbrellas. A gray squirrel chased up a pine.

Hagbottom-Smythe heaved a sigh. "Later that day Peter took me into my office under the pretext of discussing my input for the tours. Instead, he told me to my face I wasn't fit to run this place. He'd been chipping away at the society's top management and the custodians in charge of the museum to let him run the whole show. I'd known for quite a while. Once he was in the saddle, he would 'cut out the deadwood.' By that he meant me. So, I had to get the skeleton back. That's why I called you."

He toweled his perspiring forehead with his oversized hankie. "The museum is my life. But he'd already arranged for an audit, which didn't go too well either."

"I'm sorry to hear that. But surely you can't be expected to run that place with only voluntary staff. You get on with Anna, don't you? She's highly efficient, she should be paid a proper salary."

"Mh, not a bad idea. But money is scarce these days."

"True, but some investments are necessary, otherwise the assets deteriorate. Do you want me to speak to your custodians?"

A hopeful smile surfaced on his face. Then it sunk again.

"Wait until I'm finished. You might not want to help me afterward. I'm not proud of this myself, but I was desperate. After Peter had left, I approached that young man, told him what I overheard and threatened him. They all need certificates, see?"

Not Cal. Hagbottom-Smythe had been playing out of his league.

He scraped a muddy shoe against the other, but only spread the dirt around. "Uh, I believe I mentioned the standing stone."

The light switched on in my head. "So, it was you who gave him the inspiration to loosen the stone's foundation and drop it on the tourists?"

Hagbottom-Smythe's eyes widened. "Oh, no, no. Who do you take me for?"

*An idiot, but not unlikeable.*

The curator waved his hankie in agitation. "I gave explicit orders the stone should fall at night. So, people would wake up and realize Jedd wasn't quite on top of things as he pretended. That would have changed things quite a bit. But that little monster nearly caused a disaster."

Cal's taunts in the manor rang out in my mind. "Not what he wanted either, hah." "He" being the curator, it was all becoming clear. From a moral perspective, what Hagbottom-Smythe had done was clearly wrong.

"Ah."

"He didn't dig deep enough to topple the stone there and then. He just left it to chance and risked lives." The curator's voice shrilled on the last word. "And not only that. He used Peter's spade and hid it in my shed to implicate both of us. He even gloated about that when I confronted him."

The idiotic spade. Nothing but one big misdirection.

Once more, the curator mopped his brow. "I feel guilty."

I kept quiet. By opting for petty revenge, he'd most likely triggered a dangerous individual. But given Cal's personality, the guy needed little to blow, or so Sarah said. And the curator stood little to no chance against a bully like Jedd.

*To err is human.*

Hagbottom-Smythe must have interpreted my expression correctly and shuffled around, his gaze absorbed by the nearest puddle. "Mrs. Coldron, believe me, I never wanted Peter to be killed. Just ...stopped. Cal totally overreacted."

That wasn't quite the right word for murder. "I believe, Mr. Hagbottom-Smythe, Cal wasn't very good at listening."

"No, I realize that now. But I was desperate, absolutely desperate."

That sounded horribly familiar. "I suggest you contact the officer in charge of the case. Tell her what you told me. As you say, it won't change anything. But it will give her the full picture and you some closure. And I'll talk to the custodians."

"Thank you, I'll do that. You're a decent person, you know? I'm in your debt." With a quick nod, he walked away.

"Hey." Another black umbrella floated up, the man who carried it dressed to match.

Chris.

My heart did a happy little skip and hop. "Hey yourself. Are you finished, then?"

"Ta-dah. First release of the database, yes. More to follow later. Listen, I've had quite enough of the village, the hexing, the murders. And the coding. I need a break. How about if we go away for a couple of days? Just you and I. I think we deserve a treat."

"Love it. Where shall we go?"

He winked. "I have something very special in mind."

*A honeymoon?* I called my imagination to order.

"But I can't leave the B&B—"

"Yes, you can. I asked the Simpkinses, and it appears

bookings for the next week are sparse. Only the odd salesperson, and a Belgian couple. They can handle them on their own, they said. Come on, say yes." His eyes twinkled with boyish mischief.

"I love surprises. Okay. Yes."

"You'll love this one even more. Let's just slip away, before there's another hexing disaster, or the next villain shows up. This place seems to breed an amazing variety of the buggers."

He hooked his arm through mine, and our umbrellas collided.

He burst into a snicker, and I followed his example. As one, we turned our backs on the wedding party, the churchyard, and all those remains, peacefully at rest where they belonged.

# Acknowledgments

I would like to thank Susan Brooks for all the support Literary Wanderlust has given me. You absolutely rock!

Also, I'm very grateful to my fellow authors in the LOL-35 and Scribblers' Society groups for their insights and kind feedback.

A very special thank you goes to my husband Keith, who acts as alpha reader, critique partner, sounding board — and who takes the occasional rant in his stride. Thanks dear.

# About the Author

Lina Hansen has been a freelance travel journalist, teacher, belly dancer, postal clerk, and science communication specialist stranded in the space sector. Numbed by factoid technical texts, she set out to write the stories she loves to read— cozy and romantic mysteries with a dollop of humor and a magical twist. After living and working in the UK, Lina, her husband, and their feline companion now share a home in the foothills of Castle Frankenstein. Lina is a double Watty Award Winner, Featured Author, and a Wattpad Star.

*Out of Body* is the third book in her Magical Misfits series of mysteries. More information and Lina's blog can be found at www.linahansenauthor.com or connect via Instagram @linahansenauthor or Facebook @linahansenauthor.

www.ingramcontent.com/pod-product-compliance
Lightning Source LLC
Chambersburg PA
CBHW061755190726

48289CB00007B/1966